Church Bound

A Bride in Fake Diamonds

Emily Tomko

Emily Tomko
April 14, 2013

Also by Emily Tomko:

COLLEGE BOUND: A PURSUIT OF FREEDOM
THIRTY-ONE THOUGHTS ON PROPHECY

Scripture quotations taken from the New American Standard Bible®, Copyright © 1960, 1962, 1963, 1968, 1971, 1972, 1973, 1975, 1977, 1995 by The Lockman Foundation. Used by permission.

Copyright © 2012 Emily Tomko

All rights reserved. No part of this book may be reproduced or transmitted in any form or by any means, electronic or mechanical, including photocopying, recording, or by an information storage and retrieval system.

www.EmilyTomko.com
https://www.facebook.com/AuthorEmilyTomko

Acknowledgments

Thanks to the Society of Authors as the Literary Representative of the Estate of John Masefield, and to the Augsburg Fortress for granting permission to quote Dietrich Bonhoeffer.

Thank you to Charity Meals for feedback, as well as general awesomeness.

My gratitude to Jake Kail, Joanne Miller, Andrew Bennett, Derek Prince, Allan and Rose Chambers, E. Daniel Martin, Don Lamb, and all my spiritual family at Lifegate Church for teaching and pouring life into me.

And a special thanks to my husband, Craig, who comes home from work and eagerly reads my manuscripts, even when it's baseball season.

This book is dedicated to the Meißners – my wonderful German "family" – as well as all my pals from the Bremen program.

"Suchet den HERRN, so werdet ihr leben." (Amos 5.6)

New York State of Mind	1
Back at Durst	6
Two Roads Diverged	13
Growing Pains	17
Arranged Marriages	25
A Scare	31
The Waiting Game	36
Revelation	47
Milestone	52
Close Encounters	61
A Cup of Woe	71
Germany	77
Xani	89
Auf Wiedersehen	101
Bremen	109
The Slough of Despond	122
Stalker	132
Wilderness	141
Respite	149
Back in Bondage	157
An Encounter	165
Warfare	173
Lost in Translation	181
Culture	191
Amsterdam	200
The Sinful Mile	205
Springtime	213
The North Sea, and a Baptism	228
Petra's Story	240
A Series of Surprises	251
Prelude to Farewell	265

Chapter One

New York State of Mind

"How did the world get along before there was flavored coffee?" Anise sighed, taking a sip from her enormous disposable cup. "I feel so sorry for everyone who died without experiencing it."

"And Swedish fish and peach iced tea," I agreed, popping a red gummy in my mouth.

The air had that rich smell of damp earth as we lounged on a patch of grass in west Central Park. Insects buzzed about gaily as their tiny brains acknowledged that the long winter was finally over. Grand, ancient trees spread out canopies of green, matching the mossy lawns and shrubs surrounding them. A cluster of azaleas created a fuchsia splotch amidst all the shades of sage and emerald. At first glance, we might have been in the middle of the countryside, except for the medieval-looking twin spires of the San Remo building looming just behind the treetops.

We were mid-way through our fourth semester at Durst – celebrating a stretch of spring break this sophomore year in The Big Apple. Anise had interviewed the day before in the Financial District for a summer internship, and I had taken the train up to spend a couple days meandering around as a gawking tourist. We were using her mom's elegant apartment in Manhattan as home base.

Each city seems to have its own individual personality and feel – an aura that is distinguishable to the visitor and the native alike. New York gave me a sense of overwhelming awe – towering concrete mirrored in millions of windows; herds of flesh in sync on the sidewalks, at once both compressed and isolated; the swirling realization of millions of minds converged within a miniscule amount of space. And mammoth materialism. "New York thy name's 'delirium,'" floated the line of a satirical poem to mind. I could at once understand both loving it and hating it.

New York was a city where anything at all could happen, and nothing at all would be surprising. Witnessing earlier in the day a man in a baseball cap stretched out in a lawn chair smack in the middle of Broadway, lounging while taxis and voices shouted all around him, hadn't seemed at all unusual. Nor had the three leggy women in their micro minis and stilettos seemed out of place as they sashayed down 72nd Street in between baby strollers and businessmen.

"I wish *my* legs were that ripped," I'd remarked quietly to Anise just before the women were absorbed by the rest of the crowd on the sidewalk.

Anise had peered over the top of her sunglasses for a moment. "They're men so they have an advantage," she concluded. "Transvestites."

The city was thrilling – and yet it had a sense of starvation about it. Like it was hungry, always looking for new ways to feed itself. It contained everything under the sun, yet still it wasn't satiated.

In fact, most of the people we'd seen that day had actually looked physically underfed. Striking, half-emaciated women grasping handbags heavier than themselves strutted on stilt legs down the sidewalks. Sometimes little terrier dogs hopped alongside them, earnestly hurdling trash that came into their path. Even the men had looked gaunt, thin in the face and limbs, seemingly unsuited for any task requiring strength or vigor.

Stretched out now on a blanket in the park, I watched as a man tossed a miniature football to his little boy, who completely missed catching it.

"Can you imagine being a celebrity and living in this town?" Anise asked dreamily. "Open doors to the glitziest clubs, treated like royalty in the most posh restaurants . . . riding around in your limo and ruling the city like you're part of some exclusive dynasty? Everything at your comfort and command, and everyone wanting to catch a glimpse of you?"

"I think I'd love it for about two weeks and then get ridiculously bored," I concluded, flipping my dirty blond hair over my shoulder.

"Really? Oh, no way. Not me. Too much to do, and you'd be doing it all first-class."

"I guess it'd be fun for a while," I conceded. "But where's the challenge? Everything at your fingertips, no obstacles and more money than you know what to do with. After a while I think it would feel stale. What do celebrities do? Groom for hours in preparation for a potential run-in with the paparazzi, or for a party where people who probably don't even like them will be studying them to see if they had any plastic surgery done since the last time they met?"

Anise snickered. "What I'd like most is access to the best clubs in every city in the world, and having every hot man wanting to dance with me." She leaned back, cradling her head in her hands. "And whenever some guy would start giving off creep vibes — acting like I owed him some special attention or something — then I'd have my personal bodyguard take him by the clothes and bounce him across the floor!"

"Wouldn't it be weird to be famous?" I mused. "Everyone would recognize you, but you wouldn't know them. So people would stare, and you'd look back, wondering how you knew each other, and then you'd realize, 'Oh, yeah I forgot. I'm famous. I don't know them.' But they'd have all these ideas about you already and see you really as somebody you're not."

"I think I could tolerate an A-list celebrity lifestyle," Anise said. "Champagne and caviar, valets and Versace. But I guess they do have to go to work. They say acting's hard work."

"Ha!" I disagreed. "Acting hard work? *Tedious,* maybe. Outtake after outtake, and a thousand different shots of the same thing. Now migrant work in 95-degree weather where the pay is peanuts and the language is foreign and nobody thinks you're special — *that's* hard work."

"Oh. Well I wouldn't want tedious work, either. I guess I'll just have to be a socialite."

We laughed. The little boy in front of us finally caught the football from his dad and it filled me with sudden exuberance. A guy and girl formed a single silhouette under a lamp post, and were planting staccato kisses on one another. A saxophone player was emitting some doleful notes a short distance away.

"Unchained Melody," I remarked sentimentally.

"What?" Anise said.

"The song he's playing. I always sort of envision myself slow-dancing to this music with God."

"I've never, ever, ever imagined dancing with God," Anise said incredulously. She didn't say anything for a few moments, and I went back to listening to the achingly sweet melody. She spoke up again. "When I do think of God, I always kind of picture Him as the headmaster at boarding school, sitting in his office at the end of a really long, dark hallway. You don't know what to expect when you finally get to where He's at, but you know He's not going to be happy with you."

"That's a painful picture of God!" I remarked. I was silent for a moment, reflecting. "If anything, He'd be delighted that you finally stopped by."

"You sure are sure of things, aren't you?" Anise remarked cryptically.

I guess I am, I thought, but I did not say anything.

I gazed at Johnny Saxophone in his tweed jacket and jeans and wondered how much money he made on an average day, and whether the mellow notes floating out from his cool, relaxed posture belied a gnawing desperation for the shekels passers-by might throw him. I wondered whether he had grown up in the city, and if his parents had stayed together and his childhood had been happy. I wondered whether he had any children of his own, and what came into his mind when he heard the name "Jesus."

The shadows were lengthening and Anise stood up to stretch, indicating our imminent departure. I studied the San Remo again. It had a peculiar personality, I thought. Anise had said that it was one of the most sought-after addresses in The Big Apple for the rich and famous. Its Gothic-style towers were reminiscent of a cathedral, looking very much as though they were urging New York's mass population to look towards the heavens. Yet the base of its architecture resembled all the office buildings neighboring it. It seemed to be a mismatch. It was as if the San Remo had aspirations to be a church, wanted to have a higher purpose, but in the end had given up or gotten confused, so that its foundation had taken on the nature of the corporate structures surrounding it and had made it common.

Tonight was our last night in the city, and a club was in the plans for the evening. Like celebrities, we would spend the next few hours prepping in a frenzy of make-up, clothes, perfume, glitter, and hair irons for a fleeting night in the restless, pacing city. Anise and I made our way out of Central Park, as the white exterior of the famous San Remo darkened and sunset drew near.

Chapter Two

Back at Durst

It can be a little surreal to look back on one's life a year earlier and remember what was happening, and then compare it to the present. As I now neared the close of my sophomore year and looked back on my freshman days, it was as though I had been living in a dark and shadowy dream a year ago. Having been awakened from this nightmare stint in the *Twilight Zone*, I was finally free to walk around in the light and gulp big breaths of air.

Something revolutionary had happened as a result of my prodigal wandering and return. Perhaps from feeding on the proverbial husks of pig food for so long, I came running back to the Lord with a voracious appetite for His Word. While the burden of college work had previously sucked up any desire for extra reading, I found that I suddenly couldn't get enough of the subject of *Him*. In addition to the Bible itself, I read everything from C. H. Spurgeon to A. W. Tozer, from Fenelon to Francis Chan. When I wasn't reading devotionals or some internet link I'd found, I was reading commentaries.

Kendra, my beloved friend from school days, and in many ways my Jiminy Cricket, was a regular and rich part of my life. A year ago we were barely speaking. Now, the idea of being away from her encouragement and wisdom, or being unable to share some breaking spiritual revelation with her, was unimaginable.

She had warned me shortly before we'd parted ways for the second summer that back at Durst, my secular college, that besides all the temptations, I'd be labeled a prude and a goody two-shoes, and even misunderstood by my close friends. I already knew that my Christian worldview could invoke poor grades from professors who might tolerate other religious philosophies, but who had a disdain for Christ.

"Will that sway you from following Him, Molly?" she had asked me.

It was easy enough to say, "No, never" while I was sitting there in the fortitude of her farmhouse, away from the seduction of campus and the foes of my faith. But her words played over and over in my mind, and I came home later that night and opened my Bible to the gospels. Jesus' declaration jumped out at me in Luke 9:62, that "No one, after putting his hand to the plow and looking back, is fit for the kingdom of God." A shudder went through me. What a terrifying pronouncement. What purpose or promise could there possibly be in life if *I* looked back, like Lot's wife? If I returned to last year's follies, then I was a fool – unfit for His kingdom!

Though I'd just spent the entire evening with her, I had called Kendra again.

"Pray for me again, would you?" I had asked. "I know we did before I left, but we need to do it again. I'm uneasy right now. It's all or nothing with Christ. There's no in-between. It is so easy to get ensnared. I don't want to lose everything again."

Kendra agreed, proclaiming me free, walking in the truth, and committing me to victorious living in Christ. "Many will see your works, and will put their faith in Christ," she declared. "Remember that you are blessed when people insult and ridicule you for His sake."

Repeating her prayer over and over myself like a banner, I had returned to Durst for my second year. Immediately, I had sought out a church, and decided to visit where many of the other students attended. With its friendly congregants, relaxed service, and likeable pastors, it was a similar atmosphere to my home church.

Caitlyn and Anise and I were sharing a suite sophomore year, and it had worked out pretty well. We weren't snarling or escaping to other campus buildings in avoidance of each other, and we had a lot of fun in between the heavy studying and writing and reading. I had thought it would have been good to be living with some of the people from the Christian fellowship, but that wasn't an option at the moment.

Caitlyn continued to return from every break and summer vacation with a staunch commitment to her boyfriend Dave, but that resolve usually waned within two weeks and there'd be a new guy in what I called the Caitlyn Circuit. She did not have a reputation for being promiscuous – rather, she pulled men in but generally kept them at a certain distance, until one or the other tired of the flirtation. I had come to understand that she deeply craved the attention she was given and was insecure when it was diverted elsewhere.

Anise garnered equally as much attention with her dark beauty and smashing fashion. Yet she was very unlike Caitlyn, who sported J. Crew neutrals and girl-next-door good looks. Anise didn't seem to thrive on all the attention, nor did she manipulate. She could even *flirt* with integrity, I thought once.

If I was the ugly friend, it seems natural that I should have been jealous of both my beauty queen pals. But it never hurt me to hear Anise complimented or admired. Rather, I was proud of her. The line of simpletons at Caitlyn's beck and call, on the other hand, at times produced in me a kind of contemptuous pity for them, and at times a creeping resentment towards *her*.

Nevertheless, in spite of these occasional feelings, I loved Caitlyn dearly. She was a lot of fun, and was not incapable of having introspective and meaningful conversations. To suppose that she was a heartless or superficial creature due to her ways with guys would be to misjudge her.

Reflecting now on Graeme, my freshman year boyfriend (and first real boyfriend ever, for that matter), was now just, well, goofy. When I first returned to school in the fall of sophomore year, after a summer of his slowly waning pursuit, it was like viewing him through corrective lenses. Why had it never occurred to me before that his eyes — which I'd always previously thought to be irresistible — reminded me exactly of a goat's? His frame, which was considerably thinner than it had been, had all the appeal to me now of embracing a hat rack.

There had been the occasional awkward encounter as our paths crossed on campus, but by homecoming weekend, it was apparent that he was sporting a new girlfriend, and that realization made whatever leftover tension there might have been between us dry up like a drink ring on a coffee table.

My grade point average had climbed from the previous year's as I discovered the deep satisfaction of persistence and steadfastness in working and studying "as unto the Lord." Of course, it wasn't always a picnic in the park trying to balance a university workload, and I had my moments of angst. But papers and exams were a different challenge entirely when I sensed that the Lord was with me in all I was doing.

Only once had I gone to a fraternity party this year — a total trend reversal from last year. It had a dance theme, and I only went at Anise's imploring. It was a strange blend of fun and amusement and consternation — to dance and to watch the effects of alcohol on everyone else and then to remember my previous life when a sloppy freshman dropped her beer down my dress. Throughout the evening, though, my mind kept returning to a story Kendra had told me of a local minister she knew of who had gotten in trouble with his congregation once for simply pointing out that the Bible instructed believers to dance before the Lord even more than it did to clap.

Mostly, my free time seemed to be an even pull between the Christian fellowship and my roommates, and rotated around each group's calendar of events. Which was a little peculiar in itself. I seemed to have two sets of friends. Two kinds of mindsets. Two worlds, really.

Being a true disciple of Christ at Durst felt like trying to grow a garden in Sodom. It didn't seem as though any truths could take root amidst the hostile conditions of cynicism, depravity, and unbelief. Even Caitlyn and Anise hadn't proved to be eager to receive the good news. Although both had said they were interested in visiting church or a fellowship event with me, when presented with opportunities, there were always reasons why they couldn't make that particular time.

"What am I even doing here?" I had messaged Kendra one evening in late November. "This school does have the best studies for my major…and I do have a good group of friends here. But spiritually, what am I doing here? I've been back a whole semester and I can't see how my being here has made an impact for Christ."

"If you're seeking Him with all your heart, listening for His voice and ready to act when He tells you to do something, then that's really all that matters," Kendra had replied. "Keep looking to Him. The breakthroughs will come."

Threaded through the questions of life and the demands of college was my relationship with Hank. The boy from high school continued to hold my interest beyond all others. The distance of college had afforded the pleasantness of an undefined relationship – a male friendship that was *just* a friendship – and yet, at the same time was infinitely more than that on my end. But what was it for Hank?

It was never discussed between us that we were both single. Nor did we talk about relationships looming on our individual horizons at school. So I was no less than devastated to learn that Hank would be spending most of the coming summer in Los Angeles, as part of an opportunity to apprentice with a well-known artist. It was a wonderful chance for him, and I was glad of that. But I was sorry that he wouldn't be around. And what hope did hometown me have against a whole city full of glamour and celebrities and women who didn't ascribe to the possibility of body fat?

"Lord, blind him to skinny blonds and give him an aversion to fitness models," I prayed fervently, pitifully, whenever I thought of the summer.

"You will keep him in perfect peace whose mind is stayed on you, because he trusts in you," Isaiah 26:3 promised.

"If that's true, why do I want to throw up whenever I think about what could happen?" I said out loud.

The thought came to me that perhaps I was not looking to the Lord as much as I claimed.

Instinctively, I said aloud, "I trust *You*, Lord. I just don't trust Orange County."

Had there been an opportunity for a *defined* relationship with Hank, would I even have wanted it at this stage in life? Both of us not halfway through college, burdened with school demands, and separated by hundreds of miles? Or would I be like the hound madly chasing the mail truck that, when the chase is over and the vehicle stops, absurdly has no idea what to do with it?

It seemed a terrible quandary to live in a culture where everyone solemnly warned you not to marry too young, half the population served as a warning not to get married at all, and compounding everything, your spirit was in a raging battle against the desires of your flesh.

"Living in a cloister would seriously be so much easier," I messaged Kendra grimly one night. "Do you think nuns get catty?"

"You wouldn't be happy in a convent," she countered. "Remember how ready to get back you were after just one weekend on a ladies retreat?"

While I was at a much better place in my journey than I had been a year ago, I was far from having arrived at my destination. I struggled a lot, and not one day seemed to go by that I didn't agonize over having messed up in some way.

In Biology I remembered learning about a particular kind of coniferous tree that doesn't lose its leaves seasonally like other trees do. Instead, the dead leaves hang on the branches all throughout the winter. It isn't until spring comes that the new buds beneath them push off the dead stuff. That was illustrated to me how He was transforming me as I daily was in His word and as I listened and meditated on the lyrics of the worship songs to Him and took in the sermons on Sunday and Friday night fellowship. As I took on His nature, there was less and less room for anything in me that wasn't of His Life.

I again found myself regularly at the pianos in the practice rooms of the college, singing, banging away at the keys, and creating a cacophony that I trusted was music to God's ears. In particular, I loved playing and singing the old hymns – they were so rich, so lyrical, and so brimming with biblical wisdom. One of the verses from the familiar "Trust and Obey" really arrested me:

> But we never can prove the delights of His love,
> Until all on the altar we lay.
> For the favor He shows, and the joy He bestows
> Are for those who will trust and obey. [1]

What if those lines were true? What if total obedience to His leading and His commandments ushered in a new realm of just *being* with Him that was unimaginable? If it were true, then the opposite must also be true – that anything less than complete surrender to Him must mean living in a frustrated, sub-par state of underlying dissatisfaction.

---

[1] John Sammis, "Trust and Obey" 1887. Copyright: Public Domain

Chapter Three

Two Roads Diverged

The home stretch from Spring Break to the end of the year was once more upon Durst. For most graduating seniors, it meant that they'd be flung out of the college playpen and into the crazy, chaotic world of adult independence. Responsibility. A career. Rent. Insurance. Alcohol to be purchased with one's own resources.

For me, it was a reminder that I was already half-way through my college experience and I felt like I had little direction as to what I was going to do with my life. I was pursuing languages because I was better at that than anything else, and because I had been told that a liberal arts degree was a passport to loads of career choices. But this really felt like eliminating what I'd be terrible at rather than forging a course in life.

"What would you do if you didn't have to worry about money? If you could do anything that you wanted?" This was what people always asked. What a question — if money weren't a factor, what would anyone do? Eat Fritos and watch Jane Austen movies and then go to the gym to work it all off. For an occasional thrill, I'd fork Mrs. Eldridge's yard or rearrange real estate signs around the neighborhood while everyone was sleeping. When I'd get bored, I'd fly to Europe for a few weeks. Why would people preface anything with "If money were not a factor"? It was like suggesting, "What if you didn't need to eat to live. What would you do?"

I paid a visit to career services, hoping that this might spark some ideas as to what direction I should take — or avoid. Inside the limestone walls, framed posters hung of models wearing spectacles and suits and looking very successful at whatever it was they were doing. Inspirational photography featured climbers scaling alpine heights with single-word captions like "Pursue" and "Dream."

Miss Viviano, the woman with whom I'd scheduled my appointment, greeted me. She had curly, carrot-colored hair and wore orangish-red lipstick.

"So . . . what would you do with your life if money were not a factor?" Miss Viviano asked, sitting down from across me.

I stared back at her.

"What do you enjoy doing?" she tried again.

"I like to write."

"Oh! You like to write. Prose? Poetry? Copy?"

"More like satire. I enjoy making fun of things that pass for normal in society," I said. Miss Viviano continued to stare at me wordlessly, so I added, "I enjoy reading satire, too."

Miss Viviano smiled tolerantly at this profession. "Well, what would you say are your academic strengths?"

That was easy. *Not physics.* "Verbal cognitive skills – language arts."

"And where do you see yourself in ten years?"

Ten years? I'd be pushing thirty and ancient. Hopefully Jesus would return by then.

"Um. I don't know. It's foggy. I mean, I really have no idea."

"Your major is in German language and literature. Do you plan to teach?"

"I wouldn't mind teaching, but I really don't like kids." I cleared my throat, tried again. "Well, it's not that I don't like kids. I don't like the way they behave. Or don't behave. And then suddenly you're disciplinarian, psychologist, and mediator all wrapped in one. I just don't think teachers get to teach much anymore." I fiddled with a button on my cardigan. And I'm afraid I'd smack a student eventually and get suspended. So no, I don't want to teach."

I left Miss Viviano and the career center's inspirational posters feeling worse off than when I'd arrived.

"Maybe I could drive truck," I wrote half-seriously in a letter to Hank (he still corresponded with old-fashioned snail mail, and I liked this in that it still kept a comfortable distance to our relationship). "Listen to tunes, stop at greasy spoons all across America and eat French fries, travel . . . I could be independent and wouldn't have to deal a whole lot with people."

"The interstate would get boring pretty quickly," Hank replied. "But I'm sure drivers would love to see *you* pull up at a truck stop."

I took some career tests online. There were all sorts available: the kind that base you on one of four types of personalities, the kind that compare you to animals, the kind that suggest other people probably find you dull at parties . . . there were the kind that show graphs with different colors and predict you could be successful as a high-power attorney but would go broke as a hog farmer.

A verse in Proverbs sprang out at me as I was reading late one night. "A man makes his plans, but the Lord orders His steps."

"Lord, you brought me this far," I said, switching off my light and pulling the sheet up to my head. "I'm trusting that You're ordering my steps even now, when I have no idea even what my plans are."

✸✸✸✸✸

It was strange. I loved Anise and Caitlyn dearly, and we could get to laughing over things together until my ribs ached and my nose ran. But I felt very torn. Something was missing in those moments, and more and more I longed to be surrounded by other Christians. Not just Friday evenings at fellowship, or

Sunday mornings, but at lunch and dinner and even when hitting the gym.

"There's an instant depth that a relationship goes to with a fellow believer that simply isn't there with someone who doesn't know Christ," Kendra agreed when I wrote to her about it. "Christians, as they say, are truly 'blood brothers and sisters.'"

It dawned on me that that was what I was really missing. I wanted to talk to other people about Jesus. Just *talk* about Him. Think about Him. Hear what He was up to in their lives. Hear what He was saying to them. Share with others what He was revealing to me.

I read in Acts 2 how the early church functioned. "They were continually devoting themselves to the apostles' teaching and to fellowship, and to the breaking of bread and to prayer . . . and all those who had believed were together and had all things in common." Their whole focus in life was four things: learning about Christ, spending time with other believers, eating together, and praying. Because they had Christ in common, they also shared everything else. From those verses, it sounded as though the first church functioned more as a family than most families do.

Housing arrangements would be up for grabs soon for the following school term, but the decision with whom to room would bypass me for now. I was leaving for Germany in August, and would be spending my junior year overseas.

Chapter Four

Growing Pains

"Do you ever picture yourself as an old person?" I asked Kendra. We had gone for a run way out in the country, past the cornfields and the mildly curious cows, who paused in their chewing for a moment to gaze at us. The ground beside the asphalt road was cracked and hard, and we occasionally dodged some roadkill. The air smelled of dampness and manure and vegetation. I think I'd swallowed a few gnats.

"Not usually," she replied. "Why?"

"I don't know. Working around these elderly people at Shady Oaks, now and then I try to picture myself in sixty years. So many of them just sit there, staring at nothing. They have all the time in the world, and they just sit there. Doing nothing. It's depressing. I hope I'm a feisty old lady."

"You'll probably be the kind who hides the other nursing home residents' Depends," Kendra assured me.

"But seriously, if you knew that you had just a couple years maybe, and then someone would be putting you in the ground and throwing dirt on you . . . wouldn't it just make you think about death? About meeting your Creator? And wouldn't you want to know everything you possibly could about Him, about eternity, because this was your last chance?"

"Well, sure."

"But so many of them — almost all of them — sit in front of blaring televisions wrapped in a shawl, and just *sit* there. I don't even know if they know what they're watching. And — and I just think, that if I were an old lady, I would know that it couldn't be too much longer till I would breathe my last breath…and *what then?*"

"But it's no different really from younger people," Kendra reasoned. "Even the ones who are able-bodied enough to be out doing something just sit there – in front of a TV, in front of the computer, in front of a bar. They're not conscious of their own mortality. Most people are ruled by their flesh. They cater to their physical bodies, and they put off the spiritual until tomorrow. Everyone figures they have another day. Not many people think about the possibility that tomorrow might not come."

Pastor Lawrence, leader of the church I'd been attending while living at Durst, had invited me and another student from fellowship to his office just before the last week of school.

"We want your ideas about how to recruit more college-aged students to start coming to church," he had said to me and to Chad, the male representative. (Chad had once bravely stood up to Ms. Jankowski in our Durst calculus class freshman year to defend his Christian belief.) "This seems to be a group that kind of falls between the cracks once youth group is finished. We have a young adult group, but it's dwindling. Truth be told, it's always been a bit anemic. What can we do to make church relevant for your age group?"

Chad had offered some ideas about an alternative service for young people with a different feel to it, as well as implementing a coffee shop at the church.

I sat there in silence, thinking about his question and trying not to be sidetracked by his dirty glasses. Pastor Lawrence always had smudged lenses, and each time I saw him I had an urge to yank them off his face, spray them with solution, and rub them clean on my shirt.

Finally I answered, "Fellowship of the church *is* relevant to our age group. The Bible is relevant. Prayer is relevant. They're not only relevant, they're life itself. Now that I'm reading my Bible again, it's even clearer to me that last year, when I'd wandered away from Him, I was lying in a patch of ground while shovelful after shovelful of dirt piled on top of me."

Pastor Lawrence nodded and peered at me through his hazy spectacles, waiting.

"Christ is life itself," I continued, gathering my many and weighty thoughts. "And He *is* the Word. To try to prove the relevance of the Bible is to try to prove the relevance of Christ. The world out there is dying. Either someone realizes it or they don't. And — and I don't know how we as humans can make another person see that he's dying if *he* doesn't."

Pastor Lawrence had nodded slowly. "I agree. But your generation is the one that is slipping away from church the most. What do we do to rescue them? *Make* them see?"

My mind had gone to the book of Acts and the early church. "I don't know," I'd answered, shaking my head. "But surely somewhere in the Bible is the best answer for that."

Pastor Lawrence had thanked us for our time and had shaken our hands. "Have a great summer." To me he had said, "Best of luck in Germany. And keep our discussion in mind. Let me know if anything hits you."

*****

Hank had come to say goodbye one evening in early June. Dusk was closing in and the evening was warm and fragrant with hyacinths. We went for a walk down to the little creek that ran past the old elementary school that we'd attended as kids. I threw pebbles in while we talked, until the mosquitoes ruined the mood and we returned to my house, each taking a perch on the front porch.

"I'm close to caving on the whole social networking nerdiness," Hank told me as we sat under another dusky, summer twilight. "All my instructors are pushing it as an essential platform for my art. I don't know if I can hold out much longer. Might as well succumb to peer pressure sooner than later."

I said nothing to this, but was sorry to hear it. Hank represented the lone holdout against the modern age — the only person of our generation whom I knew who wasn't updating his status or tweeting or posting music lyrics every five minutes. The only one in touch with a quieter, gentler, slower time.

"It's hard not to get caught up in the way the rest of society functions, much as you might loathe it. Unless you become a hermit. And first I have to sell my art before I can afford to be a hermit."

"I don't know that I'd want to be a hermit," I replied thoughtfully, standing up to stretch. I hopped down the two steps from the porch lightly to kick my sister Anne's soccer ball, which had been left in the front yard. "But I wish the world could just stop for a few minutes, sometimes. Long enough to let everyone get off and just *think*. No one knows how to think for themselves any more. Someone else does it for you. And the chaos increases and the world goes faster and faster, and people think even less. It's like riding some sort of never-ending, nightmare merry-go-round."

"You got that right," Hank agreed, getting up off the porch slowly and following me. He reached down to snap the stem of a Dianthus and held it out to me, smiling. "We'd better stick together 'cause we're the only normal ones. Everyone else has lost their minds."

As I reached for the flower, my eyes met the moonlight brilliance of his. I stopped breathing. Hank had The Look.

Holy Hannah, he's going to kiss me, I thought.

"Molly, is that you out there? Who's that young man? Are you alright?" Mrs. Eldridge's voice cut through the dreamy atmosphere like a scythe, dissolving its romance. The neighborhood watchdog. She was wading out through her front lawn in a nightgown that looked like it might have been hand-sewn back in the days of covered wagons.

My insides slowly imploded as the moment turned from ethereal to toxic. I took a half-step back from Hank. I didn't know whether I wanted to strangle Mrs. Eldridge right there in her nightie or thank her for keeping me virtuous. The moment of a lifetime was ruined.

"Good-bye, Molly," Hank whispered, giving me a quick, warm hug, before turning around and walking toward his car. I watched him get in and pull away from the curb, accelerating out into the darkness, even as his brief scent of musk and tobacco lingered with me.

*****

Stop eating resolution" – July 15th is national refuse-to-eat day. To protest rising food costs, we are all agreeing not to eat for an entire day. That way, farmers will feel the ramifications of millions of Americans not buying food and will lower their prices. Express your outrage not in words, but actions!

"It's making fun of those people who buy into the campaigns suggesting everyone refuse to buy gas on such-and-such a date in order to lower prices at the pump," I explained to Kendra.

"Oh, right. I get it. What's your other one?"

"Lawmakers to extend family medical leave act to include pet adoption."

"What's the family medical leave act?"

"That law where you can take long stretches of maternity time from your company but they still have to pay you for not working."

"Oh."

I sighed. "It's getting more difficult to write satire because the real news is so over the top these days. The world is nuts. People are nuts. It's hard to make fun of what they do. They make fools of themselves and nobody's much shocked. No one has any shame. Either of these headlines could be true. In fact, by next year they'll probably both be true."

"Well, send it to the editor anyway," Kendra encouraged me. "What does it hurt?"

I signed my pen name to the articles – Eliza Emma-Gee, an allusion to military weaponry. I arranged the cursor over the "send" button. I squinted my eyes shut for a moment as I clicked the mouse, and opened them as the screen changed to tell me enthusiastically that my message had been sent.

*****

One of the strangest things for me to reconcile after "coming back" as a prodigal was the group I called the "in-between" Christians. The Half-Hearted. These were the individuals – friends of mine through school or church or college – who professed to know Christ, spoke of Him from time to time, publicized it on their social networking statuses (and sometimes even forcefully) yet said and did things on more than one occasion that raised eyebrows.

I had spent a year of my life marked by disobedience and godlessness, even degenerating into drunkenness and promiscuity. I had been the lowest of the low, and was not in a position to judge others, I realized. On a scale of the shocking, my wandering was far more reprehensible perhaps than the transgressions of some of these Halfies. Yet during this time, I'd never wanted to drag His name down with my lifestyle and proclaim myself to be one of His followers. I was conscious even then that I *wasn't* following the teachings of Christ, and there were people watching. I was always aware of this.

Whereas I had lived in abject sin, the Halfies did not seem so flagrantly wicked. Yet it was worse somehow to me that they held up His name, all the while subtly compromising Him. Whether through the occasional "coarse talk" that Paul warned the church of, or through volunteering the fact that they attended questionable movies, or in the case of their gossip that sometimes leaked out about other believers, the Halfies had one foot in the sanctuary and one in the world.

There were even pastors and others prominent in church leadership, I began to take note of as I read their various books and blogs, who wandered comfortably into this gray area. This to me was especially grievous, for it led others to think that the behavior wasn't really *that* terrible. After all, if a pastor used occasional crass talk or the sketchy colloquial of this generation to get a point across, might it not simply resonate better with his audience? Was it really compromise, so much as bridging a gap?

"Who may ascend the hill of the Lord? Who may stand in His holy place?" Psalm 24:3 asked. The following verse gave the answer: "He who has clean hands and a pure heart, who does not lift up his soul to an idol, or swear by what is false."

Holiness was necessary for fellowship with Christ. It was also meant to be a trademark of His followers. The question therefore wasn't whether something was permissible. But rather, was it holy?

I didn't believe that discerning this about the Halfies was even the same as judging them, because what I often observed in their lives wasn't necessarily sin as defined in scripture. It wasn't a sin to have a drink. Yet to go out boozing was ungodly. The Bible did not forbid smoking. Yet addiction to anything was bondage. Television was not outlawed under the Ten Commandments. Yet much of what was broadcast was dark and grisly and harmful to the soul. Nowhere in the Bible did it say not to attend certain movies. Yet clearly most films not only didn't glorify God, but they tore down His truths and mocked His followers. Somehow, somewhere, a line was crossed. The Halfies seemed unwilling to decide whether to go all the way with Christ, yet they refused to hang out exclusively with the world and reject Him. It was something different entirely than falling into occasional temptation. It was worldliness. Stunted growth — a failure to mature. This disturbed me much more than the riotous sinners.

"If thine eye be single, thy whole body will be full of light." If this were true, and it had to be because Matthew 6:22 said so, then cutting out the doubtful areas of one's life was not a sacrifice so much as a trade up for something much better.

One missionary to our campus fellowship put this in transverse, making a statement that rattled around my brain long after he'd left: "If your non-Christian peers don't think you're eccentric, or at least a little weird, you're living a compromised Christianity."

Well, I was pretty confident most people thought I was a little odd. Whether they attributed it to following Christ or not, I couldn't be sure.

Chapter Five

Arranged Marriages

"You know, maybe there's something to arranged marriages after all," I said to Kendra one evening as we slurped down some Italian ice. I'd attended her church youth group where a missionary had shared with us about life in two different African nations in which he'd ministered, and he told us all about the courting process where a native man had to go with other male family and present a really sweet gift to the girl's father in the first meeting, *just* to be granted access to a second such meeting in which he might ask for the hopeful opportunity to court the daughter. If the father said "nope," it was all over. Neither the guy nor the girl would ever even think twice about seeing one another again.

"Think about it," I said. "Your parents pretty much do all the hard work of fixing you up, and the dowry doesn't get blown in a single day with a commercialized wedding like it does here in the States. If things go sour between you, you can always blame your folks for your miserable life." I grinned.

"You'd trust your parents to arrange a marriage for you?"

"No way. My parents would choose a nerd for me. I just know it. He'd have some good Christian credentials and be a nice sort of chap, but there'd be no sex appeal."

"Maybe you underestimate your parents," Kendra argued. "They'd want grandchildren, so they'd look for somebody reasonably handsome."

"I don't know. I picture standing at the altar with a real Poindexter. But the point is, it seems like marriages in more 'primitive' cultures have just as much success, if not more, than the ones in the West where the kids get to decide for themselves. With the high rate of divorce and infidelity, plus all the domestic abuse, our methods really haven't led us to better choices in the matchmaking department."

"How did we get on this topic again?" Kendra wanted to know.

I treasured the fact that I could have conversations with Kendra about stuff for which others would have recommended me to the psych ward. Just the day before, I'd wondered aloud to her whether angels on assignment ever shook their heads in the midst of their duties. The Bible said that they were learning about the nature of God by observing church assemblies, so what did they think when they saw congregants falling asleep, texting, and doodling? Or how about guardian angels who got a close-up of man, made in God's image and loved madly by Him, flicking a booger out the car window. Did they ever wonder what God sees in mankind and secretly want to call off work?

Now that the overload of college studying was finished for the school year, I had more time to devote to the handbooks on the Bible that I'd bought. I had always figured, perhaps with more than a little wicked pride, that I knew my Bible fairly well compared to most of the kids I'd grown up among, thanks to my parents' relentless instruction and encouragement to read it. But now, for the first time I was discovering that I really didn't know it nearly as well as I'd once imagined.

Never in all my nearly twenty years of Sunday school and sermons and Bible studies and Good News Clubs and Vacation Bible School could I recall it explained to me that pretty much everything in the Old Testament had deeper, allegorical meanings behind the stories themselves. That we were to understand Old Testament chronology and history as having actually happened, but that the reason it had been included in the Bible was to foreshadow what would be fulfilled under Christ's New Covenant.

In other words, one handbook explained that the Old Testament was laden with symbolism and full of types — real people, places, and events that had counterparts in the New Testament and were given to be examples for us. Like Noah's ark was a type of Christ, where the righteous entered in and flourished unharmed while the unbelieving world around them was destroyed.

While I knew that the blood of the lamb applied over the doorways of Israelites' homes was symbolic of Christ, no one had ever explained that Egypt was a type for the world. To be in Egypt – in the world – was slavery, and so God's people had to be led out. He alone had the power to deliver them. It was the same for us.

Even more astonishing was to discover that the Israelites crossing the Red Sea was a type of baptism, and I Corinthians 10:2 said as much, plain as day.

"How did I miss all this?" I wondered. "Why didn't someone explain this? It makes so much more sense now. And it *means* so much more."

I was beginning to see that the Bible was crafted logically, even flawlessly. It was poetic, it was prophetic, and at the same time, it was the truest psychology I had ever read on human relationships.

In addition, I read apologetics because I didn't want to take anything for granted. The more I read apologetics, the more that it hit home that God was big enough for the questioning, big enough for the skeptics.

Sometimes, however, I'd come across a scripture that didn't make sense, or that seemed to directly contradict another scripture. And I'd suddenly get a little panicky, wondering if my faith would go down the drain with this one verse. But God was showing me that the more I studied His word, the more He would bring to light my understanding of the passage. Verses that once puzzled me or caused Christians to get into hefty debates would at some point be crystallized if I was willing to press in, seek, and wait on Him. Sometimes, the answers to these puzzles came when I least expected them, or had forgotten about my confusion over the particular passage.

But knowing that I lived among a world of scoffers — those who questioned but weren't looking for the answer, and were in fact looking to refute the declarations of scripture — encouraged me to study the works of agnostics and atheists. That is, I read the works of the intellectual naysayers who had really done their homework. I read Josh McDowell's *Evidence That Demands a Verdict* and waded through the weighty intellectualism of journalist Lee Strobel's *The Case for Christ* and consumed C. S. Lewis's *Mere Christianity* with relish. I devoured in one week during breaks at Shady Oaks and after work Paul Little's *Know Why You Believe* and *Know What You Believe,* followed by Ravi Zecharias's *Jesus Among Other Gods.*

"Lord, *how* can people not get this? There's nothing else in the world that even remotely makes sense — for our very existence, but also for the way we *are*. In three thousand years, the nature of man has not changed. Your Word holds true."

"The message of the cross is foolishness to those who are perishing," I Corinthians 1:18 answered. Further confirmation came from 2 Corinthians 4 in that "the god of this age has blinded the minds of unbelievers so that they might not see the light of the gospel." And suddenly I remembered last year as a freshman, when I had walked away from Him, when I had hardened my heart with deliberate sin. I remembered distinctly how I had opened my Bible and read the words and felt the cynicism — even rebellion — rising up in me toward His word. I shuddered.

How good it was to come back that summer following sophomore year to my home church, and see those old familiar faces, beaming and welcoming. These warm people who had known me since the days of animal crackers and orangeade, and who had been my family growing up. I was in fellowship with them again, but it was different than it had ever been. The feast that the prodigal son partook in with his Father's friends must have tasted so much sweeter after he'd returned home than all the times he'd sat at His table before he left.

Having been digging so deeply into scripture, I was eager to share with others the treasure that I had mined. I was certain that many of them had arrived long ago at what I was just beginning to uncover, but I wanted to gaze at it with them.

To my disappointment, at most church events and socials, we talked very little about Christ or spiritual things. Conversations even with adults older than me revolved around jobs, sports, travel, and secular books and films. Very rarely was Jesus mentioned, or His redemptive work in our lives. When I broached the subject, I sometimes felt that I was getting too "heavy" and making the other person a bit uncomfortable.

Plopping down in a rickety lawn chair next to one of our elders at a church picnic one June evening, I targeted him as a listener to my excited babble. He was a merry, kind-hearted gentleman whose eyes smiled whenever he looked at you. All of us "younger folks" loved him.

After a few pleasantries I remarked that I had been reading that morning in Colossians. "In the second chapter it says that He has transferred us into His glorious kingdom of light. Isn't that wild? 'He has transferred us.' We're already there! Eternity has already begun, and we're living it. Isn't that amazing?"

He looked at me, smiling and faintly nodding but not saying anything. A couple semi-awkward seconds crept by between us. Finally he spoke. "So I hear you're taking off to Germany in August."

I thought maybe he hadn't heard me and so after we talked about my upcoming semesters abroad, I tried again to strike up a conversation about Christ, but in a different vein.

"So I've been reading in different places how almost all the biblical prophecy concerning Israel is being fulfilled right now, and according to scripture, once it happens, the end will come and He will return. I know He could come back at any time, but isn't it amazing to think that we could hear the trumpet sound any moment? Even if it's five years away till He comes, isn't that incredible?"

The lines around his eyes deepened and he chuckled quietly. "Well, sure. But, you know, people have been talking about this same thing since I was your age."

Then His return must be all the much nearer now, I thought to myself, sinking back into my lawn chair. That's hardly a means of dismissing its relevance, but rather seeing the even greater urgency *now*. I said nothing more. I felt a little as though someone had taken a candle snuffer and placed it right over top of me.

Chapter Six

A Scare

"This coffee has cream in it! I don't take cream in my coffee – I take whole milk! Get it away from me!"

I sighed. Surely I should get paid more than minimum wage for this abuse. Old Gladys. Your hearing's gone, your eyesight's fading, but your taste buds rival that of a cooking contest judge. Imagine that, I thought as I marched from the dining room into the kitchen with the rejected coffee.

She took it half decaf, half regular, whole milk, and precisely 1½ teaspoons of cane sugar. If this recipe wasn't followed exactly, she'd sniff it out in a second and let you know. She'd get so incensed about her coffee being right, and yet I'd witnessed a staff member trying to help her by holding her bag as she walked from the dining room to her room, and Gladys had snapped at her for being patronizing.

"So many of these older people aren't well," my mom often said when I recounted my work stories. "Try to remember that when they're rude. Imagine how it must feel to be in perpetual pain or discomfort. Many of them are lonely and their families don't come to see them."

No wonder, I thought now as I re-entered the dining room with another mug of coffee and set it down in front of Gladys Grumplefart.

"How's that?" I asked, softening my voice and trying to muster real kindness.

Gladys took a sip and made a distasteful face. "It's not hot enough. I like my coffee hot."

"Should have made it scalding," I muttered as I turned to make a second trip back to the kitchen.

"What did you say?" Gladys asked in her crackly voice.

"I said 'it's all my fault,'" I replied.

"Yes, it is," she agreed.

I glanced back and saw that she was loudly declaring to her deaf neighbor how incompetent the staff was around here. I wonder if anyone will mean the nice things they say at her funeral, I thought.

A letter had come from Hank — one of his usual ones, full of witty little caricatures, and sparse in the way of news. "The scenery out here is so different — I keep thinking I'm on the set of *The Rockford Files,*" he wrote. I picture you getting annoyed with all the vegans and ordering hamburgers in front of them just to set 'em off. But it's obvious for those who live here, 'West is blest and east's the beast, and never the twain shall meet'" he wrote, slyly misquoting Kipling.

"Until Hollywood and Wall Street stand together, at God's great Judgment Seat," I wrote back, contributing to the parody rather wittily, I thought. "Someday I want to do a road trip out there." With you and our passel of neurotic kids, I thought to myself, coloring a little at the mix of humor and hope I harbored over this. I was not so blinded by *amore* to miss seeing how pathetic it was that I carried such a steady torch for Hank, and for so long. I'd really have preferred to be a femme fatale, spreading out my affection over multitudes of men, always leaving a trail of tears in my wake. But being a vamp didn't dovetail nicely with the Christian walk. And anyway, in my generation, it was a big health risk.

When I wasn't working or running or reading my Bible, I seemed to be spending a great deal of time conjugating German verbs. I pored over them in a lounge chair afternoons as I sunbathed, and stuck little post-it notes with German words and their English translations all over the bathroom mirrors and above the toilet roll.

A peculiar thought came into my mind that I should start learning Spanish. But I dismissed it almost as quickly as it entered, and didn't think much more about it.

Durst was hosting a forum on preparation for living abroad the following year, so one evening I drove back to campus, which, in summer now seemed like a ghost town. The forum was supposed to ease culture shock and I guess make sure the college kids weren't playing the role of "Ugly American" while they were overseas. There were six of us Americans headed there together, with all of us on various summer speech programs, eventually converging in the northern city of Bremen for our school year.

After a video, there was a question-and-answer segment hosted by two native German guys who were affiliated with the college. They were both named Klaus, and when I raised my hand at the end of the little film we saw, I asked what they could tell me about the specific region of southeastern Germany where I'd be going for my three-week summer language course.

"Bavaria? You're going to Bavaria? Haha! It's like the *Texas* of Germany," the larger Klaus laughed derisively.

"Well, what's the matter with Texas?" I said quietly, a little startled at the reaction my soon-to-be destination had gotten.

"They think they are their own little country, they have these awful accents . . ."

"They are so old-fashioned," Little Klaus added, smirking. "And wait till you see the traditional clothing they wear sometimes."

I couldn't tell if the Klauses were talking at this point about Texas or Bavaria, but it sounded charming to me. Some of my anxiety faded as I thought of going to Germany.

At the moment, my plans were to be away for eleven months. The German university term didn't end until July. My parents and I had talked about my flying home for Christmas, but the opportunity to travel the continent instead during this break might not come again, and even if it did, would be considerably cheaper now with a student rail pass.

Again the thought would come to me that I should learn Spanish. I had no idea why. But the thought was more insistent now — it wouldn't leave so easily. One evening after work, I went to the local library and checked out one of those book-and-CD sets that promises to make you speak like a native within a month, even if you're not very bright.

"Why are you learning Spanish?" my dad wanted to know, listening to me one night repeating after the cheerful señorita on CD. "Aren't you going to Germany in less than two months?"

"I don't know, I just feel like I should start," I replied.

"It makes sense to me to stick to one thing at a time, improving your German as much as possible since it's your major, and since you're going to be in the country for nearly a year. Besides, what if you start confusing the two?"

"You mean like I'd start speaking 'Spangerman'? I don't think it's likely. Spanish and Portuguese maybe might be easy to confuse, but German's too different, especially with their verbs coming at the end of the sentence half the time."

"Well," my dad shook his head in an act of resignation. "Do whatever suits you. It doesn't make sense to me, though."

It didn't make sense to me, either. But I continued plugging away at both the Spanish and the German.

A call from Caitlyn showed up on my cell phone one evening when I got out of work, but there was no message. I was surprised to see that she had called, as her hometown — and her boyfriend Dave — seemed to absorb her completely whenever we had a break.

Turning the key in the engine of my car, I dialed her right back.

"Caitlyn?"

"Molly? Molly, can I call you right back?"

"Okay," I agreed, letting my phone drop into the console.

My cell phone rang thirty seconds later.

"Hey, what's going on, Caitlyn?"

"Oh, not much."

"Yeah? How's your summer going?"

"Oh, pretty good. Um, listen . . . Molly? Would you want to come visit?"

"To your place in New Jersey? Yeah. Sure. When?"

"This weekend?"

"Can't. I have to work."

"Oh. Okay." She sounded really deflated.

"Caitlyn, you alright?"

"Um. Yeah. I'm sorry to bother you."

"Caitlyn, what's wrong?"

"Nothing, really. I'm sorry to trouble you, Molly. We'll catch up when it works better for you, 'kay?" Her voice had a note of false cheer about it.

"Caitlyn, *tell* me."

"I'm fine, I . . ." Caitlyn's voice cracked. "I think I might be pregnant."

Chapter Seven

The Waiting Game

I left the very next morning at seven, and spent the whole three hours to Caitlyn's house listening to worship music and praying for wisdom, and simultaneously imagining every horrible outcome in the world to the situation.

Would Caitlyn have to drop out of college? What would her parents do? Would Dave support her? He seemed like the steadfast type, but with this kind of pressure exerted on a relationship . . .

What if he *did* walk out on her? What if she got an abortion? What if she had to live with that scar for the rest of her life? What if *he* dropped out of college and they got married and they grew resentful and tired of each other?

I counted it the mercy of God not only that I'd found someone to take both my weekend shifts, but that my parents had miraculously not roadblocked my sudden and cryptic need to drive to New Jersey. Since this involved borrowing one of their cars, this forbearance towards me was even more surprising.

How I wished as the mile markers flew by that I could call Kendra and unburden my heart a bit, ask her to pray for me. But Caitlyn had begged me to promise not to say a word to another living soul, and I would honor that.

Anise would have been a comfort to have around, but her summer internship at the moment had her at a trade show in Chicago. And so there was me – inexperienced, inadequate little me – and God.

Any other time it would have been an adventure to be driving this far, to a place I'd never been, and all on my own. But as my car gradually slowed from the interstate to state roads, and finally to county routes as I neared Caitlyn's town, I barely perceived any of the scenery around me.

When I arrived at Caitlyn's home, she greeted me at the door with an edginess about her pretty face. She looked pale. Her eyes telegraphed gratitude at my coming, before I was whisked in front of her parents in a whirlwind introduction of strained pleasantries.

"We're heading out," Caitlyn called over her shoulder to them, grabbing the keys.

I held my breath as we got into her car and shut the doors. Not a word was spoken until we were a block away.

"Thank God you're here," she said, letting out a long breath. "I'm a wreck." She took a deep breath. I waited.

"I was late this month and you know I'm usually like clockwork. I also had some other . . . symptoms. So, yesterday I drove all the way to Chesterfield, which is twenty miles away, so no one I know would happen to bump into me buying a pregnancy test."

A car cut us off. Caitlyn swerved but otherwise didn't react.

"I bought two pregnancy tests. The first read negative. The second showed positive."

I quietly exhaled, only realizing then that I was barely breathing. "Have you told Dave yet?"

Caitlyn swallowed and looked straight ahead. I didn't think she had heard me, and I was about to repeat my question.

"Molly . . . it's not Dave's," Caitlyn said quietly.

I was shocked. But I said nothing.

"Senior week . . . well, you know Rob and I were kind of dating . . ."

Rob Ketchum – handsome, arrogant, and with more unearned money than he knew how to spend – had been a frequent fixture in our suite. He had left an unfavorable impression on both me and Anise. Caitlyn had defended him as a nice-when-you-get-to-know-him sort, but neither of us had

had much desire to know him better. I always secretly referred to him as Doorknob Rob to Anise.

I didn't know what to say in response to Caitlyn's bombshell. All I could think of was Uncle Billy in *It's a Wonderful Life* saying, "This is a pickle, George! *This-is a pickle!*"

"Molly, you *can't* tell a soul!"

"You know I won't." We were both silent for a moment. "Have you told Door- um, have you told Rob?"

"No. He's on vacation with his family in Nag's Head, and I haven't heard from him since he left last week. Besides, I didn't want to say anything until I'm one hundred percent sure."

"Are you going to take another pregnancy test?"

"I want to get a blood test. I don't know anything about this but I went online and found out that there are labs that will do the testing and get back to you within a day. But the closest one is in Philly. Will you go with me?"

"Of course."

Caitlyn let out a sigh of relief. "Thank God you're here. Besides, I can tell my parents we're going to the city and it won't look nearly so strange as if I were driving there by myself."

Caitlyn put a call in to her parents as we drove. I only half listened to the feigned lightheartedness of her explanation for our sudden road trip. I was praying.

You promised in James that if anyone lacks wisdom, we should simply ask. So I'm asking God, because I have no idea what to say or do that could possibly be helpful in this situation.

We didn't say much on the drive to Philadelphia. What is there to talk about when the direction of your whole life hinges on the outcome of a single, irreversible pronouncement of a lab test?

I helped Caitlyn navigate the unknown area we were driving through, until we finally reached a small, square building that looked somehow so formidable.

Inside, I waited while Caitlyn filled out a bunch of paperwork. There were several guys in the waiting room staring at her, but for the first time I can remember, she was completely unconscious of their attention.

It seemed like a whole day went by before a woman in a white coat called Caitlyn back. When Caitlyn stood up to go back with her, the woman gave me a questioning stare. "She's my best friend," Caitlyn explained, to my amazement.

It was only then that it occurred to me that Caitlyn could have asked any of her other close friends from home to come along with her. Likely, they knew Dave and so that might jeopardize her secret. Still, I was surprised at the confidence she obviously placed in me, among all the people that she might have asked to accompany her.

We made our way back to a tiny room where Caitlyn was given a ball to squeeze while a nurse tightened a tourniquet around her forearm. We both averted our eyes as the needle went in and the blood came out.

"You should receive a phone call within forty-eight hours," the nurse explained, writing something on a piece of paper and sticking it around the vial of blood.

"I don't know what I'm going to do with myself until then," Caitlyn moaned once we were outside, sitting there without starting her car. "This is like waiting for a death sentence to be overturned."

I wanted to tell her not to worry, that she shouldn't anticipate the worst. But how was that possible? How could anyone think of anything else in the world besides the prospect of an unexpected, unwanted pregnancy looming?

Evidently on the same wavelength, Caitlyn voiced my thoughts. "I have to walk myself through the worst possible scenario. I have to prepare myself for news that the test is positive."

"I'm with you all the way, Caitlyn. Whatever I can do, whatever happens."

"Molly . . ." Caitlyn started to say something then stopped. "Promise me you won't think I'm a terrible person."

"I would never think that," I assured her.

She took a deep breath. "I've been thinking. I mean, I could never ever get an abortion. I couldn't live with myself. Remember what happened with Karyn Helm?"

Karyn had been in our freshman class, and a rumor had gone around that she had gotten pregnant, but that she and the baby's father had gone somewhere and gotten rid of the baby during last year's winter break, before her parents could discover her pregnancy. She had suffered an emotional breakdown early into our sophomore year – a breakdown that those in her circle of companions had whispered was linked to her abortion.

"I've been wishing so badly that it was Dave and me facing this together – I mean, as tough as it would be, it'd be so much easier if it were *his*. I- . . . I know I've played the field a little at school, and have had a few different relationships . . . but I'm young and it's natural I'd want to have fun before settling down. I've always known that after I had my carefree season, Dave and I would end up together. And, well, if I *am* pregnant, what I'm trying to say is . . . well, there's no reason that Dave needs to think this baby is anyone's but his."

"Caitlyn!"

I saw her chin go up and her mouth tighten in a gesture that allowed for no dissuasion. She turned to look at me squarely. "Molly, you *swore* you'd keep my secret. You promised, and you can't say a word."

"You would let everyone involved in this situation believe a lie for the sake of not having to face consequences? You'd let Dave struggle to support you and then maybe someday even marry you based on a lie? Do you think that marriage could possibly be a success? Do you think you'd have even one moment's peace until your secret was exposed? Every time you so much as looked at Dave or at your child, you'd be hit with guilt!"

Caitlyn let out her breath, the sudden puff making her bangs flutter and then resettle.

"Not to mention the issue of practical things like medical history and—"

"Alright, Miss Has-It-All-Together," Caitlyn cut me off sharply. "What am I supposed to do? Have a miserable life trying to get child support and balance custody with a man whose only interest is in a college fling, and at the same time sacrifice the love of my life over one lousy mistake?" She burst into tears.

"Lord," I prayed silently. "Wisdom, please. *Now*, please."

I looked at her and the most tender and strong gentleness came over me. I took a deep breath. "Caitlyn, the Lord has a plan for your life. You're on His mind right now. He longs to take you in the shelter of His arms." My hand instinctively went to her arm. "I don't have the answers for the next year, or the next couple years, if things don't go the way that you had always pictured. But He has answers for every tough question you're facing now, and I know all His purposes for your life are good ones. Because *He* is good. He is beyond-our-wildest-imagination good."

She was still sobbing, and I rubbed her back for a few moments until they grew fainter.

"You know, God's a lot like this GPS. There's a destination, and the destination is *Him*. We take a wrong road, and it leads to a dangerous area, or a jam, or a dead end. Or else we're just hopelessly lost. But like the GPS, He's always meeting us where we're at, and always seeking to redirect us back to the original destination – to Him. He sees the whole picture, and we never run so far or so fast that we can lose Him. And whatever the hurdles, whatever the obstacles, He is ready to lead us to that good place of His presence."

Caitlyn sat quietly, sniffling a little, but not saying anything. I continued, "He says He'll give those who seek His face 'a crown of beauty in exchange for ashes, and a garment of praise instead of a spirit of despair.' His promises aren't just words on a page that mean nothing. He is as good as His word, and I know it firsthand."

"When I was little, my grandma used to tell me stories from the Bible." Caitlyn smiled, staring at some point in space past the steering wheel. "I still remember them. God seemed very real to me back then."

"He *is* real. He is real whether He seems like it or not. He is near whether it feels like it or not. And the God of those childhood stories is big enough to handle the grown-up problems of life. And not just to handle them, but to bring you through them with outcomes and blessings that you could never even dream up on your own without Him. He doesn't just help us with life. He *is* life."

Caitlyn grabbed a tissue from the console and blew her nose. She sighed. Slowly, she sank her silky hair back against the headrest. "I'm not going to try to fool Dave. I'm scared and I guess I'm just being really selfish about this."

I quietly released the breath I hadn't realized I'd been holding.

She started the ignition. "You want to get something to eat? All of a sudden I feel hungry."

"Sure," I replied.

"Molly? Thanks for being a good friend."

*****

The rest of that day and night, Caitlyn continued to ask me questions about God and about my faith. She would be focused on that for a while, and then she would withdraw and I could tell she was shifting back to her immediate problem.

Her mind seemed to be on a pendulum, swing back and forth between her circumstances and her Creator.

We were lounging outside the next day, sunbathing, me reading a book and Caitlyn paging restlessly through magazines, when her cell rang. She drew herself up tightly on the chair as she saw the number on the phone screen, and her voice shook a little as she answered it.

"Yes? Yes, this is Caitlyn . . . Yes . . . Are you sure? Alright. Alright, thanks."

I watched all this with a tight chest. She slowly sank backward into her lounge chair, covering her face with her palms. She rocked back and forth, ever so slowly. Finally, her voice came out, muffled, from within the tent of her hands. "Molly. Molly, the test came back. It was negative. I'm not pregnant."

*****

I drove home praying that this open door – Caitlyn's vulnerability, and then oceanic relief and gratitude – wouldn't swing shut before the Lord could do a work of redemption in her life. It seemed that people turned to God for crisis intervention, but then forgot Him as soon as the danger passed. Just like the Israelites of old, we hadn't seemed to gain much in the area of steadfastness. I'd told Caitlyn I was available at any time to talk with her more, and suggested if she was interested, she might want to get connected with a local church in her area, which Durst's fellowship might be able to help with, as there were some Christian students in her area. I figured that the next step was hers, wishing desperately for her to take it, but realizing that the measure of her spiritual appetite wasn't something that I could control.

When I returned to Pennsylvania, there was a message awaiting me in my inbox from the editor of the satire web site to which I'd submitted samples of my writing. It said:

"Eliza Emma-Gee. Terrific work. Show us more. Please submit an article on a hot topic of your choice. And welcome to the staff!"

It was signed Paul de Sanguine

I did a little dance around the room. Then I sat down to let the creative juices run as I thought of my first piece. They loved my work. I was no doubt a genius. Probably I'd have a career in this and make millions. The snobs from school would weep and gnash their teeth at the thought that they weren't nicer to me when they had the chance. The world was a shining, beautiful place. I did a back flop of exuberance onto my bed.

Since I was lying down, maybe I'd just stay there for a few moments. Maybe just close my eyes a little. I hadn't realized how utterly exhausted I was until just that moment, from all the driving, but also from the emotional rollercoaster of the weekend.

*****

One evening, visiting Kendra's church, I was challenged by one of the Bible teachers who likened reading commentaries or books *about* the Bible as baby food. Somebody else had processed it for consumption. Sometimes the starter food was necessary, but a strong, satisfying element of chewing and savoring was lost which could only be experienced from reading the Word firsthand. This challenged me, and this same person had given Kendra some guidelines on meditating on scripture which I was now following, like a toddler taking her first steps without holding on to someone's hands.

That week, I was reading through the gospel of John – carefully, savoring each verse like a morsel. Sparks seemed to be flying off the pages whenever Jesus spoke. It seemed now when I read my Bible that I was seeing things in very familiar passages for the very first time. This was not the Jesus of my

Sunday school classes. At least, not how I had come to know Him, as the calm, serene, unruffled Jesus who floated from one distant spot to another, even-keeled and stoic, teaching good. The Jesus I encountered now in the gospels was in-your-face, polarizing, astonishing, sometimes seemingly tactless; and yet at the same time He was captivating, irresistible, deeply emotional, compassionate, and tender-hearted.

But there was a disconnect somewhere. As I read about what Jesus said and did in the gospels, and what He commissioned His disciples to do, it was worlds away from what our Sunday church services resembled – and in fact taught. Rather, church seemed to be spiritual culture shock after reading the Bible. It reminded me of an episode of *Star Trek* in which governing documents had been left behind on a planet, but years later when the crew returned, the natives had taken the wisdom of the documents and used them selectively so that there was almost no resemblance to what the founder had wished them to be. Not only that, they had twisted the truths in such a way that those who were to benefit from their freedom instead were enslaved.

The Christianity of my home church – and so many other churches I'd visited over the years – seemed to be boiled down to a "do good, try harder" mentality. There were so many people who were willing to show love to the downtrodden through service projects and other sacrificial acts – which were all noble ideas – yet few if any, myself included, were doing what Jesus spent most of *His* time doing, and which He specifically commissioned His disciples to do in Matthew: heal the sick, raise the dead, cleanse the lepers, and cast out demons.

There was no way to win an argument in my mind that Jesus somehow didn't mean what He said – that we were just to disregard His commission and His example and instead serve the gospel buffet style, with the main dishes being good deeds done in the flesh, lightly sprinkled with some watered-down tidbits from the Sermon on the Mount.

First John 3:8 confirmed this, in that it stated "the reason the Son of God appeared was to destroy the works of the devil." If we were already in His kingdom, according to Colossians, then it wasn't a matter of waiting to destroy those works until Heaven. It was time for Jesus' followers – His church – to access that power now.

Increasingly, I grew troubled over this disconnect. I knew that my own church was committed to helping the poor through dinners and food drives and donations and everything else. Many families had benefited from our service within the community. Plus, we supported overseas missions. It was good stuff. But where was this core commissioning of Jesus? What was the church doing that couldn't be done by the local civic organizations? And why had I grown up in the church and never saw any of this in the Bible until *after* I'd fallen away from my faith and returned?

One summer night after I'd been pondering all these questions, I woke up in a sweat from a vivid dream in which there were all these babies crawling and playing on the floor. They were gurgling and smiling and cooing and trying to stand. Suddenly, from out of nowhere, cats appeared and began pouncing on the babies, knocking them to the ground, biting them and causing them to wail. My pastors – both the college pastor and my home church pastor – were in the dream, too, but they stood there, distracted and talking, as the cats came. I lunged toward the nearest cat, and as I grabbed it, saw to my revulsion that it was oozing pus. I flung it away from the babies with all my might, and in doing so, awoke from the dream with a gasp.

Chapter Eight

Revelation

Despite my eyes being opened to scripture in a brand new way, living at home seemed to bring out the sinful nature in me pretty quickly with my attitude toward my parents. After being away at school, the home environment felt constraining again, even though I wasn't living like a wild child. My parents and I regularly bumped heads. While I loved them, I felt like I spent most of my breaks anticipating the moment that I could get away from them again.

Kendra had invited me to attend a two-day conference with her in July, to be held not far from where we lived. It was to be replete with worship leaders and speakers who were all grand poobahs of the Christian faith, or at least that's how I interpreted what she told me. She was beyond excited at the prospect of our attending; I was going with only the sincere hope that it wouldn't be cheesy.

I had no reason to suspect that it would be goofy, except that I pictured some of the people I occasionally saw on Christian television speaking, and not all of them came across as very, well, *humble* as Christians ought to be. If these people were Christian celebrities, would they smell of Hollywood?

The conference was held in the large, bare rectangle of a conventional hall, rather than a church. The worship music lasted for almost an hour, and then the first speaker was introduced for the morning segment.

She took the microphone but did not speak. She did not even look at the audience. She stood there for several moments, head down, with four thousand pairs of eyes glued to her. Then, wiping her eyes, she knelt to the floor. We waited. The worship band was no longer playing, so there was just silence. Four thousand people, and no cleared throats, no coughs, no pages rustling, no whispers. It was a loaded, charged silence. I closed my eyes.

All of a sudden, I had an overwhelming awareness of the presence of the Holy Spirit. I became aware that people were praying — whispering — communicating worship to Heaven. The room was filled with a low, sustained hum. It grew louder, and then it had different pitches in it. The sound was otherworldly, and reminded me of the string section being brought into tune by the conductor of a Broadway performance I'd seen. Exuberance. Expectation. Exaltation. I simply lifted my hands, palms upward, in an act of worship. Silently, I began to pray.

After an unknown amount of time had gone by, the woman began to speak. She was praying, fervently, passionately, sometimes half-singing the words into her microphone, and she was praying the exact same thoughts to God that were in my mind at that moment. When she had finished, she paused and then addressed all of us. "Sometimes," she said, "it's a lot easier just to start talking than it is to wait on Him."

As she asked us to open our Bibles and she spoke out of the gospels, her words hit my spirit like rain drops pelting the dry earth after a long drought.

The rest of the day went that way, with me sitting on the edge of my chair, face lifted, drinking up the words that seemed to be falling right out of Heaven. It was so good to imbibe something so refreshing — like taking a single sip of cool water after being in the heat, and when it goes down your throat you realize suddenly how parched you really were, and you just want to guzzle.

At lunch, Kendra sighed and said, "Isn't it wonderful hearing such anointed teaching? It seems like so many times we get spoon-fed doctrine and *good ideas* and five-step programs in our churches. Sometimes, a whole sermon can come to a close without hearing the name Jesus. This — what's been spoken today — this is *life*."

When we returned from lunch, praise music was playing. Kendra excused herself to return a phone call, and I sat there alone, raptly taking in the music.

"Excuse me, Miss?"

I turned to stare into hazel eyes with kind lines around the perimeter of the lids. They belonged to a gray-haired man whom I'd never seen before. Beside him stood a woman of about the same age.

"Yes?" I answered.

"I'm Tom. This is my wife Charlotte, and we're part of the ministry team here. May I ask, do you have a gift for learning languages?"

Surprised, I looked around to see if Kendra had directed him to me. She was just outside the conference hall, smiling and gesturing on her cell phone in her usual animated way, oblivious to me and these people.

"Um, yes. Well, sort of," I replied.

The man's friendly smile widened. "I happened to see you sitting here, and as I looked at you, sensed the Lord giving me a word of knowledge. Would you mind if we prayed with you?"

I nodded, not sure what to think of these amiable strangers.

When Tom and Charlotte began praying, salt water started squeezing out from under my eyelids. I wasn't sure why, because nothing that they said was particularly sad. They were praising God and thanking Him for my life, for my compassionate heart, for the next leg of the journey I'd soon be embarking on. Things they could have known nothing about, but were praying as if they were old friends with a roadmap of my life. I wiped my eyes.

Charlotte said, "I sense this gifting in languages He's given you is to fulfill a specific ministry. It will be used to bridge a gap between peoples and cultures to advance His kingdom. You will be a spiritual parent to many international children."

As we were driving home that night, Kendra and I went over and over all the delights of the day, from the worship to the rich teaching, to the testimony of someone who had professed to being barely able to walk without agony when he came in on account of back pain, but who bent over to touch his toes.

"I just can't figure it out though," I said to Kendra. "How did that guy know about me and foreign languages?"

"He was given a word of knowledge," Kendra explained.

"Yes, I know that's what he said," I replied a little impatiently. "What does that mean?"

"Well, I'm still learning about this, but I think it's a manifestation of the Spirit."

"Kendra. *What* is a manifestation of the Spirit? My knack for languages isn't going to help me much when I can't understand English."

"It's like a visible evidence of something that is spiritual."

"Okay. I'm following you now at a comfortable distance."

"Manifestations are talked about in one of the letters to the Corinthians, I think."

I searched my Bible for several minutes, then let out an "*aha!*"

"First Corinthians 12," I announced. "Here it is."

I read the whole chapter out loud. Then I turned to Kendra slowly. "Do you realize that I have heard the second half of this chapter – on the members of the body – preached and taught probably twenty dozen times in my life, in Sunday school and in church and on retreats and at lock-ins and at Bible camp . . . and do you also know that I have never *ever* not even once heard the first half of this chapter – verses one through eleven even mentioned?"

Kendra just looked at me, waiting. I stared back at my Bible. "No wonder I had no clue what a 'manifestation' was."

That night, I read the whole chapter 12 of I Corinthians, from the first verse to the last, over and over and over again. And as I did, something else dawned on me.

The next morning, as we drove for the second day of the conference, I recapped my findings to Kendra. "Why is it that every sermon, lesson, devotional, you-name-it I've heard or been taught or read on the members of the body has been boiled down to something like, 'I'm the member of the body who takes out the trash at the church, and even though I don't preach, my job as a hand is just as important as the mouth.' That's not the context of this passage at all."

Kendra nodded slowly. "You mean, like the people teaching this passage are treating spiritual gifts as though they are a set of job skills . . . or natural abilities."

"Exactly." I ran my fingers through my hair and rapped the car window restlessly with my knuckles. "I'm starting to get a vague sense that we've missed out on something really wonderful and really valuable, and been given something cheap instead. I don't just mean with this one passage of scripture. I mean church in general." I gazed out the window, pondering it. "It's like a woman finding out suddenly after many years of marriage, the diamond her guy gave her was just an imitation. But it wasn't the *husband's* fault – he had paid for the real thing – just somehow in the transaction, someone else had slipped in a fake. And for a long time was able to pass it off as the real thing."

Chapter Nine

Milestone

The second day of our conference was even greater than the first. I felt like the water had seeped down deep into my soul and satiated some languishing, desolate places, and yet it had made me thirsty for even more.

The worship was different than what I was used to. It wasn't about contemporary or traditional, because both kinds of songs and hymns were part of these segments. The worship, the leaders emphasized, was about offering a sacrifice to God – about honoring *Him* and singing of *His* great worth, and ministering to the Lord first. It flowed freely, and on different occasions someone sang a spontaneous song, with the instruments effortlessly harmonizing with the vocals. Having attended old-fashioned hymn sings, as well as eardrum-dulling Christian rock concerts, it was evident that both forms of praise could be more about the music than it was sincere, heartfelt worship to God.

I sat through the second day of the conference awestruck by the testimonies of the various speakers. Many of them shared about supernatural encounters, about healings they'd witnessed firsthand, and miracles. What struck me perhaps even more than these claims was the offhand, matter-of-fact way that these ministers of the gospel described the specific people and places with whom they had worked. It was very second nature to them to be working in the supernatural. For myself, I don't know if I had ever once seen something happen that defied the laws of nature. Were the testimonies of these people to be completely trusted?

Though I myself had not experienced a miracle by definition, I did not harbor cynicism or scorn towards their stories. Something in my spirit believed that this was entirely possible in today's times. I had heard a story once long ago from one of the elders in our church who shared how he was working on a building that had a faulty roof, when a great storm came up. He cried out to God not to let there be damage done to the interior of the property on which he was working, and he testified that it poured down rain for miles that one afternoon, but there was a perimeter of about half an acre all around the homestead on which he was working that was completely dry and untouched. There was no other accounting for it, he testified, than the hand of God.

Of course, in other countries people always seemed to be claiming miracles. A friend who'd gone on a mission trip to Ghana had once shared about a woman from the village church who had AIDS. She had tested positive for it several times in the local clinic. Later she was introduced to the gospel, and then asked those who shared it with her to pray for her for healing. She went back to get tested at the local clinic, and after two times, her results showed negative – no AIDS. She took the test again and again and still, it was AIDS-free. The missionaries said that day after day, she stood outside the village clinic, waving her old medical tests and her new ones, loudly praising God and testifying to other patients of God's healing power and faithfulness.

To me, the most thrilling stories coming out of the conference that day were about Muslims all over the world. One speaker, with an international ministry, said that Muslims by the thousands were being saved after having dreams of and visitations by Jesus. He told a story of one town, where all these Iranians had a dream on the same night in which they were told to come to the town's center and they would receive the bread of life. One by one they individually left their homes and quietly converged at the city square just before one in the morning. Meanwhile, on the same night a man smuggling Bibles into the country was driving by cover of night, when suddenly, his car broke down . . . right in the middle of that same town where everyone had come out to receive the bread of life.

"Why haven't we heard about any of these things?" I whispered to Kendra at one point. "All these mind-blowing testimonies going on around the world, and I've never heard even a hint at anything like this!"

"I don't know," Kendra shook her head. "Do you suppose the pastors even know about this?"

"Maybe not. This blows away what we usually get on a Sunday."

Amid all the wow factors of the conference, one of the messages that stayed with me most was from a man who talked about thanksgiving. He explained that since the Old Testament was a shadow of the substance that was to come with Christ and His New Covenant, according to Hebrews 10, that the sacrifices that were made by the ancient Hebrews still have implications for us today.

Specifically, one of the sacrifices was for thanksgiving, and it was usually made in the form of unleavened cakes and wafers. When the people made their sacrifices, it was an act of obedience to God, an act of worship, and a spiritual transaction took place there at the altar.

"The reality for believers today is that choosing to give thanks, particularly when it is difficult to give it, is a sacrifice to God in which a spiritual transaction still takes place," said the reverend. "It's not just empty words mouthed to the air. Words of thanksgiving can transform us, as well as our situations. Where bitterness could take root, thanksgiving is a marvelous means of releasing anger and redirecting our energy and our outlook. Along with that, thanksgiving releases power in the heavenly realm to see our prayers answered. Philippians 4:6 tells us to 'be anxious for nothing, but in everything by prayer and supplication *with thanksgiving* let your requests be made known to God.'"

He said a whole lot more about the power of thanksgiving, and had told some story about a woman in his church who'd had a rotten boss who stank up her life. She made a choice to "give thanks in all circumstances, as this is God's will in Christ Jesus" and instead of muttering complaints or curses about her boss, or even thinking them, she began to thank the Lord for this knucklehead in her life. She thanked God for having a job in the first place. She thanked Him for being healthy enough to work. Two weeks later, the boss broke down at work over a personal problem and went to *her* to ask for prayer (even though the boss wasn't a believer). She had an opportunity to testify and tell him how the gospel had affected her life, and he listened. He kept asking her questions about Jesus, and two weeks after *that*, he confessed his belief in Christ and asked about finding a church and getting baptized.

There were parts of the conference that were downright noisy, and a little unrestrained. There was some laughter, there was some loud praising. I saw one girl in front of me go down like a sack of potatoes when someone had prayed over her. One older woman who claimed to be healed of a spine condition actually sprinted the perimeter of the conference room, hollering hallelujahs. Kendra explained to me later that this was one of the reasons church people often discouraged the presence of the Holy Spirit – He could really upset the propriety associated with good church behavior.

Seeing the small, elderly woman running laps and whooping it up burned like a brand on my mind. She was so exuberant, so undignified in her celebration. This must have been how the paralytics and the lepers and the blind reacted after Jesus healed them. It was why the man at the Temple Beautiful didn't just bow his head, mutter a "thank you," and shuffle home. Propriety – personal pride – wasn't even a thought in the face of God's kingdom bursting suddenly into their lives.

*****

The conference marked a milestone in my life. I felt as though a door had opened, and after traveling many years through a rather narrow, confined tunnel, I was suddenly standing in a spacious place. I could suddenly see around me, and I could breathe.

People sometimes say, "God is everywhere. You don't have to *go* somewhere special to meet Him." While that is true, without having the words to describe what I was sensing, I was coming into the distinct knowledge that it was possible to experience much more of Him than what I'd imagined possible most of my life. There were people who carried His presence more strongly than others, and so there must be congregations where His presence was more noticeable, too. To say that God was everywhere and therefore we shouldn't go places to seek out His presence was almost like saying, "You don't need to go to the pool on a 98-degree day. There's water at your house." Yes, I could splash myself with some droplets and it would be better than nothing . . . but it would be much more satisfying to take a refreshing plunge into a place of total submersion.

This wave of glory carried over into Sunday morning, and I couldn't wait to share with our young adult Sunday school class some of the things I'd heard and experienced.

"Isn't that amazing?" I asked, after recounting the story of the woman who was miraculously healed of a back problem. To my wonder, stares and half-smiles from my fellow young adults were the response to my story. I felt my grin evaporating.

"Sounds like you had quite the experience," was all that my Sunday school teacher said, brightly and uncertainly.

My exuberance ebbed a little in the face of this lukewarm response. But I was too fired up to be quenched entirely.

In the service, I sang the worship songs as loudly as my voice would allow. Never did I mean the words more. And as I sang, a picture formed in my mind of God seated on His throne. The cherubim and seraphim were encircling Him, their eyes covered by their wings. Angels and saints, like waves of grain as far as the eye could see, were all worshiping before the throne. The stars and planets were circling Him, and they too were pouring forth their praise! The picture was too dazzling. Tears jutted out the sides of my eyelids – wrecked again!

If the worship brought us into His presence, the sermon pushed us away. Pastor Steve put a chart on the overhead that talked about how to grow the church. He showed a graph that had been taken from a business model that the bishop was using. He didn't open his Bible once. When he was through, he gave a short, perfunctory prayer asking God to bless and multiply our congregation. We sang the last song in a kind of anemic monotone, as though all the life had been sucked out of the service in between the opening music and then.

After it was over, a lady named Jeanette came over to ask me if I was okay. She'd glimpsed me getting weepy in the opening worship. She was one of my mom's friends, and had a little girl who sat in back of me sometimes and kicked the pew.

"Oh. Yeah. I'm fine," I smiled. "I just get just a glimpse of Him, and I can't handle it. He's so beautiful."

Jeanette smiled kindly but looked puzzled.

On the way out the door, I saw Pastor Steve.

"How have you been, Molly?"

"Really great, Pastor Steve." I eagerly told him a little bit about the conference I'd attended.

"Oh. Yes. I'm familiar with those guys," he said when I answered his question about who had organized it. He had a tiny smile that made my heart sink.

"Have you been to one of their conferences, or heard any of them preach?" I asked.

"No. But I'm familiar with their ministries." He paused, searching for his next words. "We need to be *careful* that what we're attracted to with certain people or churches isn't just emotionalism."

I considered the statement. I didn't know what it meant. What was emotionalism? Did it mean too much happiness? Or did it mean happiness without substance? If that were the case, I wouldn't want emotionalism either. But that wasn't what I had just experienced those two days at the conference.

On the other hand, were Pastor Steve and other people who were wary of emotionalism as *careful* of the alternative? Blank, joyless faces – that must be non-emotionalism. And what was the substance behind these stoic facades? Did a staid, Vulcan-like posture indicate more faith than the joyful, more demonstrative people?

Moreover, had these people who fretted over emotionalism ever experienced the presence of God on them so heavy that they wondered whether they could survive it?

Emotions were real. They were God-given. So how was it possible not to be overflowing with joy after having an encounter with the Lord? I thought of those old-time photos you see in which the husband and wife are captured on their wedding day, standing there grim and gray as statues. "We're in love and our lives are now joined together. Let's not get caught looking happy – it's not dignified."

As I left church, I felt a little like a steamroller had gone over my soul.

*****

"You really could do *something* to help out around here," my mom bellowed, spiking a dishtowel onto the counter.

I rolled my eyes. *Here we go again. Fireworks at* our *house.*

"You come home from work and turn on that computer and you're just oblivious to the fact that there are other people besides you who live in this house!"

Buffalo gals won't you come out tonight? Won't you come out tonight? I sung in my head. I began to whistle quietly.

"Are you listening to me? Why can't you lend just a *little* help around this house? It's not *my* job to serve you."

"Why do you wait until I come home tired and try to pick a fight with me?" I asked crossly. *What do you do when I'm away at college and there's no one to verbally assault?*

"Oh, *you're* tired!" my mom increased her volume. "I work too, you know, and when I come home, the trash is overflowing and the grass needs to be cut and the bathroom's a wreck, and if I don't do it, it doesn't get done!"

"Agh, I can't take this," I said, going back the hallway, hands over my head. "Leave me a list of what needs done and I'll do it tomorrow."

"There are things that can't wait until tomorrow – the lawn should have been taken care of days ago. I want you to go out and cut that grass now."

I knew I had procrastinated on that one but I was so stinkin' tired from being on my feet eight hours at Shady Oaks, hustling all day, and all I wanted to do was sink into a chair. Aggravated, I expressed my frustration at this order by slamming my bedroom door as I went to dig out my grubby shoes to mow.

When I emerged from my room, stomping down the hall in my rubbery-tough old sneakers, stained lime-green from mowing, I caught a glimpse of Anne kind of cowering in the doorway of her room. She reminded me of some frightened little animal, and seeing her fearful expression intensified my annoyance.

"Oh Anne, go mind your own business," I snapped.

Her lip quivered and her eyes suddenly overflowed. She hastily shut her door and I could hear a sob break loose.

Dang it all. Anne was so sensitive. She always got emotional when other people argued.

I went outside and started the mower with a vengeance. I mowed the lawn recklessly and rapidly, heaving and throwing the mower this way and that, causing it to sputter at times and miss whole patches of grass now and then. When I was about halfway through, all my anger got burned up in energy loss and I just felt weary.

"God, what happened?" I asked. "How did I go from being a disciple to a dumbass so quickly? Why do I soar to a new place with you, only to crash back to the earth? I think my life would be a lot more pleasing to you if I didn't have to live in this house."

All I could hear was the drone of the mower.

As I finished the yard, I conceded that I needed to go ask forgiveness from my mom and Anne. But I still was perplexed as to how I fell so fast and so far.

Chapter Ten

Close Encounters

Government encourages smoking in order to fund public health care

Both federal and state governments are launching an ad campaign to encourage Americans to begin smoking in order to fund the massively expensive health care program.

Since both the state and federal government benefit immensely from the sale of cigarettes, with states such as New York reaping as much as $5 per carton, the government is counting on more Americans to pick up the nicotine habit.

"With downsizing and so many cuts at the state level, we thought this was a wonderful way to keep people in their jobs, and provide health care for the poorest Americans," health department spokeswoman Diane Doohickey explained.

"Since the majority of Americans who smoke are poor — those living below the poverty line — then really the poor are funding their own health care by smoking. But since the system has so many demands on it now with socialized health care, we really need other Americans to join them and do their part to carry the tax burden that cigarettes provide. We're asking every American to step up and smoke! Only that way can we give people the most extensive health care out there."

I read over my work one more time and then sent it sailing through cyberspace to Paul de Sanguine. He had begun paying me a tiny commission for my articles via an online account, thanks to the advertising dollars flowing to the site. It was a strange culture indeed, I thought, to be earning currency by poking fun at one's culture, and then getting the payment from someone with whom you'd never even spoken. In fact, I didn't even know his real name.

Paul had also been zipping short, goofy emails to me here and there. His language could tend toward the colorfully coarse, but he was so funny I was inclined to overlook the way he seasoned his writing with tidbits of profanity.

When he'd asked me to send a photo of myself for the site, I responded by attaching a head shot of Mae West instead.

"I get the sense he might be flirting with me," I told Kendra. "Or at least he's wondering what I look like to see if it's worth his efforts to flirt."

Kendra made a face. "Did you tell him about Hank?"

"Not yet. I'm waiting for a graceful way to slip in that I'm planning to marry a boy who is currently living three thousand miles away, and who hasn't asked me out."

Kendra was experiencing her own romantic advances in the form of a dental student who had invited her to his church, then to a Christian concert, and then to the National Day of Prayer at the community park. He'd put the moves on her in the front seat of his car when they got back in from praying.

"I had no *idea* he was such a toad!" she told me about it later.

Mystified, I tried to imagine no-nonsense Kendra in such a position.

"What did you do?" I asked.

"I yelled, 'Unhand me, you beast, or I'll scream!' and he did."

I laughed out loud at the picture. "Well, now we know what *he* was praying for," I remarked.

"Molly, it's not funny," she exclaimed.

I straightened my smile.

"Anyway, I'm not that disappointed to see the relationship go. He had this habit of clearing his throat a lot when he was nervous that got to be pretty distracting." She thought about it a minute. "I should have known that something was up that night after the concert, because in the car he started clearing his throat like crazy, and I kept waiting for him to *say* something hugely important, and then . . ."

Meanwhile, I had decided to implement the teaching I'd heard at the conference on thanksgiving, and just start thanking God for all those things in life I usually took for granted: my eyesight, a job, education, health, lasagna, friends, public tennis courts, hot water, not living in fear of secret police or terrorists raiding our houses and church services, etc. It was amazing when I began to thank the Lord consciously for all these wonderful things how quickly I would begin to see how blessed I truly was, and the hang-ups that had snagged me and made me grouchy appeared so ridiculous.

"No wonder God hates complaining. He must find it especially detestable in Americans," I wrote about it to Hank. "Us with all our wealth and comfort and resources."

"Without a doubt, Americans do it best," Hank had replied.

I had written him about the conference, telling him some of the impressions I had, but I'd elaborated even more on the tepid reaction my stories had produced in the church friends I'd seen that Sunday. Hank had written something in his reply that really struck me.

"The same people who might be welcoming to a visitor that has eggplant-colored hair and a labret, or who would overlook the smell of cigarettes, might have a lot more trouble with someone who's oozing the supernatural power of God," he'd written in his guy-scrawl.

After I'd read his letter, I turned his words over and over in my mind, inadvertently assigning them to various people I knew at my home church and wondering whether Hank's analysis held up.

At Shady Oaks, I came armed to face Gladys with thanksgiving.

"How are you this morning, Gladys?" I asked. "Beautiful day today, isn't it?"

Gladys grunted.

Thank you for my job, Lord. Thank you that I work in a place that's air-conditioned.

"You can take this toast away. It tastes like buttered cardboard."

Thank You, Jesus, that I don't have bunions. "All right, Gladys. Can I get you anything else?"

"No."

Thank You for Gladys' life. Thank You that You have me in her life for a reason and that You dealt with difficult people, too. Thank You that You love her and have thoughts that are specific to her.

"Well, sorry about the toast," I apologized, as I whisked it away.

"Bad enough the workers here are so flaky. You'd think that at least they could get these little things right," I overheard Gladys loudly pronounce to her semi-deaf tablemate. I paused for a moment as I walked toward the swinging kitchen door, stung. Then, slowly I marched to the kitchen and began mechanically scraping the dishes. I dabbed at the corners of my eyes with the starched sleeve of my uniform. I'd traded my armor of sarcasm for one of tenderness, and the barb she'd thrown had actually nicked me. Grumplestiltskin had made me cry. Imagine that.

I was sorely tempted to thank God that Gladys was in the last years of her life, but I rejected this thought as ungodly.

Anyway, Jesus was pleased if I was "a doer of the word, and not just a hearer." It was all that mattered.

*****

Germany was coming closer. I would get butterflies in my stomach as I read through the cultural tips and then the itinerary of my summer immersion course that was designed to refine my language skills. My passport with its unflattering photo became a reality, and the sticky notes of German words were steadily growing into a wallpaper over the toilet roll dispenser.

Anne had found a tourist's pamphlet of "useful German phrases" published in the 1980s and we had read over it and laughed ourselves sick in the stomach at the illustrations and totally non-useful phrases.

"Have you a shady place?" the tourist dad in his itty-bitty swim trunks and tube socks asked the smiling proprietor of a lake resort. "Have you a bucket and spade?" asked the tourist mom with helmet hair.

"Who would ask those things in *English?*" Anne wanted to know.

"What they really want to ask is, 'Which way to the nude beach,' and 'Show me the Biergarten,'" I observed.

One evening in early August, Hank called from California.

"I know it's a long shot, but I had this crazy notion," he said. "My internship's coming to an end, and I found out I'll have a chance to feature a series I did on scratchboard at a local exhibit. I wondered if you would want to come out here to be my guest for the event."

My heart stopped. Holding the phone with one hand, I struck my chest with the other and it started again.

"Molly?"

"Oh. Well, yeah. Yes. Um, I mean, maybe."

"I thought maybe if there was a ridiculously cheap flight you could fly out next week. If you could get the flight, I'll take care of all the costs of course once you get out here."

Hank . . . in Los Angeles . . . and a guest at his art show . . . strange how you could dream about someone far away and in a certain setting, and when reality came it could be so much wilder than you imagined. Usually, it worked the other way. But this—

"Thanks for thinking of me," I said slowly, hoping my voice sounded normal and not two octaves too high. "How about I look into it and I'll get back to you."

I waltzed into the kitchen where my mom was peeling potatoes.

"I might be going to L.A. next week," I said, sashaying across the tile and nearly colliding with her, before doing a twirl. I stopped and tottered on my feet, slightly dizzy.

"What? What do you mean?"

I told her about Hank's phone call.

She smiled. "Well, I see you're pretty excited. But before you get your hopes up, I need to talk to about it with Dad."

"Talk about what," I said flatly.

"Well, I want to ask what he thinks of it. That's all."

"Um, are you suggesting there is a possibility that I might be outlawed from making this trip?"

"Molly, please don't look so upset. All I'm saying is, I want to discuss it with him."

My heart, which had raced at first glimpse of Hank's name coming across my phone, then stopped for a moment after his announcement, now seemed to be doing a slow, doleful dirge.

I went back to pace in my room like a defendant awaiting the sentence of a deliberating jury until my dad got home. This was ridiculously unfair! I was twenty years old, not some little kid! How could they suggest they had a say in this decision? I tried to put my outrage aside long enough to pray as hard as I could.

Two agonizing hours later, my dad knocked on my door and asked me to come out to the living room. I could tell by the looks on their faces that they'd conspired to ruin my life.

"Molly, your mom told me about this trip to California. What kind of airfare rates have you found?"

"Well, I'm still looking."

"What's the cheapest you've found so far?"

"Around three hundred dollars." (With taxes and fees, it was rounding up closer to four hundred).

"Since we're paying for most of your college, and an extra chunk for this summer speech course, I don't think it's wise for you to miss several days of work *plus* spend so much of your earnings on airfare. Are you even going to be able to get off work on such short notice?"

"If I can't get off work, I'll just quit Shady Oaks. I'm going to be gone for a year anyhow." I heard my own voice and it kind of had a whine to it. I was getting panicky.

"Quit without giving notice to an employer who's been good to you, been flexible with your school schedule? Don't you think that's a poor way to treat someone?"

"Dad, let me at least see if I can get off work. This is such an amazing opportunity – I mean, California! If I can't go out there, I won't be able to survive the disappointment!"

"I'm sorry, Molly. It's just too much with you about to leave for Europe in a few weeks."

I stared at my parents in disbelief, looking from one face to another. Finally, I whispered, "I don't think I can *ever* forget this one." I whirled around and stomped back to my room, shattered.

That night I couldn't sleep. Too much raw emotion, and I wondered if I might explode from the violent concoction of resentment, disillusionment but also surprised elation at the fact that Hank had wanted me to be a part of his big moment.

"I want to smash something," I told Kendra the next evening as we met for a run. "Maybe if I could wreck something — like a car — in a demolition derby. *That* would help."

"Did you tell Hank?"

"Yep. Called him while I was driving over here."

"What did you tell him?"

"I couldn't tell Hank that my parents overruled me. Twenty years old, but mummy and daddy said 'no.' So, I just said I couldn't swing it this time. That I realized I had too much to do in these last weeks before leaving, and as wonderful as it sounded, it wasn't practical."

"Oh. Did you tell him you were disappointed?"

"Well, I feel like my life's over. I couldn't tell him *that* exactly. But I'm sure he could hear the disappointment in my voice."

"How did *he* take the news?"

"Pretty much in stride," I replied honestly. "He didn't sound as though my not being able to fly out there was the end of *his* life."

"I'm sorry, Moll."

"Yeah. Me, too. It's going to take a while to get over the disappointment of this one. I feel like all my life my parents have had this heavy hand over me. When I was younger, I could understand it a little better. But now that I'm an adult, they use tuition and other monetary things to strong-arm my life for me. Why can't they just let me do what I want now and then, even if I make some mistakes? Isn't that how we're supposed to learn? They expect me to be a grown-up, yet they keep me on such a short leash. I can't wait for the day that I'm no longer subject to their totalitarianism."

Kendra laughed. "Is it really as bad as that?"

"In this situation it sure feels that way."

"But at least you'll get to see Hank right before you leave for Europe?"

"Yes, at least there's that. He'll be home for three days before I take off. Whoop-dee-do."

*****

Paul de Sanguine was making a road trip to New York, and he wanted to "meet the mind behind the headlines" who contributed to his site. He wondered if he could make a quick stop-off in Pennsylvania on his way.

Naturally, I fancied he might be a psychopath. But I agreed to meet him. I was curious about him, too, having interacted with him almost daily the past two months. I referenced a coffee shop, not in my hometown, but a good twenty-five minutes away to distance him from my house. He still didn't know me as any other name but Eliza Emma-Gee.

Meanwhile, I had begun to pack — or at least, I had thrown a bunch of items on a pile together. As I accumulated various can't-live-without treasures and clothing from around my room, my mind went back to a ship we'd toured in Jamestown, Virginia, on one of those barbarous family vacations Anne and I had been forced to undergo, when all we wanted to do was hit the amusement park one day and the beach the other. I remembered the claustrophobia of the crew's quarters, and how the captain of the ship had enjoyed a larger space, replete with velvety furnishings, some maps, books, and brandy decanters.

How very different a time in which to live, when music, books, communications, and navigation devices could all be assimilated into one single, portable electronic device and transported overseas. We really were living out *The Jetsons* on so many levels.

But I was too much of a purist to surrender real books for electronic, and so I did not use an e-reader. Half the pleasure of reading is in the heft, history, and smell of the pages in one's hands. So Emily Brontë, Colleen McCullough, Carson McCullers, Edith Wharton, and Jane Austen would be coming with me in the form of their various novels; Clive Staples Lewis would be their escort, the sole male representation. The rest of my reading, I had determined, would be whatever German literature I came across, written in its native tongue. And of course, I was bringing my Bible, which would take up a good percentage of my carry-on space. Faithful Leopold (a stuffed animal), my clothes, and my cosmetics would comprise the rest of the coveted room.

I worked my last shift at Shady Oaks that day. As Gladys was getting ready to exit the dining hall, I stopped to talk to her. Actually, I pretty much had to yell it. "GLADYS, I WON'T BE SEEING YOU FOR A WHILE. I'M HEADING TO EUROPE FOR THIS SCHOOL YEAR."

Gladys grunted. "Well, that's nice. Now they'll be hiring someone new who won't know at all how to serve my coffee."

I had to laugh. "Glad you'll miss me," I said as I cleared away her dishes.

Chapter Eleven

A Cup of Woe

I sat apprehensively in the coffee shop, awaiting Paul de Sanguine. When he'd asked me what I looked like, I described myself as a short, overweight redhead with freckles up and down my arms.

"Why would you tell him such a thing?" Kendra had asked, flabbergasted.

"So he won't know who I am. I'll have a chance to analyze *him* before he can study me," I'd explained. "If he's weird, I'll get the creep read in time."

"He could look totally normal and be a creep!" Kendra retorted. "Molly, don't you think this is a bad idea?"

"Not really," I shrugged.

"Put it this way," Kendra reasoned. "What *good* can possibly come out of this?"

Now, as I sat there scanning each face that walked into the coffee shop, I considered Kendra's logic and conceded that she was probably right. But I *did* want to satisfy my curiosity on the one hand, and on the other . . . I should have been in Los Angeles that very moment. Sunny, warm, glamorous southern California. With Hank. I would have used about anything to help put that painful thought out of my mind.

As I thought about getting up and leaving, in walked a man of twenty-some odd years, tall and wiry and dark-haired. He had a handsome but impish face, and as his eyes darted around the room, I could tell by the way his lips curled in a slightly mocking smile that this just had to be the ghost editor for whom I wrote.

His eyes locked with mine for a moment, then made their round across the room again. He looked bewildered, looked at his watch, then scanned the room once more. A second time his gaze met mine, and this time, I broke out into a chuckle. I couldn't help it.

Seeing me laugh, he took deliberate, long strides over to my table. He spoke, and when he did, his voice startled me a bit with its depth. Perhaps he was a little older than I'd guessed. "I'm supposed to meet a red-head by the name of Eliza here. You wouldn't by any chance happen to know her?"

"Is she scandalously witty and writes razor-sharp satire?"

"The same," he smiled grimly.

"Eliza Emma-Gee." I stuck out my hand.

To my amused horror, he brought the back of my hand to his lips. A couple people glanced over at our table, then looked away.

Grabbing a chair, he pulled it up close to the table and studied me unabashedly. I blushed.

"You don't exactly fit the description of the fair, fat carrot-top you gave me," he smirked.

"I hope you're not disappointed," I said gravely.

"On the contrary," he said, staring right into my eyes. I blushed harder.

"Why did you tell me such a crazy fib?"

I glanced away. "Oh, I don't know."

He looked at me with a kind of haughty admiration. "Next, I'll discover that you're an Amazon who secretly stalks her prey in coffee shops."

"Maybe," I smiled. "But by then it will be too late."

What am I doing? Man the controls! A guy's decent looking and Autoflirt is taking over! I don't want to do this! I shifted in my seat.

A bored waitress came over and mumbled a question that I interpreted as asking for our order.

"So, why did you want to meet me?" I asked Paul after she'd left, shedding my momentary coquetterie for a formal, no-nonsense tone. "Besides, of course, your fetish for roly-poly redheads."

"Like I said, I had to put a face with the genius. You wouldn't oblige me by sending a photo. Are you always so difficult?"

"I-I don't know," I answered truthfully.

"Well, whatever your reason, I find it strangely charming." He inched his chair a little closer to mine.

I grabbed a sugar packet and twisted it in my fingers. "Um, so is this what you do full time? Writing? Or do you have another job besides your web site?"

He looked at me for a moment, then leaned back in his chair. He smiled. "I teach high school social studies."

Eek. This knowledge made me recoil.

"Um, how old are you?"

He smiled. "Guess."

I blushed. "I don't want to."

"That old, huh?"

The lethargic waitress set down two mugs on our table.

As I grabbed the handle of my coffee cup, I tried subtly to scoot my chair a half foot in the opposite direction. I figured I'd take a few sips and then say I had to leave.

"Where you going?" Paul laughed. "You scooting off to another table?" To my dismay, he reached over and covered one of my hands with his.

Frozen and unable to react, I looked up to see of all people, Danny Clevenger, Hank's best friend, standing at the counter, watching me with a slightly questioning look. I yanked my hand from under Paul's and smiled weakly at Danny.

Danny took his coffee and left the register, walking over to our table. He had a look of guarded interest about him as he approached us.

"Hi, Molly."

"Danny, hi. Um, this is my friend Paul. Paul, this is Danny."

Paul stood up to shake hands with him, dwarfing Danny. I wondered wildly what else I should say. Stricken with awkwardness, I couldn't think of a single thing.

As he sat back down, Paul stretched his arm over the back of my chair. I felt myself changing colors again like a chameleon. Blood red to dead white.

"Well, I'll see you later," Danny said, shifting a curious gaze from Paul to me. He turned and walked out of the coffee shop, without a further glance.

The bottom of my stomach dropped out.

"So, who was that guy?" Paul asked.

A short time later, after practically doing a full orbit of the table with my chair to get away from his continued advances, I practically had to sign and hand Paul an affidavit swearing that he made my flesh crawl. It was all I could do to get him to leave without trailing me to my car. Having waited until his taillights were long gone before I ventured into the parking lot, I sat in my car with my head on the steering wheel. I let out a groan that would have rivaled Chewbacca.

*****

It was four days until blastoff to Germany. Hank supposedly was home or en route, but I hadn't heard from him since the week prior, when I'd informed him I couldn't come to see his art show. Since he seldom texted, and letters and the occasional phone call were his modes of communication, I wasn't too alarmed by the silence. But, it would be an understatement to say that I was eager to see him.

My parents were suddenly pretty emotional, and I worked extra hard to steer clear of conflict with them. My mom would follow me around the house, reading the Germany orientation handbook at me, emphasizing key points.

"If the state department issues a warning of escalated terrorist threat levels, you'll be extra vigilant, won't you?"

"I'll steer clear of any U.S. embassies, churches, synagogues, or McDonald's." I gave her a sideways smile. "It will be tough to stay away from that last one. Imagine the nerve of someone blowing up a McDonald's."

"This is serious, Molly. This is really hard on me and your dad. Letting you go."

"I know that, but I'm going to Western Europe, you know. It's not a war zone. Not at the moment, anyway. Chances are you'll see me again." I patted her shoulder.

"Thanks a lot," she said, grabbing a tissue and walking quickly into the other room.

I was sorry I had said it, but I just went back the hall to my room and closed the door. I didn't feel like dealing with other people's emotions at the moment.

As I scanned my poster-plastered walls and bed, it really dawned on me. In just a few days, I was leaving my home, my country, and also the church body on whom I counted. Family and friends would be four thousand miles away. I was going to be in a foreign land where common words were longer than most English sentences. And, after my month-long speech course was finished in Bavaria, I'd be living in a city whose staple food was herring.

*****

With two days till departure, I began to suspect that the silence on the part of Hank might be intentional. I decided to take the initiative and send him a text.

"Leaving in two days for Krautland. Hope your art show went well. If you're home, gravy fries at the Jupiter?"

I waited, glancing at my phone every four seconds or so for the rest of the evening. No reply.

The evening before I was to leave, Kendra prayed with me again. She specifically asked that God would send His angels to watch over me, and that I would have divine appointments all throughout my travels.

When we'd "Amened" it all, Kendra suggested I call Hank to clear up any misunderstanding.

"Two weeks ago, *you* were the one he wanted to fly out and join him for his achievement. Clearly if he's avoiding you there's been some misunderstanding. Why don't you call and try to clear it up?"

"Maybe there's no misunderstanding. Maybe he just lost interest. Maybe he met a movie star and they fell in love."

"Molly, even if he did, you have every reason to call him as a friend. At least you want to say goodbye as friends, don't you?"

I conceded she was right. I hadn't seen Hank for the entire summer. Soon I would not see him for a whole year. What was there to lose?

Heart thumping in a rapid crescendo, I dialed his number. It rang several times, and then I got Hank's brief, offbeat message. I hung up.

Chapter Twelve

Germany

I arrived in Frankfurt am Main Airport with whistles going off in my head. Sleep deprived and feeling a little like a dried flower arrangement after eight hours of recirculated air, I stumbled through passport control, baggage claim, and finally customs. Over loudspeakers and on signs and from the mouths of airport officials, German words – fast, vaguely familiar, intimidating German words – accosted me.

Drawing from energy reserves, I dragged my cumbersome luggage, in stops and starts, throughout the various airport stations. I felt very much like a bewildered heifer being herded through tiled terrain. Thinking of cattle drives made me think of American westerns and cowboys films, and I felt a wave of homesickness pass over me.

I found the trains that were departing from the airport and managed to pinpoint the one that was headed to southern Germany – specifically, I was to catch a train to Nuremberg, and from there, make the final trek to Bayreuth for my summer speech course.

As I was standing in line, about to board, a stranger ran up to me, breathlessly. "Is this yours?" he asked in English, with a German accent. I glanced at his hands. He was holding my small carry-on bag that contained not only some essential amenities like my toothbrush, but also held my computer and my Bible.

"You left it over t'ere," the stranger beckoned with his shoulder.

"Danke sehr," I said, shaking my head and taking it from him. "Thank you *so* much!"

I turned my head as I positioned the carry-on over my shoulder. When I turned around again, he was gone. I looked all around in every direction, but there was no sign of the stranger.

Thanking the Lord over and over for His watchfulness in not allowing my computer and other priority items to be lost, I headed toward the train. Just before I got on it, I had the fleeting thought that maybe the stranger was in fact not an angel, but rather a terrorist or a drug smuggler. I quickly rummaged through the contents of my bag. No visible drugs, no visible bombs.

The train was crowded but I finally found a cozy little spot that was uninhabited. Moments later, I was ousted from my comfy digs by the conductor, who pointed at something above the car and threw a word at me that I didn't quite grasp. Something about needing to join second-class seating. He pointed in the direction of the next car over, which I could see had standard, less-luxurious seating.

"Wo gehen Sie hin?" the conductor asked.

Whoa. German. Directed at me. I had to launch it back. I fumbled through my mind for the right words.

"Nürnberg, und Bayreuth danach."

He punched some buttons on his portable electronic thingy and I paid for my fare in Euros, which felt like exchanging monopoly money. I found a single, unoccupied seat and settled in next to a girl who looked to be about my age, wearing headphones. We watched as the train zipped past vineyards growing on the slopes of hills and half-timbered houses adorned with flower boxes, and teensy villages just visible past the tall grass and wildflowers. We were traveling neck and neck with what I thought must be the Rhein river. Places I'd only seen in social studies texts and in my German curriculum were now alive before my eyes. Despite my crazy weariness, I was too thrilled to sleep and miss a moment of it.

An hour and a half later we stopped in Würzburg, and beyond the perfectly lined rows of vineyards on the hills I could see a castle. I was in love.

On to Nürnberg, where I had to switch trains (this time, carefully doing an audit of my luggage first), and less than an hour after that, I was at my final destination for the next four weeks – Bayreuth.

I took a cab to the International Office of the Universität Bayreuth, marveling at the spotless city streets, the quaint architecture, and the other vehicles, which sped past us like little matchbox cars. My taxi was a Mercedes, and all the other cars seemed to be BMWs and Audis and Volkswagens. I was in an engineering paradise.

The man and woman assigned to help us *Ausländer,* or foreign students, were both very kind and spoke slowly and articulately. I realized in the midst of their briefing me on the itinerary and the town and helping me find my on-campus apartment that I was actually having a two-way conversation in German, and that was kind of wild.

My dorm room was pretty much an efficiency apartment, with its own bathroom and shower, kitchen, and a balcony furnished with two chairs and a table. The balcony overlooked a pretty courtyard, and everything was meticulously clean, I was relieved to discover. After I'd unpacked some clothing and had marveled at the funky toilet and peculiar door handles, I hooked up my adapter to my computer and was triumphant when I saw that it was charging. Then, I made a quick call to my parents. It was unfathomable that less than twenty-four hours prior, we had dragged ourselves out of bed in the sleepy darkness of a late August day, and I'd bid goodbye to my hometown and then eventually to Pennsylvania. Then I'd said goodbye to my country as the Lufthansa jet circled over the eastern seaboard and then finally, only the ocean waters were in sight beneath us.

As soon as the connection picked up and I heard my dad's voice on the other end of the line, to my surprise, I burst into tears.

"Are you alright?" his tone was full of warm concern.

"I'm just really tired," I sniffled. "And a little overwhelmed."

"Well, that's pretty understandable. You traveled a lot of miles to embark on a big adventure. It will all look brighter after some sleep."

"Yeah." I was unconvinced.

My dad added gently, "Remember what Vince Lombardi said: 'Fatigue makes cowards of us all.'"

"Yep," I sniffed. "I remember. It's just been a long day."

"Well, we sure miss you. But we're praying for you. And, I do think this is going to be an unforgettable time in your life."

*****

Bayreuth, (pronounced "Bye-royt"), is located in the northern part of the southeastern German state of Bavaria. I was instantly captured by its cobblestone streets, its mixture of baroque and rococo architecture, its landmark Moore Apothecary, and its pristine parks and gardens. Everything about it I found quaint, charming, and lovely.

The day after my arrival in Bayreuth, another Durst girl showed up – Helene – and that was a great comfort. While we weren't close friends back in the states, we quickly bonded through familiarity, and in being able to communicate freely with one another. Rather than living in student housing, Helene had opted to live with a family for the duration of the speech course to get the full effect of German living and language.

I soon regretted having paid such loose attention to history, whether it was what we'd studied in social sciences or in German class itself. What had been the conditions of the

Treaty of Versailles which had been imposed on Germany, and who were the major names in the Weimar Republic? And what was the span of the Hohenzollern dynasty, and who were the Prussian kings? At the time it all had seemed like light years away, passable only via a visa to boredom, with no bearing whatsoever on my present life. Now, as I walked through history itself, I wished I'd been more attentive to what my teachers had shared from their vaults of knowledge.

Among what would become the familiar sights of Bayreuth, there was the Krauss'sches House, five stories high and painted Pepto Bismol pink, with bay windows and a corbie-gabled roofline that looked like a set of wavy steps, and a tiny round window peeking out at the apex. Charming *Kämmerei* alley, with each structure of a different color and material, and ivy growing up many of the walls. There was a tiny, peculiar narrow home dwarfed between the more magnificent houses called the Schmales Haus, or Consumption Cottage – and it *looked* consumptive with its skinny, slightly sunken façade. I spent a great deal of time wondering about the people beyond the walls of these houses. How long had they lived there? Did they have their mortgages paid? Were their marriages happy? And, as A.W. Tozer would say was the most important thing of all, what came into their minds when they heard the word God?

The businesses were as beautiful as the homes. The Bank of Bayreuth with its large, sandstone blocks. The lovely Hotel Golden Anchor. There was sprightly Sophie Street and the colorful, lively Downtown Marketplace. There was the Old Castle with its tower looming in the background, and a statue of King Maxmillian II in the foreground, who had turned a sea green as he weathered the years.

On Maximillian Street Helene and I discovered a wonderful ice cream parlor by the name of San Remo, which reminded me instantly of the building that seemed to be a morph of a church and a business that had captured my focus last spring when we were in Central Park.

So different than America, in what was considered the oldest of old in my own homeland would have been the Jamestown colony that we'd visited on that family road trip. Instead, the streets I now walked were a thousand years old, and many of the buildings medieval. There were a half a dozen palaces and the ruins of a castle within biking distance. In tank tops and flip-flops, we were tracing the stomping grounds of margraves and duchesses.

In the university's *Mensa,* or cafeteria, I lived off of deli cuts and *Schwarzbrot,* a dark, sourdough bread. I was also introduced to *Quark,* which sounded like a Dr. Seuss word, but was a kind of pasteurized curded cheese in between a yogurt and a sour cream. I got a kick out of the way the soda machine dispensed glass bottles of cola, not plastic or aluminum. The student lounge furnishings were reminiscent of those in Stanley Kubrick's *A Clockwork Orange,* kind of retro and yet futuristic at the same time.

It was odd to realize suddenly that *I* was one of the outsiders, and like the foreign exchange students who had attended our high school and studied at Durst, I was automatically flung into a hodgepodge group of kids from other countries. We sat together at lunch, segregated from the Germans, looking like our own little United Nations assembly.

There was Marta from Malta, dark-haired and thin-lipped and freckled, and Kareem from Egypt, plump and bald, and Drago who was Serbian and cheerful and had a lisp. There was a shy Japanese girl named Akiko who didn't initiate conversations and who looked at her hands when she spoke. There were also about a dozen other students from former eastern bloc nations, the Balkans, and Scandinavia.

The speech classes were mind-numbing, lasting four hours in the morning with two fifteen-minute breaks. Our instructor was a sweet woman with straight, greasy hair who often wore the same outfit two or three days in a row, which was not the cultural abomination in Germany that it was in America, I'd later discover. After the four-hour morning speech session came lunch break. In the afternoon, we'd discuss current culture and national events. Twice a week, we'd go on an outing – a trip to a local museum, a gothic church, a castle, an opera house, or a brewery.

My favorite days, however, were those designated for a *Wandertag* – or field trip. At least once a week we'd assemble early in the morning and take off for some Bavarian city.

Bayreuth was most famous for being the home of composer Richard Wagner, a controversial figure touted for his ingenuity but infamous for his anti-Semitic remarks and his narcissism. When we toured Wagner's *Festspielhaus* atop the city mount, built to perform his operas alone, a line from Woody Allen came back to me. "Every time I hear Richard Wagner played, I get an urge to invade Poland."

The only thing I'd heard of Wagner's that I liked was his "Ride of the Valkyries," and I wondered what Hank's artistic taste would say. While I could only guess, I could kind of imagine Hank saying that it reminded him of Elmer Fudd vowing to get "that wascally wabbit," recognizing the famous composition for its association with *Looney Tunes.* How uniquely flippant and American his opinion would be – and how dear to me.

In all the excitement and wonder and adventure of being halfway around the world, I'd hardly forgotten Hank. Thoughts of him would intrude while looking at a piece of art, or my gaze would suddenly be seized by some side-burned someone who I thought was him, only to realize that this of course was impossible, that Hank was over four thousand miles away across an ocean, and after a second or two I'd see that the stranger bore no resemblance to Hank whatsoever.

Underneath everything was a resentment that I nursed whenever it nudged me, that my parents were to blame for the derailment of my budding relationship with Hank. Had they not chosen to override my trip to California, whatever misunderstanding had happened between us would never have occurred.

*****

Very peculiar to me was a recurring sensation that I'd had since my first full day in Germany, of having been there once before. I'd suddenly catch a glimpse of something — the tiled rooftops of a row of houses, or glance up to see a chapel spire protruding from a sleepy village as we took the train to Bamberg — and in the moment there was something so strangely familiar that I'd try to recollect from where the memory came, only to remember afresh that there *weren't* any memories, because I'd never been to Germany.

When our group visited the medieval city of Nürnberg for a field trip, this impression intensified. What a draw had Nürnberg on me upon first sight! With its Imperial Burg castle towers looming above us as we walked the cobblestone hill from the *Hauptmarkt* past the town hall toward its ancient fortressed headquarters. Nürnberg, with its quaint corners and unexpected alleys and gothic churches. The town evoked a deep longing in me.

"I wasn't looking for a mystical experience," I typed to Kendra late that night. *"But there's something about being there that had a pull on my soul that I simply can't explain."*

What was it that I sensed here in this city, in southern Germany as an entity? Was it simply the piercing beauty, or the pastoral allusions to a time gone by? There was an ancient, nameless call. The wistful, whimsical vapors of romance and magic, hard work and heritage. Traditions, old as the Alps, and dialects, carved out of the humanity of so many generations. But something else. Something so ethereal and yet so satisfying, and had I been able to place my finger upon it, it would have vanished before me.

I felt that if I were to live my whole life in Bavaria, I'd forever be an outsider to its inherent mystery. Perhaps it was because I was American through and through. And yet, my spirit echoed a decided response to its evocative call, causing me already to belong to it in some way.

*****

As we continued to explore Bavaria, I could hardly imagine a country containing more loveliness than what surrounded my delighted eyes. And the train rides themselves beguiled me. What a coupling of mystery and romance was embodied in a train in motion!

Breathtaking Bamberg enchanted me when we visited it. Intricate frescoes were tattooed on its ancient meeting house, a portion of which had been built partially suspended over the rushing *Regnitz* River. The city's charming old-world homes were dressed up in perfectly painted shutters and earthy colors. Dormer windows peeped out of the upper stories like sleepy eyelids, and flower boxes outside the windows spilled over with color.

Rothenburg ob der Tauber, the walled medieval city, was almost more than the senses could take in. With its arced city gates and beguiling half-timbered houses standing shoulder to shoulder, lining either side of the cobblestone streets like gracious sentries, the town felt like a stroll right into the pages of a storybook. Its world famous Christmas museum was downright overwhelming when Helene and I ventured inside. Gazillions of ornaments and nutcrackers and whirring trains greeted us. Like any good tourist, I bought an ornament there for my mother.

In Bayreuth and in Nürnberg and in all of these towns, the churches especially were intricately and breathtakingly fashioned. No expense had been spared in the details of their exterior or interior, from the awe-inspiring colonnades and pilasters, to the marbled ambulatories and stained-glass quatrefoils of the windows.

Yet as we toured each one, I wondered whether God still met people there in special ways as they came to worship Him. Did they hear from Him, and were they broken in two over the messages flowing from the pulpits? Or was it dead liturgy and mechanical ritual? Did people leave as empty as they'd come? Were they like Jesus' assessment in Matthew of being whitewashed tombs, polished and pretty on the outside, but full of decay within?

Rothenburg had a criminal museum that held legal documents from centuries past and depicted how jurisprudence operated over the last one thousand years. Items such as the ducking stool were used to humiliate and censure offenders accused of gossip or quarreling by dunking the individual (usually a woman) into the river. Other items, such as the iron maiden and the scold's bridle, I recoiled from in horror, getting an instant picture in my mind of the very victims who'd long ago suffered under such cruelty. While the rest of the group took their time mulling the various instruments of torture and some of the translated legal documents housed in the museum, I fled the darkness and bee-lined a path quickly back out into the September sunshine.

Later I would learn that most of these cities on the so-called Romantic Road had similar torture devices and relics, originally housed in the basements of their town meeting halls. It didn't take much discernment to see that administers of such types of "law enforcement" were guiltier than the accused. Supposedly the punishers often included the townsfolk themselves coming out to jeer and even beat the offender, sometimes to death. How wretched to be alive in such a time, I thought, and especially for the women. Just as awful to ponder was the knowledge that such barbarism was ongoing in our times in various parts of the world.

"Sounds awful," Kendra wrote in agreement when I described it to her. "There's a reason that time was called the Dark Ages…when the true church virtually disappeared, and was counterfeited with a heretical, anti-Christ 'church' instead."

Lest I should get too excited about escaping the medieval times when heresies reigned and civilization was at its blackest, Kendra added to her thought.

"You know, I always picture these coming Last Days being like that for Christians."

*****

Navigating another culture using a language different from one's own felt like trying to rollerblade in the wrong sized skates – awkward and intimidating and even hazardous. However, the Germans were generally very gracious at our attempts to tackle their native tongue. I soon realized that my German was poor compared to most of the other students in the group, but I took some small satisfaction in the fact that it was slightly better than Helene's.

While Helene had chosen to live with a family to enhance her language experience, the couple with whom she lived didn't talk.

"They're nice enough," she'd say. "But they don't say much of anything to me, or to each other really. The wife puts out breakfast for me in the morning, and the husband goes in the living room and reads his paper. I come home in the evening and they say 'N'Abend'' and go on reading their magazines and papers and eventually I say in German, 'Well, guess I'll go to bed now.' I don't know much about them, except that they have a son who's at university in another town. I got that from asking about ten questions one day."

Helene and I experienced our first *Volksfest* in one of the district's villages. The *Volksfest* was a kind of carnival combined with a town fair combined with lots of *Maiselsweisse,* a local wheat beer. Some of the attendees were wearing the traditional *Lederhosen* — or leather pants — and wool alpine hats. We didn't know which aspect of it to find more intriguing: the fact that radishes and white sausage with mustard were served as the main delicacy, or witnessing the chicken dance being done in sync with the oompah band.

Under billowing tents of blue and white checks, representative of the Bavarian flag, long tables stretched out in every direction where people drank beer by the liter. As the fest wore on, they began to dance on top of them. Helene and I linked arms and decided to get in the spirit of the festivities a bit. After a few songs, we opted to leave after watching Drago pull an inebriated Kareem away from a potential fistfight and helping him into a taxi.

"I'm zonked," I said, after we watched the cab pull away. "Think I'll head back to the dorm."

"I'm heading home too," Helene agreed. We began walking in the direction of the bus stop.

"Ladies, you're not leaving yet?" the words followed us in German.

Chapter Thirteen

Xani

Helene and I whirled around at the same time, as though we were synchronized. The voice belonged to a young guy who had a shade of bleached-blond hair that was at odds with his dark brown eyebrows. He smiled and I determined he was somewhat cute. "The party is just beginning!" he said.

We stood there, staring at him, deliberating the proper response. All at once another young man stepped forward from just behind Brown Brows. This one was the better-looking of the two. He wore a baseball cap and had eyes as blue as the color in the Bavarian canopy billowing above us.

"This is Alexander," Brown Brows said. "I am Markus."

Alexander took off his cap and put it back on in a kind of nervous gesture, and I saw that his head was shaved to the level of blond stubble. "You can call me 'Xani,'" he said, pronouncing it like *Zonny*.

"We saw you with your friends there," Markus gestured toward the table where Drago had just finished his beer and was waving us goodnight. "And we thought maybe they were your boyfriends and we didn't want to be rude." He smiled again, kind of shyly this time. "But we didn't want to miss saying hello. Can you stay a while?"

I could see that Helene wanted to stay, and so I kind of half-heartedly agreed. We sat back down at the table.

Exchanging the usual pleasantries we explained where we were from, and why we were in Bayreuth, and how we were smitten with Bavaria, and we kind of semi-apologized about how crappy our German was, and they reassured us that we spoke excellent German, etc.

After a while, Markus and Helene were talking together, and Xani and I were in a dialogue. He told me that he'd been to the states once, to the southwest, and how he had family there from his father's side.

"Germany could fit two times into the state of Texas, I think," he said, still smiling. "It must be cramped to come from the United States to here."

"I adore Germany already," I said. "I hope Bremen is as nice as what I've seen so far."

"You're going to Bremen? When?"

"Our program starts middle of next month."

Xani said something to Markus, but it was so fast that I caught only the word "Bremen."

"Bremen?" Markus scowled slightly. "You're leaving here to go live among the Fischköpfer?"

"Fish-heads?" I repeated.

"Yes, that's what we call them."

"It doesn't sound promising," I murmured to Helene in English.

"We only have ten more days in Bayreuth," she explained to Markus.

"Well, we'll have to make plans again very soon," Markus said, gazing at Helene. "What are you doing tomorrow afternoon?"

"Not a thing," she said, lowering her eyelashes a little.

"We'll come get you." Markus looked at me. "And you'll come too, right?"

"Oh, well, I don't know," I said. "I think I need to run a few kilometers around the city tomorrow and work off all the sausage and *Kartoffeln*." I patted my hips.

Xani spoke up. "Please come."

"Thanks, but maybe another time," I said shyly.

We left the guys after Helene exchanged contact information with Markus. I took the bus back to campus, and after getting the key in the door, I flung off my shoes and sank immediately into bed. I didn't wake up again until light was coming through the window of the balcony

My second Sunday in Bayreuth, I had attended a local church by myself. It had been very liturgical, and I had barely understood anything that had been said. I felt like I was so busy concentrating the whole time on when to spring up, when to sit back down, that all in all I'd felt more like a jack-in-the-box than a worshiper. Communion was administered differently from how my home church had done it, and I missed the cue for when it was time to eat the wafer. Realizing everyone else had already eaten theirs, I had awkwardly slipped mine into the hymnal (which I'd later repented of, thinking it an unintentionally sacrilegious gesture). I'd decided not to repeat the church experience for a while.

The morning following the *Volksfest*, after I'd spent an hour in my Bible and in prayer, I went for a long, achingly satisfying run around the Hof gardens. I had just showered and pulled on some clothes when there was a knock at the door. I opened it to find Helene standing there, and just behind her were Markus and Xani.

"We've come to get you," she grinned.

"Oh, you guys," I groaned in English, shaking my head. "I thought I might actually study and be productive today."

"You will be," Xani grinned, picking up on what I'd said. He stepped into the room as I opened the door wider. "Being with native speakers helps to better understand the language."

He was really quite good-looking. I hadn't imagined it last night. *Good thing I'm immune to blond guys*, I thought.

Markus and Xani had packed a lunch and took us to the grounds of the beautiful Eremitage, or Hermitage, founded by Margrave George Wilhelm in 1715. On these grounds was a castle, eventually taken over by another margrave, and later expanded upon when he presented it as a gift to his wife. His wife was Margravina Wilhemina, a title and name I found poetic, and an argument against what Hank once declared as

German being "a language created strictly for barking orders at someone."

"Can you imagine giving your significant other a *castle* as a present?" I murmured to Helene, staring at the beautiful, Baroque structure spreading out on the hillock. "'You know I hate shopping, Honey, so here ya go – I got you this. Happy anniversary.'"

The hilltop setting was all loveliness and romance. Amidst the meticulously manicured lawns and bubbling fountains, late summer breezes stirred the trees and ruffled our hair, carrying to our senses the fragrances of exotic botanicals.

Xani and Markus knew each other primarily through hockey, and they were a year younger than me and Helene. Both worked full-time and lived at home with their parents, and Xani had an older brother who still lived at home, too.

It wasn't unusual for German adult children to live at home and to be dependent on their parents up until their mid- to late twenties, Xani told me, and he knew a decent amount of guys who were hitting thirty and hadn't been kicked out of the nest.

"Too expensive to live on your own," he said. Then in English, smiling, he said, "The tax man cometh."

It was another cultural norm in Germany for households to have only two children – Xani told me he knew only a few families that had three children, and no one personally who had four or more, which astounded me.

Helene and I dialogued pretty poorly in German, often asking the guys to repeat things like we were old-timers, hard-of-hearing. Sometimes they had to switch to English to bail us out. Like everyone else in Germany, Markus and Xani had both studied English since they were in *Grundschule,* or elementary age. I got a kick out of the way they pronounced our names, saying Helene as "Hey-lean" and mine like "Moley."

Sometimes you take a snapshot of your life in a single instant, and it can seem very surreal, like you're switched with someone else. That's how it felt now, sitting on the grass in the late summer sun, eating bratwurst and broetchen with two German men, on the grounds of a palace.

After we walked around the symmetrical gardens and saw a water display, Xani said that he knew someone who owned a couple of horses, and asked if we wanted to go riding Tuesday. Helene quickly agreed, and I was intrigued by the idea as well. When we left Xani and Markus and boarded the bus back towards my dorm, Helene prattled on and on about Markus. It was clear that she was already bonkers for him.

"So what you do think of Xani?" she finally asked me, as we were nearing her stop.

"Oh, well . . . he's nice."

"You can tell he really likes you," Helene said.

"Really? How can you tell?"

"Oh, you can just see it. Anyway, what guy would spend his whole Sunday taking a girl to a castle if he wasn't interested in her?"

"Well, but maybe Markus wanted him to go so that it wasn't just you and he and be all awkward."

Helene gave me a knowing little smile. She stood up as the bus came to a halt. "See you tomorrow morning, bright and early for speech class."

*****

"I wish so much I had one of these," Drago said, holding up my U.S. passport. "I'll trade you." He held out his crimson-colored one toward me.

"You should find a nice U.S. girl and marry her and get your passport that way," Marta teased.

"Bah, the United States used to be on top of the world, but they're quickly coming down," Kareem sneered, spreading *quark* on his bread.

Quiet, Kareem-puff, I thought. *Only us Americans are allowed to criticize our country.*

We were sitting in our usual designated place in the cafeteria, and were comparing passports and snickering at each others' photos.

"No, I still say this one is the ticket," Drago affirmed, tapping his forefinger on my passport.

The little conversation about passports and national identity seemed to coincide with my devotions, because that night I read in my Bible in Philippians Paul's assertion that "our citizenship is in Heaven, from which we also eagerly await a Savior, the Lord Jesus Christ." What a thought to know that one was a citizen of Heaven! Not an immigrant or an alien hoping to be someday naturalized, but an actual, current citizen with a legal right to be there. I read the verse over and over, asking the LORD to speak to me through this scripture. He brought to mind the other passage in Colossians that said how we had already been transferred to His Kingdom of glorious light. There was a cross-reference in my Bible to Ephesians 2:6, and I looked that up as well. It said, "And God raised us up with Christ, and seated us with Him in heavenly places."

"Raised us up . . . seated us with Him." Past tense. God already did this and we were already there.

This was all news to me.

It was finally sinking in that the Bible was telling me that I was already in Heaven somehow. I didn't comprehend this, and had never heard it discussed in church. I didn't even know exactly what it meant. But I knew that such a truth had huge implications – life-changing, mind-blowing implications.

*****

Meeting Markus and Xani was like a door opening up to another layer of our Germany experience. It was not only the native perspective that they gave, but the fact that they doubled kind of as tour guides and secret service agents both at once.

Helene and I unexpectedly ran into the two of them Monday afternoon after class had dispersed for the day and we'd been doing some shopping. I had been drawn to a bowl of individually wrapped chocolates in a local store, and I asked how much they cost. The shopkeeper gave me a price. When I later showed it to Xani, he pointed to a word on the wrapper that said it was a sample, and not for retail sale. It was a German word with which I wasn't familiar, but sure enough, when we went back in the store, there was a sign at the counter above it that labeled it as a sample from a local *Konditorei*, or bakery. Xani ripped the shopkeeper apart for trying to charge me for something that was free, and he told the guy not only to give me my money back, but to give me something else as well or he'd tell everyone in town that he was a cheat, as well as the owner of the Konditorei who'd given him the samples to advertise. I ended up walking out of the store with a tiny woodcarving of Bayreuth's coat of arms – free of charge.

A new door to language comprehension opened as well in meeting Xani. Studying verbs and adjective endings and memorizing noun genders in German was all well and good, but I'd never before realized what a role idioms played in language. A person could know every single word in a sentence but still not understand the meaning if an idiom were used. I also was learning the raunchier ropes of *Umgangsprache*, or slang. Especially when I was a passenger in Xani's car.

Xani had asked me that Monday if I wanted to accompany him for a "test drive" on the Autobahn that afternoon. I readily agreed. Since it was clear that Helene and Markus were already off walking together in a world that included only the two of them, I knew she wouldn't mind if we split up.

We went to a car dealership, and to my surprise, Xani was given keys by a man there who didn't seem to question his age or ability to afford a new vehicle. We got into a beautiful, if somewhat cramped, Porsche. As we got further away from the towns, the Autobahn stretched out wider and straighter.

At one point, Xani pointed to a sign with a white circle and some diagonal lines going across it. "Know what that means?"

I shook my head.

"No speed limit here. Want to go a little faster?"

"Yes!"

I watched as the needle of the speedometer climbed up to 140, then 180, and finally over 200 kilometers per hour. Mentally, I tried to convert that into miles. I gripped the handle of my door. It felt like we were flying, like the wheels weren't even touching the road. The needle went up to 220. Trees whipped past us and I pictured my parents back in the states receiving word of my death. The needle tipped and finally hit 240. We were going 150 miles per hour. Pure exhilaration. I let out a shout.

Xani slowed the car a little after that to a leisurely 145 kilometers per hour. I collapsed back in my seat into a heap of laughter.

"Wahn-n-nsinn!" I yelled, using the best German equivalent I knew of for the word "awesome." It was so difficult to be cool in another language, particularly when one wasn't really all that cool in English. "Let's do it again!"

As Xani applied more pressure to the gas pedal, I snickered to myself as I thought of a single sentence from my Germany orientation handbook: "IT IS NOT ADVISED THAT YOU DRIVE ON THE AUTOBAHN." I could see why. It had already become clear that, besides the speeds at which they traveled, whether on the bus or in a car or on a bicycle, the Germans universally preferred using their horns to using their brakes.

*****

Tuesday after class was over, we went horseback riding. From a ridge, we looked out over the wide, spacious valley to pools of canary yellow meadows, set in surroundings of jade green fields. Eventually, we entered the damp shade of a canopied, woodsy setting, and the rustling of forest sounds enveloped us. Markus explained that we were in the foothills of some mountain range bordering the Czech Republic.

Presently, we got down on foot and Xani held the horses while Markus took us to a little clearing. Before us was a giant rock, a boulder really, circular in shape at its base, with three enormous layers of rock on top of it. On the rock was a sign that read: TEUFELSTISCH. Devil's Table. Indeed, it looked as though some unholy minions might sit down there to dine, and beckon naïve passersby to join them. Or worse, the idea popped into my head of midnight sacrifices being committed atop it.

*****

Later that evening, I reflected on the whole experience to Kendra as we talked online:

"For most of the horseback ride, I was behind Helene, and every time that Helene's horse ran, mine took off after it at the speed of light. It was scary, holding on with every ounce of strength for dear life, but it was awesome. I was yelling at the thing, 'Whoa!' 'Stop!' 'No!' but my words were getting lost in the wind. And then I was realizing, 'Oh, wait – this horse doesn't speak English.' Finally I yelled 'Nein! Nein! Nein!' But to no avail. The crazy horse went about nine times faster."

"Did Helene manage to stay on?" Kendra wanted to know.

"Oh, yeah. Compared to me, she was a regular equestrian. We were galloping so fast though, I was sure that if I *did* fall off, it would be instant death. And that was kind of a rush."

"Between the autobahn and German horses, it sounds like your guardian angels are doing overtime."

"Kendra," I abruptly switched the subject. "Why does a nice girl practically have to give the Gettyburg Address of Chastity the minute a guy pays her the least amount of attention?"

"Yeah, I know what you mean," Kendra messaged me back, her reply zipping halfway around the globe in a single second. "And you make a fool of yourself if you try to set boundaries and he says all he ever was looking for was a friendship."

"Exactly. And I guess there's an off chance some guy really does just want to pal around and that's it. Unlikely, but vaguely possible."

"What brought this to mind?"

"I've been having such a blast here. Being in this exotic land where there's something so strangely familiar about it all. Taking a Formula One style joyride on the Autobahn. Almost losing my life on a horse. Going out to a Biergarten afterward and just savoring the breezes and the sights and the funky food. And, the fact that my companion for all this just happened to be a hot guy did not detract from the experience."

"Oh. Do you have feelings for him?"

"Eh, feelings schmeelings. He's handsome and entertaining and there isn't a girly thing about him. But whatever that amounts to, I'll get past it because I'm leaving here in five days. But I'm having such a good time. I want to have fun. I can hardly turn down all these experiences with a 'No, thanks. You might hit on me.' And last night when he walked me back to my dorm, he *did* plant one on me."

"Molly–"

"A little cultural exchange," I wrote.

[Pause]

"So something is expected from me," I continued, typing fast to get the frustration out. "And I've just been trying to dodge it as long as I can. But it's really annoying that a girl constantly finds herself in this position. Like the fun is over before it's officially begun. What do you do with that?"

[Long pause on Kendra's end]

"Kendra?"

"I don't know, Molly. Only dating Christian men is part of it, I guess."

"You mean like your church boy who took you to the concert," I replied, a little vindictively.

"Ouch," Kendra wrote back.

"I'm sorry. I don't mean to be unkind. But I wasn't dating. I was trying to avoid anything romantic. Maybe they should just have an app on phones, so that when a guy smiles at you, you can hold up your phone and it says 'NO.' Or if he does you a favor or shows you a kindness you hold it up – 'Thanks . . . I'm waiting till marriage. NO.'"

"Well, maybe that's a *little* extreme," Kendra opined.

"Besides all that, did you ever realize how hard it is to make friendships with other females? It's extra tough when there's this big language barrier. How am I supposed to develop relationships while I'm here? And if I hadn't had a relationship of some sort with a native person, I'd never have experienced any of these amazing things."

[Pause]

"Anyway, going back to dating . . . there's not a whole lot of visible difference between the two breeds sometimes – secular and Christian men."

"Yes, but with a guy who doesn't know the Lord, it's just asking for trouble," Kendra replied. "A committed Christian might falter, but the fact that he's struggling at all and not just giving in is a sign that there is a war between his flesh and his spirit. I think of the verse 'What does light have in common with darkness?' And remember that analogy of how a believer, who's been renewed and given life, going to find a nonbeliever for a mate, is like going to the cemetery in search of a spouse. They're dead without Christ."

I remembered the stark picture Kendra's youth pastor had painted of unequally yoked couples.

"Still," I said. "I need answers to these questions. Is living life as a Christian automatically dull? I can't believe it, because Jesus isn't dull. Yet He's created us – or me anyway – to desire fun and excitement and even risks. But I feel like I'm supposed to constantly keep a lid on that somehow. What do I do with that?"

Chapter Fourteen

Auf Wiedersehen

Helene and I went to a hockey game where Markus and Xani were playing. Xani had told me in English before the game, "For you, I score big goals!"

Especially flattering was when Xani *did* score a goal and turned around and grinned at me. It was kind of provocative to watch a guy throwing his bulk around a hockey rink, knocking into the other players, shoving, and clashing sticks. It was a little reminiscent of wildlife locking antlers and vying for female attention during mating season.

Hockey was something I'd paid little attention to back in the states, but found the brutality of it a little more interesting to watch than soccer, which I was discovering was a national obsession in Germany.

"You'd enjoy soccer if you understood it," someone had once tried to convince me back in the U.S.

"I understand it. I've played it. And watching it is like watching paint dry," I had replied.

Sitting there in the hockey arena, I remembered suddenly that I was missing the beginning of the American football season, as well as the baseball championships. Not that either of those sports was something I was consumed with back at home, but the knowledge that family and friends would be watching it so far away, and without me, now made me just a little sad.

Xani invited me to go to a club following the hockey game with him, Helene, and Markus. I really wanted to go, but this time, the practical won out. I figured there was no sense in throwing myself into an atmosphere of sweaty dancing and heavy drinking with a hot guy who couldn't be anything more than a hold-at-a-distance friend. I declined.

He drove me back to my dorm and walked me to my room.

"I really like you," Xani said softly as we got to my door.

I flushed. Dang, this was hard. He had proven me wrong about my universal indifference to blond guys – and, he was a nice person. Why couldn't he have a misshapen nose, or a big goiter growing out the side of his neck?

"Well, I–" I stopped. To attempt this in another language was to add injury to insult. "You have been so kind to me. I'm leaving soon and I really have been trying to avoid any romantic involvement."

"Well, we don't need to think so far into the future. There's tonight and Bayreuth." He said the last part in English, and the little rhyme made me smile in spite of myself.

"I'm sorry. I just am not interested in getting involved right now."

"You . . . don't find me attractive," he pronounced.

"Well, no. I mean, *yes*. I mean, that's not what I mean."

He took a step toward me. Bottle rockets went off in my stomach.

"Look, Xani." I stared at a point on the ground, feeling the hot blood rushing to my face. I've enjoyed every minute of our time together. But I'm only interested in friendship at this point. Truly. That's it."

He stood there deliberating for a moment in my doorway. Then he gave a slight nod of the head and said, "Alright. *Gute Nacht.*"

"Good night," I replied quietly, watching him walk down the hallway of the dorm. I closed the door.

I paced my tiny room for several moments, and rubbed my head as I sank onto my cot. I picked up the vocabulary lists I had intended to go over – some in German, others in Spanish – then tossed them aside. I couldn't think of anything in the world that interested me at the moment to do, so I absently ate an entire *Milka* bar and went to sleep.

A day went by, and there was no word from Xani. The afternoon and evening following our morning speech class seemed strangely long and lonesome as I was left to myself. Xani and Markus had previously asked me and Helene if we wanted to drive into the neighboring Czech Republic with them. Another exotic land to see, and only two days until the end of our speech course. But when the second day came and went, and there was still no sign of him, I was convinced that Xani had lost interest when he discovered that he wasn't getting anywhere with me.

Helene was sympathetic and certainly a little sad that whatever brief, sexually tense friendship that had transpired between Xani and me was now at an end. Our little foursome had created quite a few memories in less than two weeks, and she expressed the feeling of loss in my not being part of it. But I had a distinct sense that even *she* was impatient with me in some fashion. That she found me somehow temperamental. Or simply peculiar. Or was that just my imagination?

Either way, she was going to the Czech Republic tomorrow with the guys, and I was staying home.

*****

September was swiftly drawing to a close, and so was my time in Bayreuth. The summer speech course ended, and was celebrated heartily by students and staff alike with a party in one of the university's lounges.

Packing up my clothes and books and knick-knacks two days later, I bid goodbye to my little dorm room overlooking the courtyard. It was a splendid, sparkly, dewy morning, just on the cusp of autumn – the kind of day that belies the chilliness ahead. After handing in my key, I wrangled my luggage onto the bus and rode it back to the *Bahnhof*. As we turned down the now-familiar streets, I sadly said a silent farewell to the city of Bayreuth and its Old Town and the cobblestones and San Remo's ice cream and old greenish King Max II. As I waited for the train, I thought fondly and a little wistfully of Xani, though common sense told me I shouldn't. Finally the great long streamlined train swooshed before me like a rocket on wheels. It would take me first to Nürnberg, where I'd make my connection to the line that would transport me all the way to my new home away from home for the next ten months: Bremen.

*****

Of course, I couldn't travel to Nürnberg without spending some time there again. The Old City had stolen my heart. So upon arrival, I checked my luggage at the station, figuring on taking a later train, and walked, down Königstraße past the American fast food chains that greeted me like familiar faces, past pretzel vendors and street musicians and the view over the water of the picturesque Holy Spirit Infirmary.

Nürnberg had fountains popping up here and there and everywhere. My favorite was the *Schöner Brunner* (Beautiful Fountain) with its jutting gothic spikes and its seamless golden ring, supposedly placed there by an apprentice to the architect, in an effort to display for his master his own genius. One was supposed to turn the ring three times and make a wish.

Particularly arresting, though, was the *Ehekarussell*, or "marriage carousel," which was quite grotesque. It supposedly depicted the various stages of marriage life, from love's early days of enraptured passion to grim death. With its six stark scenes, including the matrimonial duo yanking intertwining chains around each other's necks, the fountain was hardly a selling point for wedded bliss.

When I got to where I could see the tall, gothic towers of the medieval St. Lawrence Church, I thought it might be interesting to go pray there. So I went in. After several minutes of trying to devote my thoughts to God, I finally gave up. Although there was a sanctimonious hush within the ancient walls, the presence of tourists milling in and around me created a spectator atmosphere rather than one of worship, and I couldn't concentrate.

I took a seat in a café called Zeitlos, or "Timeless," and dined on *Nürnberger Wurst,* spicy, finger-sized sausages, with, of course, a side of potatoes and also *Spargel* (asparagus). ("Spargel" was a word that always cracked me up whenever I saw it, and sounded like it should be muttered three times by an alien, right before shooting green slime over its victim.) It was amazing to me with such heavy, rib-sticking diets, accompanied by equally hoppy and heavy beers, that the Germans could stay so trim. But then again, most of them walked or biked so much more than Americans.

Leaving Zeitlos, I meandered through Weissgerbergasse, a beguiling street that felt like a backdrop for a storybook romance. There was a salmon-colored stucco antique book shop neighboring an array of half-timbered houses. Some of the homes were festooned with intricate scroll or gold leaf, and here and there an oriel window would pop out, catching the eye. Banderols dressed up the tops of window frames, and everywhere delightful flower boxes undergirded them, overflowing with greenery and posies.

There were places I still wanted to see but hadn't the time, like the Nuremberg Toy Museum, and the German National Museum, and to explore some more streets. When we'd visited with the speech group I'd toured the Albrecht Dürer House, renaissance home of the artist famous for his "Praying Hands" and his apocalyptic woodcuts. I had set off an alarm during the tour, leaning a little too far over a roped-off exhibit to get a better look at Dürer's table settings, and all the other tourists had stared at me. I received what was probably a rebuke from the austere-faced guide, but due to my novice German, the admonishment was lost on me.

Passing the home of Dürer, I took a quick jaunt up to the Kaiserburg, the medieval fortress our speech class had visited once before on one of our afternoon outings. Inside the imposing walls was this impossibly deep well that gave me goose bumps whenever I peered down into its fathomless depths. You could drop a penny down in it and listen but never hear it make a sound. That's how deep it was. Tradition held that this was the same fountain in which the princess dropped her golden ball in the fairy tale "The Frog Prince."

Within the Kaiserburg is what known as the Double Chapel, equipped with an upper room and a lower room, as well as an open area. The upper room was designed for the Kaiser and members of the royal family, while the lower room was for the common folk. The design of the entire fort depicted a hierarchical culture among the German people, with certain places that only royalty could go.

"How very different is Your Kingdom," I whispered to the Lord. "In which the weak and the despised and the lowly and last are the strong and desired and exalted and first. You really turned everything upside down."

From the Kaiserburg, I could see out all over the town, over the red roofs of its houses, and the green spires of the various cathedrals. What a lovely, dear town was Nürnberg.

Reluctantly, I left my view of the city and began the journey back to the train station. You could set your watch by the German trains, I already knew, and I'd have to keep stepping to make the last one north. I stopped only for a moment to turn the golden ring three times in the Beautiful Fountain and made a wish for success and happiness in Bremen.

✭✭✭✭✭

It would have been nice to have a traveling companion, but Helene was lingering until the absolute last minute in Bayreuth so that she could be with Markus right up until the start of the Bremen program. To her surprise, she had been invited to lodge at his parents' place, after knowing him not quite two weeks.

Taking in the scenery that darted past my window, I listened to conversations around me, sometimes picking up only pieces. In school, I'd been near the top of my class in German, but I realized now I was about at a pre-school level when it came to speaking with and understanding the natives. It was very different to be flung into the colloquial, rather than hearing the familiar accents and cadences of one's teachers and professors.

When we stopped in Kassel, a slender man sat down across from me. He had wire rim glasses and a pronounced underbite, giving him a look like an intellectual bulldog. After a while, he started a conversation. As soon as he discovered that I was an American, he began eagerly drilling me about my country's foreign policy. I didn't feel much like taking the stand, so I answered his intense questioning with pleasant, clipped phrases. When he asked me why the United States insisted on policing the world, I just stared at him, picturing myself giving him an atomic wedgie.

Eventually, I took some of the fire out of his rant by articulating the best I could in my intermediate German that a country should always act in its best national interest. Should it act in the best interest of another country whose citizens are being slaughtered or terrorized? The best authority would be the citizens of said country.

Underbite Urkel either didn't know what to say after this, or my German was just that bad that he didn't understand what I'd said. He sat back in his seat and we both watched the scenery go by in silence, until he exited the train in Hanover and I bid him a polite *Aufwiedersehn*.

The student handbook had warned that the Germans would engage us in political dialogues, in part because they knew our government and global news far better than we ourselves did, but also because of recent American foreign policy. The handbook had instructed us not to take it personally, and that the Germans tended to be direct. I wish I could have asked whoever wrote the handbook whether these Germans drilled other nationals in such a way. To reciprocate this behavior back home to a visitor from another land, to me, would be deemed hapless ignorance.

Suddenly and irrationally, I wished that Hank were there with me. He would know exactly what to say, how to parry with such people in a way as to neither lower the flag nor take the bait. I realized with a choke in my throat that I very much missed him.

Chapter Fifteen

Bremen

Bremen was a harbor city on the Weser River, located about 35 miles south of the mouth of the North Sea. From the moment I was herded through the fluorescent intestines of the train station and spit into the gray outside, the atmosphere of the region was instantly and unmistakably different than in southern Germany.

Once more, a kind stranger helped me as I struggled with my luggage, and as I made my way past the peep-show booths outside the train station to where I was supposed to catch a bus, he had waited until he knew for sure that I knew where I was going before disappearing into the crowd.

The days following my arrival in Bremen were a swarm of instructions, orientations, and deciphering public transportation. One by one, our American group of four arrived and settled in Luisental, one of the areas in Bremen that housed most of the university dorms. A quiet girl by the name of Maria was in the same building as me; the other two, Helene and Tabitha, were in two neighboring buildings. Our student dorms were about a twenty-five minute trek via a walk to the bus stop, then the bus ride itself, from the University of Bremen. It was a bit of a challenge to learn this larger city with its bus schedules and S-bahn, or Streetcars. Then there was the added challenge of timing the trips from Luisental in conjunction with our classes at the university and also the Goethe Institute, which was located in another part of town. At the Goethe Institute, we'd be taking language classes to continue hammering out our German. I would soon discover that a lot of my life in Bremen would constitute waiting in a foggy mist for a bus or a tram.

My dorm room was similar in size to the one I'd had in Bayreuth, minus the balcony, which it turns out had made an enormous amount of difference. The lack of it, combined with the austere feel of the room's white cinder-block walls, contrived to give the room the feel of a sanitarium. The only color in it was the stiff magenta of the ugly drapes thrown across the single window. I had a kitchenette stocked with some basic cookware and utensils, a low, built-in cot for sleeping, and a bathroom with a private shower. The water pressure, I soon found out, was equivalent to the trickle of a knotted garden hose.

We were given cell phones that made it feasible to call locally – and most importantly, our fellow Dursties. We were responsible, however, for our phone bills, and international calls were expensive. The dorm also had internet access, which we were urged not to overuse, as it would be the temptation to shut out our new life and immerse ourselves in the familiar. For 40 Euro, I bought a second-hand television.

A small grocery outlet was within a short, brisk hike of the student dorm (albeit through quite a lot of mud), and Tabitha, who'd arrived from her speech course in Heidelberg at the same time I did, accompanied me on our first venture shopping. Amid the overwhelming variety of German food and unfamiliar labels, I found Pringles and a package of Oreos, and I felt very blessed.

One of the first things we had to do in Bremen was to register our residency as noncitizens. This involved, among other documentation, filling out what was known as a *Meldebestätigungsformular* and making sure that we had our *Studentenversicherung*, or health insurance, documented and handy.

"Some of their words look like they fell asleep with their fingers on the keyboard while typing and just kept going," I wrote Kendra.

The University of Bremen had a 1970s industrial look and feel to it, and perhaps that's why I didn't feel the warmth toward it that I did Bayreuth's. The first time I walked into its library, I nearly cried. The *Bibliothek* was huge, overwhelming, and everything, of course, was in German. Not only that, but we weren't allowed to bring backpacks or any other type of bag with us; instead – immediately upon entering – we had to check everything in these blue plastic bags. It was reminiscent of airport security all over again. Not like your average trip to Durst's library where you wandered in, found a cozy corner, and feigned study in the comfort of your books and notebooks and some smuggled gummi bears.

The presence of graffiti and political signs everywhere might have also contributed to the cool atmosphere I felt toward the school. The Communist Party seemed to be very active, and had left their mark throughout the concrete and pavement. With words like "tyranny" and "revolution" it didn't leave me with a down-home feel. A vendor that sold baguettes and meat kabobs had been vandalized with a message from an animal rights' group that equated the business with murder.

Back at Luisental, I set about trying to make my room feel like home, tacking pictures to the wall and setting up photos of my family, and of Kendra, Anise and me, and Caitlyn. I hung up a Bavarian flag I'd purchased in Bayreuth across the far wall, and Mae West reigned above my oversized table-desk. Near the student housing was a flower shop, and I bought several plants to cheer up the room, vowing not to kill them as I placed them in front of the window.

From the time I first arrived in Bremen, the weather did not change. It was overcast and cool, and seemed determined to remain so. Through mud and bog we plodded to the bus stop. Picking over slugs and soggy ground we trudged to the grocery outlet. After six straight days of this cloud and mist and cold, I began to feel pretty glum.

When Helene arrived, my spirits were uplifted considerably. We both agreed on the superiority of where we'd just come from in southern Germany, and began to reminisce about "old times." Helene filled me in on the days since I'd departed Bayreuth.

"So I stayed at Markus's place, and he eventually went back to bed, so I just kind of hung out in the living room, watching television with his parents. I didn't know what to do. Finally, his dad said to me, 'Aren't you going back there with him?' And I was like, 'Um, okay?' And when I went back to the room, Markus explained that it was totally normal for guys and girls to share a bed under the parents' roof, even if they'd only been dating a short time. He said if I'd asked to stay elsewhere, his parents would have thought I'd had two heads.'"

"Creepy," I said.

"Yeah, in America, my own parents would have *killed* me for doing something like that – even if we'd been dating a year!"

"No kidding," I remarked, imagining my own mother's aneurism in such a situation. Another cultural discrepancy noted.

I waited for Helene to mention Xani – some interaction that she'd had with him through Markus. Perhaps he'd even asked about me. But though I was itching for some news, I was too proud to let Helene know how interested I was to hear about him.

Our program leader, Ulrich, was a bearded, bespectacled gentleman who spoke quietly and seemed unflustered with his duties of escorting a flock of American females around a foreign country and keeping them out of harm for a year. One college credit that we would earn while in Germany was under his tutelage, which was the cultural immersion program.

Bremen did have an *Altstadt* like Bayreuth and Nürnberg, and like the other cities, this Old Town had delightful crannies and old-world houses and all kinds of boutiques and shops. The name of the district, and its oldest street, was known as the *Schnoor* – which, of course, totally cracked me up.

"The disadvantage to this much more enchanting part of the town is that it's a good 30 minutes away from the dorm by bus. So an excursion out that way is really a trip," I explained to my parents in an old-fashioned hand written letter that I sent a week after my arrival.

Perhaps, however, the most difficult adjustment of all to my new surrounds was the population itself. Ulrich had explained emphatically to us that the northern Germans tended to be more reserved and less outgoing than other regions of the country, but that once they got to know you, they were friends for life. In interacting with them, this quickly became apparent; well, at least the latter part. Their dispositions made it even more of a challenge to break the ice as an outsider and get to know them.

"Oh, Leopold," I whispered aloud one night to my old stuffed mouse, before trying to find some sleep. (Despite efforts to personalize my new surrounds, I still felt a cool dread being there, thinking the room had all the warmth of a mausoleum). "I don't know if I can take ten whole months with these Fischköpfer."

*****

I was trying to see the merit in Bremen, and to find some affection within myself for it. After all, it did have some charming streets when one happened to be in the Old Town; but everything was shrouded in a curtain of mist and damp and drear. My student dorm with its cheerless interior and swampy grounds felt like an outpost. The constant daily drip of precipitation — or *threat* of precipitation — took away from the enchantment of the nearby Weser River. All I wanted to do was get away from *wet*.

There were pan handlers and drunks in Bremen's Viertel, or "quarter" as the artsy, Bohemian district was called just a jaunt away from Center City. I would feel myself withdrawing inside as we turned the corner to where they sat on the walk, these scrawny men with haggard jowls and protruding veins – men of decayed teeth and undeterminable ages. They sat, backs against buildings, legs sprawled out in front of them, sometimes staring out into space, sometimes talking with one another. Occasionally one would ask for a handout when we hurried past them. I always gave a little something when asked, believing Jesus meant what He said in Matthew to "give to the one who asks you."

My fellow Dursties questioned me on this, pointing out that these poor people would just go use the money for drugs or booze anyway. But my response was that Jesus hadn't instructed us to second guess where the money might go, but rather simply to give. It was better to please the Lord by an act of obedience and be viewed by the world as a sucker, than to disobey His words in favor of conventional wisdom. What the poor did with what I gave them was between them and Him.

Although I was still mourning the bereavement of my satire site, the Lord provided at a time when I most needed an outlet to write. Durst had set up blogspots for all us international students, and encouraged us to keep in touch with others who were abroad in various countries by writing about our experiences.

Anise and I communicated pretty regularly, and I was eager to read her blogs about Italy, as I knew they'd be highly entertaining. But when I searched for her feed, there were zero entries.

"Write something, would you?" I implored her. "I want to read it."

"Can't do it right now," she responded. "Too many Italians, too many kinds of wine, too little time. Italy is *paradiso*."

"Must be nice," I wrote back. "We have slugs. Slugs and herring and rain."

I wrote my first blog two weeks into my Bremen stay, not thinking much about who might read it. To write, to create again, was therapy.

"Aller Anfang ist schwer!"
Luisental, Bremen – 15. Oktober

"The first step is the hardest," or "every beginning is difficult" would be the literal translation of my heading.

Classes begin this week (yes, in Germany the school year runs quite differently than in the states: mid-October we start, with a two-week break in early winter, and we'll finish out somewhere in July [gulp!]). I've one class in African women's studies, a course in the history of anti-Semitism leading up to World War II, a music class, and a course in English Literature taught by a Belfast professor (no way did I want to be that American girl signing up for the classes in English, but I need it for a Durst credit! I also figured I should take something that I know I can probably pass).

Bremen is famous for the Grimm's fairytale "The Bremen Town Musicians" – remember it? These were the four animals – a donkey, a dog, a cat, and a rooster – that ran away from their respective homes to escape death. They all had musical talent, and so they headed for Bremen, where they scared away some dim-witted robbers and established themselves happily ever after. There's a statue of the four animals from the story in the town square (they're all standing on top of each other: the donkey at the bottom, then the dog, a cat, and a rooster) and legend has it that you're to touch the donkey's front legs for good luck. There is also a huge statute of a dude named Roland – a giant –, and Bremen's protector, so to speak. Historically, Roland was one of Charlemagne's paladins, or court warriors, and was a hero of some French battle. That's about all I know. But he's kind of creepy, if you ask me. Enormous, with a vacant gaze. Ulrich told us Roland's been standing in the middle of Bremen since 1404. Poor guy.

Bremen is also the hometown of the world-famous Beck's beer. As part of our cultural excursion, we toured the factory and were given samples at the end (non-alcoholic, of course ;)). Beck's is a pilsner and for my taste, it's too bitter. (I find it ironic that not even Bremen's beer agrees with my palate.)

Discovered a wonderful phenomenon today while waiting for the S-bahn called *Knochblauchsosse* at a Turkish food kiosk. *Knochblauchsosse* is a kind of a garlic cream sauce – you douse it on wraps and baguettes (the more the better), and it is out of this world. This is a definite recommendation for an import to the United States.

Here are my top three negatives about Bremen:
- The slugs (these things are not like our slugs back home – they are behemoth. And they're everywhere you step outside Luisental).
- Cola that costs the equivalent of five dollars per glass at a restaurant, is filled up *exactly* to a metric mark on each glass, and has no free refills – boo!
- Waiting in the pouring rain for a bus, and when you finally board, it's just a humidor of body odor.

#####

"Drip, drip, drip goes my shower at full throttle"
Luisental, Bremen – 22. Oktober

Well, school began last week and I can tell you, I've no idea what happened in my first class. Four years of German in high school, plus two years of it in college, equaled zero comprehension on my part when the professor began lecturing. Seriously, I've no clue what even the general theme of that class was.

On another note, while I am very grateful to have my own bathroom and shower (no sharing with other persons!) the anemic water pressure means that it takes about a century for me to rinse the shampoo out of my hair. I've given up on conditioning altogether. Today I finally approached the *Hausmeister* to see about getting someone to fix this. (Yep, our dorm manager person is called a Hausmeister, heh heh).

Hans Hecklemeyer (the name I gave him – I'm not sure of his real name) is an unsmiling man with frizzy blond hair who sits in the safety of his office day in and day out, eyes fixed on his computer monitor. When I dropped by and told him of my plumbing dilemma, he scowled and told me gruffly that this was not his problem – that since Durst rented these rooms, I should take it up with someone there. Really, Hecklemeyer??? When I went back and told Ulrich, he told me that this was most definitely Hecklemeyer's department. Sigh. Now I must go back and argue my case with my pitiful command of a foreign tongue to an apathetic Hausmeister.

Speaking of plumbing and appliances, there is currently only one washer that works in the laundry room of Luisental – one washer for about thirty or forty students. I went in and decided to wait for whoever had their current load spinning to be finished, and then I'd nab my turn next. A French girl came in and saw me, pointed to a basket that was next to the washer, and told me in no uncertain terms that she was next. I thought that this point was debatable, since her laundry basket couldn't hold her place in line. However, I didn't feel like instigating World War III – I was too tired to fight, so I waved the white flag of my dirty sock at her in surrender and left.

My friend Anise says that I need to be more assertive with people. Perhaps she is right. I feel like I don't have the energy, though . . .

"Das ist nicht mein Bier"
Horn-Lehe, Bremen – 26. Oktober

Beer plays such an important part in the German culture that they even have an expression, "Das ist nicht mein Bier," translated literally as "That is not my beer." It means, "That's none of my business." I keep running into this sentiment, but not in the way you'd think. That is, I am discovering that many businesses literally don't want to make something their business. For example, trying to figure out my phone bill with all its fees and overhead with Deutsche Telekom – I'm on hold forever, don't get clear answers, and have no threats I can level at them because there's no alternative company to which I can switch.

Then yesterday, while browsing in a boutique, the store owners literally turned the lights out on us while Helene and I were getting ready to buy something. We didn't realize that it was afternoon closing time, and I guess they'd rather lose a sale than stay open even a minute past the posted time. They didn't even give us any warning before the lights went out!

I can only make an educated guess that some of this apathy is a by-product of socialized commerce (hold onto your hat, she's talking politics – no, no!). Professor Stiegel at Durst used to say when a student answered a question only in part, "Not quite, but good enough for government work." I'm seeing his phrase at work!

On that note, someone commented on a previous blog that I should list the top three POSITIVES about Bremen. Here's what I came up with:

1. The Schnoor – it's cute as can be
2. The Germans tend to be less casual than Americans, and I like this. They use their last names by way of introduction and have a formal version of the word "you" that is always used unless one is told differently. They also dress up a bit more – in the university, you don't see students wearing sweats, although they'll wear jeans. (But all this formality really isn't singular to Bremen – this seems to be true of the country as a whole, so I guess this might not count.).
3. Struggling to find a third . . .

"The darkest hour is just before dawn . . . right?"
Domsheide, Bremen – 02. November

Was sexually harassed near the Roland Statue by some pimply dude who was sitting there with his chortling friends. I tried to rush by and pretend I didn't hear – or understand – the vulgar words he was launching at me (why is my comprehension of German obscenities perfect, but I can't figure out what half my professors are saying?). Everyone in the whole square was turning to stare. Would've been nice if one of the onlookers had gone over and given him a kick to the chops. Where's chivalry?

Did my best to enjoy the seven hours of daylight we were afforded today. With the sun coming up a little before nine, and darkness coming upon us at 4 p.m., I was reminded of some movie I'd seen in elementary school about a girl who lived on this futuristic pioneering planet where the sun only shone once in seven years. Everyone had to stand in front of a heat lamp to get Vitamin D, and they were generally in poor spirits. It could have been filmed here in Bremen.

Observed massive PDA in the library on a scale I haven't yet seen. Must wash down the memory with a *Maiselsweisse*.

#####

When I went back later and read my blogs, Caitlyn had posted a comment on my last one. "Sounds like you're having a bit of a rough start. Cheer up, Charlie. I still love you."

Some other comments from students and friends made me realize I might be becoming the Debbie Downer of the international blogspot.

"Perhaps I should keep *two* travel logs, just like truckers sometimes do with their mileage," I told Kendra morosely. "One that shows how I'm *supposed* to feel, and one that bears reality."

"I'm still praying for you to find some kind of Christian fellowship over there with which to connect," Kendra told me. "We all need like-minded people with whom we can talk and pray, and who will bolster our faith."

Ulrich had told me when I asked him once about local churches that Bremen's demographics made it about 90 percent atheist.

"Ninety-percent atheist? That's nuts!" I had blurted out in spite of myself. Ulrich had said nothing.

A missionary who'd lived in Holland for twenty years and who'd struggled to plant churches there had addressed our congregation about his work. His assessment was that, "In Africa and India and other parts of the underdeveloped world, the challenge that you run into is polytheism. Individuals believe in multiple gods and worship ancestors, so you have people paying homage to demons and thereby inviting all kinds of destruction into their lives without knowing it. Nobody in these nations questions the fact that humans are spiritual beings – their whole lives center around it, and they're well aware of the fact that there's a spirit realm. The problem of Western Europe – and certainly that of North America – is the opposite. With a post-church culture, materialism and apathy reduce humanity to a bunch of comfortable animals that seek leisure and pleasure as their highest goal. There is an atmosphere of liberal intellectualism, which scorns Christ and exalts human thinking. The rejection of any serious interest in metaphysics means that millions of Europeans are going to Hell. But unlike Africa and India and suffering, war-torn nations, the Europeans are going to Hell quietly."

Chapter Sixteen

The Slough of Despond

As the days trooped by, my despondency deepened. Looking out of the bus into the dreary darkness as the raindrops clung to the window, I'd make my way to the Goethe Institute to sit through another three-hour block of grammar and lecture and envy every soul who was back in the United States.

From time to time, I chided myself for my bleak outlook, and would try to get perspective of my situation. I'd think of troops even further from home than me, in hostile environments, separated from their spouses and children, and with no choice to return home. I'd feel ashamed of myself and of my wimpy constitution, and then I'd compare my situation in Bremen and it would look considerably brighter – for about two minutes before I'd lose the perspective and fall into depression all over again.

I was sure, in fact, that if I simply tried a little harder I could in fact be happy. It was like there was this ceiling over top of me that could indeed be shattered to let in the sunshine – only I just couldn't *quite* muster the energy to break it.

Although I'd vowed before I left not to read anything other than German works in order to sharpen my cultural experience, I found myself wandering back to the nineteenth century of British literature as a means of leaving the reality of my circumstances. My English class was focusing on the works of Charles Dickens, and I found his *Bleak House* to be a more cheerful world than my own. When I finished this required reading, I launched right into *Great Expectations* and lived the world of Pip, followed immediately by *Nicholas Nickleby*.

After these, I read Thackeray's *Vanity Fair* before quickly consuming the ingenuity of Eliot's *Middlemarch*. It was far better to escape to the land of Victorian gentry than to exist in the present starkness of miserable Bremen.

Tabitha, Maria, and Helene had their share of complaints about our new environment, but seemed to be coping better with Bremen than I was. Maria had traveled internationally pretty extensively, particularly since she had family in Switzerland, and the culture shock didn't seem so strong for her. Her ability to navigate the language was the most superior of our little group. Helene didn't like Bremen, but was pleasantly distracted from most of its faults by fixing her attention on her growing relationship with Markus. Tabitha's chief complaint was that the Germans all stared at her – (her father was black and her mother was white, and she cited her ethnic difference as the reason. It might have been, but she was also tall and slender with a waistline the size of a funnel spout, and the attention might have been more aesthetic.) Her father had been stationed in the military in Germany and she'd spent her early childhood on a base in Wiesbaden before returning to the States. Being an army brat or just being Tabitha, she struck me as adaptable and resilient.

The three of them often urged me to go out with them on the town, whether to get out for a pint or to run an errand. But I usually found an excuse to stay indoors and bury myself in a book.

"Maniacal Bicycling and Recycling"
Bremen – 27. Oktober

The Germans are nuts about bicycles. They're everywhere. And, when the Germans are on them, they ride them fast and furious. There's a lane specially designated for bicycles in the city, and I can tell you…angels fear to tread there. While walking towards the S-bahn yesterday, I heard a bell ringing somewhere. It came nearer, and I was yanked out of the way just in time by Tabitha. If she hadn't intervened, I'd have been ground into the pavement by one of the spindly, supermodel types that flew by me on her Tour de Bremen. (These German girls seriously have about 2 percent body fat and look like stick figures in knee boots).

The Germans are also hardcore into recycling. If you think the United States has their nose up the hindquarters of the god of pantheism, you haven't seen anything until you've come here. The Germans not only have recycling bins everywhere that there's a refuse container, but they have multiple bins for different colors of glass, plus plastic. Furthermore, they don't let their cars idle for even a moment while waiting in a parking lot; they abhor any kind of waste. If there was a way to recycle a dead raccoon, they would find it.

Dogs and Wymyn
Uni Bremen – 29. Oktober

Here's another eye-opener in Germany: dogs are king. They're everywhere, including the university. People bring their retrievers and spaniels right into class with them. They ride the public transportation and sit outside the stores while their owners shop. The canines are even culturally different than American dogs. They're super-trained, and usually they don't even bark. But the Germans also will take them into restaurants on occasion, and while I like dogs well enough (and have one of my own – shouts out to Agnes), that's just gross.

I am finding out that the university structure is very different from back home in that professors many times simply don't show up to class. Whether it's an illness, a family emergency, or a hangover, the reason for the absence is seldom given. It isn't out of the ordinary to wait fifteen minutes for an instructor to show up, and then watch classmates leave one by one.

Another trend is the predominance of "wymyn" at the university – that's right, women who refuse to see themselves in any way derived from men (hence the spelling for those of you from public school backgrounds, ha). These are not your garden variety of feminists back home. These gals refuse to shave anything but their heads. In class one day, I sat across from one such mohawked maiden who was wearing a tank top. She leaned back and stretched, and at first glance, I thought she had squirrels in her armpits.

There is a lounge in the uni called the "Frauen(t)raum" – translated "women's room," with the "t" inserted for a play on words, giving it the double meaning "women's dream." This room is forbidden to men. Its atmosphere as one walks by just oozes angry estrogen. I'd hardly dare venture there myself. A peek through its blinds usually reveals a cluster of spiky-haired women in ill-fitting clothes sitting around on sofas. Rumor has it that there's a percentage of these wymyn on campus so anti-male that they refuse even to speak to men – including faculty.

The workload is very different in Germany. For one thing, there are very few assignments given in comparison to Durst. The professors seemed to have a hands-off approach, to the extent I wonder how much they care what we learn. However, we were told that we would be expected to do all the reading designated for a class, but would need to process it and come up with our own ideas based on the information presented. Critical thinking. I find this aspect of the German university system refreshing. It's challenging and a little intimidating to have to forage for the conclusions, but a definite positive.

#####

There was a comment from Anise on my last blog. She wrote, "Dogs are scavengers. They smell bad and drink from the toilet. They lick themselves and then they lick you. They don't belong in a house, let alone a restaurant."

To which someone else wrote underneath, "In defense of the dogs, they sound friendlier than the wymyn at least . . . man's best friend."

"Ich bin ein Berliner, Pa & Ma"
Luisental – 01. November

For anyone wishing to make strides in learning a foreign language, I highly recommend watching television in that tongue. It's a mighty tool. Imagine my surprise to come across *Little House on the Prairie* as I was flipping through the channels! Since the show was a childhood staple in our house, I'm already familiar with the storylines, and while it takes some getting used to the different voices (Ma's normally sweet intonations are dubbed over so she sounds like a bit of a nag in the German version), I'm getting a lot out of it. Oh, and in Germany it's titled *Unser Kleiner Farm* (Our Little Farm). Isn't that great?

Even funnier to me is the fact that they broadcast *Hogan's Heroes* on television here. It's called *Ein Käfig voller Helden* (A Cage Full of Heroes).

Now, for the scary news: I have to deliver a fifteen-minute presentation to my "History of Anti-Semitism class" *auf Deutsch* – yes, in German. I get the urge to run to the bathroom each time I think of it. It's due the second week of December. I wish it were over with.

####

Sometimes, as I'd gaze out the glazed windows of the Strassenbahn and see a little kid walking with his mom or dad, I'd wonder about the children growing up in Bremen. When they drew pictures, did they draw landscapes with green grass and gray skies? I couldn't imagine that coloring scenes with blue skies or a glaring yellow sun would be anything less than a foreign concept to them.

And Bremen had to be a meteorologist's career dream. Forecasting weather in this area was pretty much a guarantee that you couldn't be wrong. "There is a 90 percent chance of precipitation today, tomorrow, and the rest of the week, with temperatures hovering around the freezing point."

One afternoon when my professor for the African Women's Studies was a no-show, I figured a McDonald's cheeseburger and some fries might perk me right up. "Why not live up to the American stereotype?" I thought drolly. Taking the bus alone to the center of town, I went inside and then exited almost gleefully moments later under the golden arches. With my warm bag of trans-fatty goodies in hand, I suddenly realized that I was being trailed by two men.

"How's it going?" one called to me, leering.

"Okay," I said uncertainly, continuing to walk as I glanced over my shoulder.

The other dude then came around at an angle and started walking toward me so that I was cornered between the two of them, with my back to the wall. Though I was in the middle of the city, no one else seemed to be around. I was frightened, yet frozen. It felt completely surreal.

One of the men took a step towards me. His oily dark hair, black eyes, and malicious grin flashed before me like elements of a peculiar dream sequence. My throat tightened.

"Lord, help me here," I muttered out loud, in a kind of gasp. "I need you."

Instantly, the men got surprised looks on their faces. They kind of stood there for a split second, staring as if confused. I didn't know whether it was my speaking English that flustered them, or whether some heavenly phenomenon appeared, but I perceived that, although they didn't appear to move on their own initiative, they both kind of shrank back simultaneously. I slipped past them and took off running.

I didn't stop until I'd threaded my way through a loose crowd of people, turned a corner, and then finally slowed to a brisk walk in Bremen's Mitte. Surrounded by the Rathaus and St. Peter's Cathedral, I turned to peer into the loose crowds around me. My sketchy admirers were nowhere to be found.

I realized that I was shaking. Only after stuffing half of the packet of fries down my throat did it occur to me that they were cold.

I later told Anise what had happened, only after I'd made her promise not to relay the story to anyone back home. "It's hard when the only people here who are outgoing and overly friendly usually turn out to be molesters," I said.

*****

My mini-fridge was bare, save for a square of Gouda cheese and a couple cans of soda. And a bottle of mustard. All I ate, day in and day out, were mustard and cheese sandwiches. I'd nibble on Milka bars for dessert. On special occasions when some of us Dursties would get together for a meal, I'd make spaghetti (which the Germans called *Macaroni*). When we were out in the *Altstadt* I'd order something hot. Once I even tried herring. But I was making an effort to save on my grocery bill so that I could put the leftover stipend money toward train fare to Nürnberg. It wasn't so difficult, because I hadn't much of an appetite anyway.

One weepy, frigid Friday as the evening shadows were just beginning to press in, I returned from the university to see a young man outside the dorm, apparently looking for something around the entrance way.

"Did you lose something?" I asked. It was always an adventure starting a conversation in German, especially with a stranger, because I never knew how far into it I'd be able to go before they lost me.

"My phone," he replied. "I think I dropped it last night as I was leaving the party." (Thursday nights there were often lounge parties in the bottom of the dorm, and students gathered there in front of its big-screen TV to watch soccer games and other events.)

I began poking around in the tall grass near the bicycle rack, helping him to look. After several moments, I saw something metallic, grabbed it and held it up.

"This it?"

Enthusiastically, he took the phone and thanked me, vigorously shaking my hand.

"Danke, danke! Danke sehr!"

"It's no trouble," I replied, hoping his hands were clean.

"Where are you from?" he asked, no doubt detecting my accent.

"*Aus Amerika,*" I replied.

His name was Stefan and he was an engineering student at the university, and a bit older than me by my best guess. We talked back and forth for a while, with me explaining where all I'd been to in Germany, and professing my admiration for southern Germany.

"I'm actually heading out this afternoon to the train station so that I can spend the weekend in Nürnberg," I told him.

"I'm driving to my father's house near Hildesheim. I'll give you a lift to the train station there, and you can save money on fare."

Later, I wrote to Kendra: "I did a no-no. I hitchhiked from Bremen to Hildesheim, essentially. Even though the Germans hitchhike pretty frequently here, especially students, we were warned in no uncertain terms by our faithful nanny, the student handbook, that we shouldn't attempt it. So, thankfully my ride delivered me in one piece to the train station, where I picked up the rail to Nuremberg (at a much cheaper rate, yes) and proceeded there in safety."

"Molly, why?" she wrote back. "Did you consider all the terrible possibilities if this stranger *hadn't* been a decent person?"

I wished I hadn't told her. She was right to holler at me, and I conceded it was stupid. I didn't know quite how to put into words that I felt so down that part of me really didn't care who I was riding with. It wasn't as though I had a death wish or anything morbid. But . . . I just didn't care.

I spent a lovely weekend in Nürnberg, marveling at the presence of sunshine and helpful, friendly people. I stayed at the youth hostel, and my room was nearly empty, save for a couple of quiet Polish girls with demure voices and good hygiene.

*****

When I reluctantly returned to my dorm at Luisental, there was something in my student mailbox. It was an envelope containing a simple silver chain necklace. Also in the envelope was a brief note expressing the hope that my trip to Bavaria was a success. It was signed "Stefan."

I didn't have much time to deliberate what to do with this unexpected attention. There was a knock an hour later on my door, and Stefan was standing there.

Not sure what to say, I invited him to come in. He sat down in my comfy armchair and I told him that the necklace was nice but too much. He was insistent that it was a gift for me. I protested again, but my resistance seemed to injure him. Confused, I wondered if I was committing some big cultural faux pas. It was so hard to know these things. For example, our student orientation book had warned us never ever, ever to shake hands with a German while keeping the other hand in your pocket – it was considered exceptionally rude. Not scraping your plate clean at a meal was considered a cardinal sin. At a restaurant, it was perfectly normal for a complete stranger to pull up a chair and sit at your table with you, assuming the chair wasn't in use. Jaywalking was pretty much a capital offense – nothing got the German undies bunched tighter than when someone crossed a street without a signal. These were the customs, and they seemed so minor – but they constituted good manners and in some cases even the law, and we'd be judged accordingly. Perhaps the necklace was just a friendly gesture, and rejecting it was akin to telling someone to go to hell.

So I thanked him for it and we talked a little, and finally I said that I had to get some studying in before class the next day. He stood up and wished me "Gute Nacht."

As I drifted off to sleep that night, a peculiar thing happened, which was difficult to describe. During that in-between, twilight time that bridges being awake and asleep, I dreamed – no, I wasn't asleep yet so it wasn't a dream – somehow I was *taken* to New York City and I was hovering with God over the city and then we were darting around windows and alleys and tenant housing. But I wasn't with Him in my physical body. It was like my mind was with Him. He was instructing me to pray somehow – not with His words, but somehow I knew I was supposed to – for the inhabitants of New York. And as we did this – it all happened so fast – there was a sense not of the incredulous or the difficulty of getting so many millions to turn their eyes to Christ, but of the ease with which they could all be saved.

Chapter Seventeen

Stalker

November set in darker and colder than ever. Bitter winds made the walks to and from the bus stops and S-bahn feel like an arctic misadventure. There were actually twice as many hours of darkness than there were daylight, I calculated once. The Germans themselves seemed colder and darker, too. I would stare at them sometimes in wonder as I rode the bus to the Goethe Institute, marveling because they must have some sort of a choice of where to live. Would anyone other than a refugee willingly choose to inhabit Bremen?

My time that I spent in concentrated, undisturbed time with the Lord was getting further and further between intervals. I *wanted* to be intimate with Him. I missed this time terribly. But lately when I opened my Bible, a restlessness would seize me, and I'd feel too distracted to absorb the words. The less time that I spent with Him, the more I suspected His disapproval. It was as though if I did get in the Word, He might be waiting there for me alright, but at a distance, and with a frown. The guilt deterred me from my devotions even more.

All of us Americans from Durst generally were hanging out together, along with a group of British students. We would go over to each other's dorms, and often traveled in pairs or a pack together. I felt I should be trying to branch out more, meet more Germans. But again, I hadn't the energy or the will to figure out how to do it. Tabitha was acknowledged now by a German girl on her floor from whom she'd borrowed an egg during a cooking crisis, but mostly the other students seemed elusive. How did one bridge that cultural gap?

Many nights, everyone would take the bus to the Schnoor and spend several hours throwing back pints at the Irish pub. While the other Durst students often urged me to go along, I often didn't even feel like making the trip out there; couldn't see the point of weathering the cold and the buses and the non-jolly inhabitants just for a few sips of brew. Lately, I usually kept a stash of *Weissbier* on hand, so sorrows could be dissolved for a few short hours by malted wheat.

One evening in the middle of November, I did decide to push back the blues and accompany them. We sat at wooden tables in the cozy hearthstone of the pub, and I threw back one pint after another. Someone suggested Irish Flags, which were layered shots of different colored liquor that looked just like the national flag of the Emerald Isle, and with their crème de menthe, they went down smooth as you please. That sounded like a fine idea to me, so I did two.

The cloud over my head seemed to lighten and lift. I was even able to laugh to the point of tears at a story Maria told in her quiet, unaffected tones, of a fuse blowing out loudly in one of her university classes. It startled everyone in the room, including someone's retriever who'd been parked on the floor, causing the canine to piddle, which in turn caused a verbal altercation between the owner of the dog and the person beside her, whose bag of books was a casualty of the retriever's stream.

But in the midst the merriment and the clanking glasses, at one point in the evening, I caught a glimpse of a pale girl with dark circles under her eyes in one of the mirrors behind the bar who looked pitifully out of place. Startled, I realized I was staring at my own reflection.

*****

Although I'd laughingly made reference to *Hogan's Heroes* and *Little House on the Prairie* being primetime shows on television, there was quite a lot of other mainstream programming that I hadn't mentioned.

For example, right before the evening news each weekday, around dinner time, there was an entertainment style "news" show that covered – or uncovered – the lecherous. It was dedicated to stories on porn stars, strippers, and other high-quality trends. But unlike their bawdy American counterparts, this media really did uncover it all. Never mind scantily dressed – the regulations were much more lax than what they were back in the states, and (female) nudity was common.

Later in the evening, you could have your pick of pornography. There were plenty of network films and commercials that would only have aired on pay channels at home. More than once, I neglected to flip the channel when I should have, and to my shame would find myself watching the whole vile thing to the end.

I had often heard it said of Europe's view of sexuality and nudity that "it just isn't a big deal" like it is in the States, insinuating that America is somehow prudish or Victorian but certainly lagging behind its sister continent in mindset. When I thought about this well-worn cliché in depth, I reasoned that the Germans certainly were more casual about sexuality because it was displayed more openly and gratuitously, but I didn't see how that was to be viewed as necessarily a standard to emulate. That is, based on my own brief experience in the country, I didn't witness that the human body in general – and females in particular – were respected more because of the national outlook on flagrant sexuality. In fact, I would have readily said the opposite – that the casualness encouraged lewdness and cheapened human interrelationships just as much as it did back home.

For my own part, the in-your-face nature of the lascivious culture was more temptation coming at me like a hook. The fact that it was common didn't make it less enticing, but more. So the argument that "in Europe, sex is just not a big deal" seemed like another vacuous cliché made by those who didn't think through their thoughts.

Upon reflection of all this though, my qualms lay not so much with the European view on sexuality as it did on Americans' overall inability to think through a cliché before declaring its axiomatic truth. What did it matter all the media outrage over our bodies becoming flabby from lack of use – machines doing everything for us? It was far worse that we'd let our minds become mush in an age when politicos and pundits and blogspots and blowhards processed all our thoughts for us.

Mine was a generation, I conceded sadly, that relied entirely on stand-up comics in order to stay informed of current events.

*****

Stefan was beginning to become more of a fixture around my dorm room, and his presence was starting to wear on my nerves a bit. After coming home from a dark day of fog and chill and bus fumes and slugs and dour-faced wymyn, all I wanted to do was curl up with a book, or check to see if there was any fresh correspondence from back home. I was becoming increasingly reluctant to put on my happy hostess face and converse with Stefan.

There were some oddities about him, too. Once when he came, he had an intense cluster of zits all over his forehead, but nowhere else on his face. He pointed to it, laughing, and said that he had a big presentation for class and that stress made this happen. It was, frankly, a bit freaky. Another time, he was sitting there recounting some story about people who were laughing about him in the university. Recalling it, he clenched the sides of the armchair and said, "But they'll see. I'll show them."

It was this last incident that made me decide to roll up and stow away the welcome mat when Stefan came calling. Since he had once done me a favor I truly wanted to be kind in return, but the creep readings were registering too high.

The next time that I was in my room and there was a knock at the door, I didn't answer it. I'd debriefed all the Americans that if they were coming over, either call ahead or do a code knock of staccato sequences which I'd demonstrated (oh, the lengths to which we go to avoid stalkers!). Eventually, I heard Stefan's footsteps retreating from my door down the hallway and I breathed a sigh of relief.

In Nürnberg that weekend I stumbled upon Jameson's, a pub in the Altstadt. After putting back some pints and pub grub, I befriended a small group of Irish waitresses and bartenders who worked there. The Irish accent knocked my socks off, and coupled with their fantastic sense of humor, the whole bunch of them made delightful company. I stayed at the bar until closing time, when they introduced me to a 1950s style American diner elsewhere in the Altstadt. We sopped up the suds with coffee and burgers and fries, until I made my way back to the youth hostel around four in the morning.

A U.S. army garrison was located not far from Nürnberg, and often the soldiers would take the train to town on the weekends. At first, I chatted with some of these guys eagerly and found comfort in the shared language and nationality. But even this contact remained superficial and came quickly to a close. Most who were on the train, I learned, were lured to Nuremberg for its Red Light District. It hardly set the stage for meaningful conversation.

Returning from Nuremberg that Sunday evening, key in one hand and my travel bag in the other, I was greeted with a bunch of flowers outside my door in a vase. With them was a note – from Stefan. I sighed. I pitched the note in the trash can after reading his declaration of having missed me. Scary Scary Stefan, I thought . . . why can't you leave me in peace and *Ruhe?*

✶✶✶✶✶

Dresden was a city in eastern Germany, capital of the state of Saxony, and close to the border of the Czech Republic. Kurt Vonnegut's *Slaughterhouse Five*, I had once read, was based on his firsthand experience of the Dresden air raid. It was a city that had been so heavily bombed by the British and the Americans in World War II, that 90% of its town center was destroyed. I remembered a veteran who'd lived through it recounting its horrors to one of our Durst German classes — that you simply could not fathom such a hell on earth. The very air was on fire.

Much of it had been restored in the last half century, and one would hardly believe the before-and-after photos. A shiver had passed over me when looking at pictures of the city center taken in 1945. Skeleton buildings with their guts blown out stood like matchsticks in a vacant, ghostly landscape. Now, Dresden was a rich arts and cultural center once again. It was here that Ulrich was taking our group for an excursion.

The day of the trip I felt achy and slightly feverish. I relayed a message through Helene that I wasn't up for travel. Disappointed, I spent the languishing hours in bed, watching German soaps since my eyes hurt to read. But the German soap operas seemed to make my head hurt worse.

Stefan somehow discovered that I was still in my room and I felt too faint to put on a performance. Upon my opening the door and wearily explaining my situation, he returned twenty minutes later with soup, crackers, and soda. I thanked him weakly and after watching him arrange everything carefully on my desk, he finally left.

Lying there chilled and alone and feeling more wretched than ever, with nothing but lousy semi-intelligible soaps for company — and a stalker for my nursemaid — I was thinking what a pleasant thing death might be.

✻✻✻✻✻

"The first cut"
Uni – 12. November

We had a spirited conversation on male circumcision today in my African Women's Studies class. It's a long story how we got onto the topic, but there is a sixty some-year-old woman who takes the class and she was especially intrigued to discover that this habit is practiced so widely in the United States (in Europe, it is not). "Perhaps I need to find an American man," she joked.

"Is my German so *schlecht?*"
Universally – 14. November

Alright, I'm just getting a wee bit irked now when I ask a question *in German* for directions, etc., and the German who I'm addressing replies *in English*. Happens to all of us Americans on a regular basis. And besides the insult factor, it's just really not encouraging.

On another note, my music professor assigned us to groups and we have to do a mini-presentation on eighteenth-century opera. I'd struggle to make this happen in English. It's like being presented with an opportunity to win a badge of makeajackassofmyself. How thrilled are my fellow group members going to be that they have to speak slowly and use itty-bitty German words so that the token *Amerikanerin* can understand?

#####

Stefan must have finally realized that I was dogging him, because one evening when he knocked and I sat still as a mouse in my room, instead of the retreating footsteps, I heard the sound of something sliding beneath my door. Quietly as could be, I tiptoed over to the door. There was a note that read, "Molly, I know you are in there because I can hear your television. Stefan"

In disbelief, I phoned Helene and told her about the note. "My only German friend is a whack job," I concluded.

"What are you going to do?"

"I don't know. Not invite him over for champagne and herring, that's for sure. I'll keep avoiding him until he gets the hint."

Stefan, however, was *not* satisfied with what I perceived as my strong hints that he'd become an overbearing nuisance. In the days that followed, he continued to knock on my door and leave notes, and one night very late I even saw the light from a flashlight darting around my window and curtains. When I received two bizarre post cards in my mailbox depicting some macabre exhibit of corpses in Berlin, I decided perhaps Ulrich needed to know.

Embarrassed, I explained the whole situation from start to finish to Ulrich. I had Stefan's number (which he'd given me the first time he drove me to Hildesheim). Ulrich said that he'd call him.

*****

Two days later, Helene and Tabitha were hanging out in my room when there was a knock at the door. Supposing it was Maria, who we were expecting, I said "come in."

Stefan burst into the room. His presence was a complete surprise to me, for after my conversation with Ulrich, I'd already completely forgotten about him. His face was white, livid.

The three of us girls stared at him, all frozen where we were. I was standing in my kitchenette where I'd been slicing an onion, with a knife still in my hand. He was actually trembling.

"Who was this guy who called me, Moley? This guy who said I should leave you alone?"

Mutely, I stared at him.

"What was this for? I don't know what you think you are doing! You made a total ass of me! Don't worry, I won't bother you again!"

His face was crimson, and when he'd finished his speech, still shaking, he stomped out of my room. He slammed the door behind him with a force that made the three of us girls jump in sync.

Helene, Tabitha, and I stared at each other in shock for several moments. Finally, exhaling slowly, I spoke. "Well." I dabbed my forehead with a paper towel. "Always nice to have some pre-dinner entertainment. *Quark,* anyone?

Chapter Eighteen

Wilderness

Thanksgiving, and a Study Buddy
Luisental – 28. November

All of us Americans celebrated Thanksgiving in the lounge of Luisental. The turkey turned out pretty decent but a little on the dry side, and one of us (won't say who) lost her grip on the canister of minced garlic while cooking, so the mashed potatoes were sinus-blasting. None of us managed to find a pie pan in all of Bremen (the Germans don't eat pies, but instead are more into cakes) but Tabitha's mom sent three dozen pumpkin cookies the day before so we had those. We went around the table and shared one thing for which we were especially thankful. Mine was that Christmas is less than a month away. By December 25, this dreaded presentation will be *hinter mir* – behind me! I'll also be exchanging Bremen's forlorn chill for an exploration of Austria, Switzerland, and Italy with my much-missed friend Anise.

In other news, the Uni Bremen has this program in which you can sign up for a study buddy – a native German with whom you can converse and thereby mutually improve your language and cultural understanding. You submit your name and information and then you fill out a questionnaire that tries to match you with someone who has similar interests. It's a bit like a dating web-site, but in this case, I specifically requested someone of the same gender. Anyway, they finally "matched" me (I was seriously concerned whether any students here would have anything at all in common with a neurotic *Ami* (the

German nickname for American) like me, but apparently, they found someone. Or, maybe there was one poor unmatched soul left and they just decided to throw the two of us suckers together, I'm not sure. Her name is Julia (pronounced "Yulia" in German) and we've emailed back and forth a couple times, and are meeting for our first "date" as soon as the holiday break is finished, haha.

Clubs and Club Sandwiches
Bremen – 2. Dezember

Had my first exposure to a German club last night. It wasn't all that different from an American one except for the dancing. The Germans have a rhythm all their own. The best way that I can describe it is kind of like an angry square dance.

Speaking of clubs, that's another thing I'm missing about home: club sandwiches. One would just really taste good right now. Cold cuts. American cheese. Crisp lettuce. Rye bread. A side of potato chips. And a milkshake to wash it down.

Glüwein
Bremen – 7. Dezember

During the Advent season, most major cities in Germany have what's called a *Weihnachtsmarkt* (Christmas market). The whole town center is lit up and decorated, and small booths are set up that sell various goodies and Christmas ornaments and other sundries.

Nürnberg's *Christkindlmarkt* (literally, Christ Child Market) is world famous, and I was a starry-eyed spectator of it this past weekend. I wish that everyone reading this could be miraculously beamed there for a moment and glimpse the sights and hear the carolers and smell the spicy mix of roasted almonds and *Wurst* (sausage) and *Glühwein* (a warm, red mulled wine served especially at Christmastime). In the background, the Frauenkirche overlooks the festivities with an air of majestic approval.

I went a little overboard with my spending this past weekend, and purchased some *Kerzenhausen,* which are small, beautifully hand-crafted Bavarian houses that hold candles. While I'm not really a fan of *Lebkuchen* (gingerbread), I bought some just because the tins in which they were sold were so adorable, featuring various landmarks in Nürnberg.

Bremen also has a Christmas Market in the city Mitte, and what a sight to see the town square ablaze with lights and colors. Even grim old Roland with his pupil-less, wary glance has a festive glow to him. I have gone every day since it opened and bought a nutcracker or an ornament or some cookies. (This is the only time of year that the Germans really bake and sell cookies.)

Werder Bremen
Weser Stadium – 9. Dezember

After a great deal of cautionary debriefing and warnings against the violence that can ensue during a European soccer game, coupled with an admonition not even to *jest* about cheering for the opposing team, Ulrich took us all to a Werder Bremen match (Werder Bremen is the town's local soccer team). It was bitterly cold and we were all bundled up and huddled together way up in the nosebleeds, but despite all that, there was an element of fun to it. It was quite a sight watching the fans in the depravity of their full-blown *Fußball* idol worship – it was rather reminiscent of a Philadelphia Eagles game I attended (particularly since their colors are green and white). Only the Germans are more hardcore.

A package arrived from home today – it was full of notes and Christmas cards and verses written by people from home. My mom encouraged people to send something, and gathered them together and shipped them to me. Very thoughtful and uplifting.

One sentiment in particular made my day. It was expressed by my grandfather on the interior of a flowery pink card that my grandmother sent. He wrote in German, "Viel Spaß. Besündigen nicht." Translated, "Have fun. Don't sin."

"Ve don't like dese Americans"
Uni-Bremen – 12. Dezember

Beethoven's "Ode to Joy" is resounding in my head right now – my long-dreaded presentation for "History of Anti-Semitism" class is finished! My topic was on the events and mindsets in America leading up to World War II, and highlighting some of the jerks who perpetrated this nonsense. While I know I made some grammatical mistakes, mixed up some adjective ending . . . overall I think they understood the general theme. I spoke for about twenty-five minutes and afterwards there was a discussion time and somehow, I got through it all *auf deutsch*.

Tabitha and Maria are in this class, and having them there was a relief to me. However, immediately upon the dismissal of class, I could tell that they were both upset about something. When I asked what was wrong, Tabitha said, "We'll tell you when we get outside." So I held my breath until we were alone, and Tabitha and Maria proceeded to exclaim, fuming, about the anti-*Americanism* present in our anti-Semitism class.

Apparently, while I was giving my little spiel, the two of them picked up on all kinds of side comments, smirks, and nods coming from the other students. During the question-and-answer segment, I *had* noticed that there seemed to be some unfriendly fire for the Americans, but in my enormous relief to be through with the presentation, I didn't pay it much attention.

So, I guess chalk another one up for Bremen's welcoming, accepting environment!

#####

There's an oldies song by Lou Christie called "Two Faces Have I" and that was essentially the life I was living. My blogs reflected my uphill battle to some degree, but I tried to lace them with sufficient humor to convince my readers that I was plodding through.

But if there was such a thing as actual homesickness, I could be hospitalized for it. I was so lonesome for the States, for my family, for Anne relaying the latest of the high school gossip while my parents shared tidbits of their workday dramas. I missed everyone and everything.

I also missed my hometown, and news and radio and television programs broadcast in English. I missed my dog Agnes — dear Agnes, who was always so excited to see me that she had to do at least seven laps around the house before she could settle down enough to greet me. I even missed Shady Oaks, and gladly would have traded places with an employee to endure the familiar verbal harassment from Gladys. I realized that I even missed her.

Thanksgiving and Christmas were very dear to me, holidays I'd always spent surrounded by family. To know that I wouldn't be with them to celebrate was compounding the dreariness of being in an unhappy, unfriendly place. When my parents and I spoke, I was very careful to put on my game face and be brave as possible when I often wanted to bawl like a baby. It would do no good whatsoever to have them realize how miserable I felt. I was glad that they couldn't see me in person. Although I hadn't been running for several weeks, I had lost considerable weight. My arms were actually looking gaunt, and my jeans were sliding down my hips when I walked.

I'm turning into Frau Bund-the-Flagpole, I thought once, thinking of my German professor from Durst as I sized up my frame in the mirror.

Once one of the British girls had made a sarcastic remark implying that I might have an eating disorder. It stung a little, especially since she was even skinnier than me. I wasn't trying to lose the weight. In fact, I didn't care one jot or tittle about whether I gained or lost. I simply had no appetite.

Social networking on the internet was losing its appeal. All of it seemed a reminder that America was thousands of miles away, friends and family were enjoying life, the holiday season was in full gear, and here I was alone.

Pushing me further down this funnel of malaise was the notion that I *should* be happy. It was self-pity or a character deficiency in adapting or some other flaw in myself that kept me from seizing this opportunity to live abroad and maximize it to the fullest. This reproach, instead of bolstering my resolve to "snap out of it," was like oil slick on the slopes of the shallow pit I seemed to be in. The surface wasn't *so* far away, but the harder I resolved to climb out, the more I failed, and the more my own guilt pressed down on me.

The Durst girls on my program were definitely a source of comfort to me, although I perpetually sensed that I was restricted from them by some vague, nameless circle. Perhaps this was just because of my overall despondency. Who wanted to keep company with Eeyore? Or perhaps it was in part because our conversations rarely went as deep as I would hope. Or maybe it was because my worldviews and my very life were stamped. Even though I wasn't living or talking a demonstrative Christianity, or exhibiting outstanding piety, the mark was there nonetheless. I was beginning to see that by its very nature, the cross offended on a level that most non-Christians weren't always consciously aware of, but rather dimly sensed, and that conviction could be felt on an intangible plane even if the Christian's conversation had seemingly nothing to do with faith.

My present mental state revived a memory from childhood. I had been maybe three or four years old at some county fair where my parents had taken me. I was playing with the other kids in one of those ball pits and jumping all around and swimming in the thousands of brightly colored plastic spheres. When I had had enough of the action and was ready to leave, I realized suddenly that I couldn't quite get out. Every time I'd start to make headway, I'd fall back. The jumping and diving of the other kids around me contributed to the chaos. And at first I wasn't scared, because I knew my mom and dad were nearby. I could glimpse them. But after a few moments, with these plastic balls having a similar effect as quicksand, pulling me back to the earth the moment I gained any ground, I suddenly began to grow alarmed. Eventually, I had erupted in a mess of fright and frustration after a bigger kid had accidentally stomped my hand in the process, and the attendant had had to fish me out and deliver me, sobbing, to my parents.

If only there were another believer with me, what a boost it would be. As Ecclesiastes says, "Two are better than one because they have a good return for their labor. For if either of them falls, the one will lift up his companion. But woe to the one who falls when there is not another to lift him up."

"I've fallen and I can't get up." That should be the real title of my blogs from Bremen, I thought. And what a tragic place that is to be.

"From here to Silvester"
Luisental – 15. Dezember

I am officially on break until right after Silvester, which is the term for the German New Year, when classes will resume right where they left off. Again, very different from Durst and many other U.S. colleges, where we're on break for over a month, and upon return, a whole new semester begins.

Tomorrow, Helene and I are off to explore Munich (hurray for being back in Bavaria), and then it's a whirlwind tour of some more of southern Germany, Switzerland, and finally, a rendezvous in northern Italy with Anise for Christmas (she is celebrating with her extended family and invited me to join, which was super nice).

Merry Christmas to all . . . if you're at home and you're with family, remember how lucky you are.

#####

    Maria had relatives in Switzerland with whom she was going to spend Christmas, and Tabitha was returning to Heidelberg to celebrate the holidays with her host family from the summer speech course. Helene and Markus were still very smitten with one another, and she was spending Christmas with his family in Bayreuth.
    Helene filled me in on some news about Xani. Evidently, he had been suspended from the hockey team for drug use. Markus had complained for some time that he was becoming a different person, and the two weren't really hanging out together any more. I received the news with sorrow. I'd only known him ten days, but I hated to hear of such a vibrant soul getting tangled up in addiction.

Chapter Nineteen

Respite

A Blog from Prague
Prague – 2. Januar

Yes, this is a blog from Prague! I'm in the capital of the Czech Republic, and I can honestly say that this city has blown away the others I've seen in sheer splendor and grandeur. Many people told me that Prague would outshine Paris and Vienna, but I had to see it to believe it. With its bevy of ancient bridges and splendid buildings and its castled skylines, Prague is a mural of unending beauty and wonder.

It is also a haven for pickpockets, and this includes both individual thieves and corporate ones. Anise and I discovered the hard way that restaurants particularly in the area of the town square enjoy ripping off tourists with misleading advertising and other tactics. Last night, our waitress incorporated a 25 percent gratuity in the bill, and then added tax on top of that (which we'd understood was already included). Having the disadvantage of not knowing the language was a major handicap. However, what the young girl waiting on us hadn't figured on was *who* she was trying to scam. She may as well have teased a tired tiger than tried to pull a stunt with Anise. I'm a little reluctant to tell you the details of what followed (I was actually frightened as a witness to it all). Suffice to say, there was quite a scene and it took place in about three languages and we were pretty much thrown out of the establishment – but happily, the personnel did not succeed in their extortion.

How we ended up in Prague is a story in itself, and we owe it all to the Italian unions. Apparently, public transportation strikes are a popular pastime in Italy, and workers do it regularly. Fortunately, they usually announce a day or two ahead of time when and where they're going to strike, and so people can prepare – nice of them!

Since the Italian rail workers had announced a strike, Anise and I decided to forego our original plans to travel from her relatives' place in Lombardy to the Italian coast. But I am getting a little ahead of myself.

Following our last day of class in Bremen, Helene and I packed up our bags and headed south to Munich, the home of BMW and Oktoberfest. Munich with its lovely city gates and its Marienplatz and its awe-inspiring churches and romantic palaces and gardens made a dear impression on us. And what a difference in the countenances of the inhabitants, compared to Bremen: friendly, helpful, shiny happy people! Of course, we couldn't go to Munich without a visit to the Hofbraühaus, and that made an impression as well. Where else can you go to feast on something called Schweinhaxl (knuckle of pork), sit at communal tables with people from all around the world, and watch Japanese men turn bright red as they drink a few ounces of beer. All this against the backdrop of an oompah band playing "Country Roads."

Following a whirlwind tour of some of Munich's sensational art museums, Helene and I headed for Füssen, another heartthrob town at the end of the so-called "Romantic Road." Originally, we had wanted to visit Neuschwannstein (the ultra-famous castle on which Disney's Sleeping Beauty castle was modeled) but (sob!) it was closed. However, there was no shortage of sights in Füssen, including St. Mang's Abbey and

Hohes Schloß, or High Castle. Words escape me in trying to convey the loveliness of Füssen, especially since it had snowed and everything was particularly idyllic. Lines from John Masefield came to me as I looked up suddenly and glimpsed the snow-capped Alps rising up beyond the castle ramparts:

"I cannot tell their wonder nor make known
Magic that once thrilled me to the bone[2]"

This loveliness stabbed me through the heart, and it continued all throughout our travels through Bavaria. But as Masefield went on to say, "All men praise some beauty . . . and fail in what they mean, whate'er they do." I simply can't articulate the way the landscape and the culture of southernmost Germany pierces my heart.

If you were paying better attention than I usually do to history, you might remember me mentioning King Maximillian II, whose verdant statue stands before the castle in Bayreuth. His son was King Ludwig II, otherwise known as Mad King Louie, or the Swan King. Louie was quite the interesting cat; I remember this from the days of high school German. You get a sense of this when looking at a photo of his wild eyes and bad hairdo. While he was born in a palace and indulged, it sounds as though his parents weren't exactly nurturing, warm fuzzy folks, and so Louie grew up isolated and often escaped to a fantasy world. He had wild ideas and lofty notions about himself, and was pretty much obsessed with building castles and landscaping their grounds, and listening to the music of Richard Wagner, of whom he was a patron. He indulged his carnal nature, however, at the expense of his kingdom and his

---

[2] John Masefied, "Ships," in Harriet Monroe and Alice Corbin Henderson, eds., *The New Poetry; An Anthology* (New York: Macmillian, 1917), 211.

subjects, and became only a puppet figure when Bavaria was taken over by his uncle, a Prussian king. At the age of 40, he was diagnosed as certifiably insane and unfit to govern, and four days later, was found drowned in Lake Starnberg, along with his psychiatrist. His death remains shrouded in mystery.

I share all this because it's simply interesting to me. Here was a man who had everything his heart could desire — a man no doubt envied by the peasants of the German countryside. Yet he couldn't or didn't want to handle the state responsibilities into which he was born. He died young and tragically, presumably murdered. He was flashy and egocentric, and would not let strangers onto his grounds. Yet he left a mark of beauty on the world, and millions have since paraded through his homes upon his death, to gawk at the offspring of his imagination. His legacy of wondrous castles and gardens dots the Bavarian landscape to this day.

I wonder if another king's words ever resonated with him, "I enlarged my works: I built houses for myself, I planted vineyards for myself; I made gardens and parks for myself . . . [yet] I hated all the fruit of my labor for which I had labored under the sun, for I must leave it to the man who will come after me."

Another reminder that life is "Vanity of vanities, and a chasing after the wind."

Okay, well I think that's plenty for now. I've given you a dose of history and philosophy, poetry and theology. Anise is motioning to me that our ever-present drill sergeant, otherwise known as Time, is tapping his foot impatiently. We've a train to catch.

Tschussi!

#####

The last blog that I wrote generated more comments than any other. There was one comment from an unknown user. "King Louie does sound like another Solomon, or maybe a prototype for Elvis." It was signed simply WholesomeInFolsom.

More Globetrotting
Luisental – 4. Januar

I left off with a crash course in the history of King Ludwig II. Well, after our one-day stay in Füssen, Helene and I parted. She took off for Markus and Bayreuth, and I continued alone through Switzerland, with a brief but spectacular stop in Interlaken. Every direction and angle one can look outdoors in this region of Switzerland is a potential postcard.

I had the fright of my life when I decided it'd be a neat idea to take a gondola ride in the Alps. The Swiss *pack* these little cable cars until you wonder whether the cable won't give way under the weight the entire time you're in it. It was a thirty-minute ride from our starting point to the end, with the gondola traveling about five miles per hour. For the first twenty-five minutes, it was pretty much sheer terror. When I glanced down, the only comfort that I had was that death most certainly would be instantaneous. The long, anticipatory fall would be horrible, but I'd die so quickly upon impact that I'd wake up in Heaven before I could remember what had happened. This was my single thought process for nine-tenths of the ride, and I kept my eyes closed.

Then, for the last three minutes, when I opened my eyes and saw that we were about to approach our destination, I relaxed and was able to take in the wonder of the ride. When our guide pointed out the Wetterhorn, a famous mountain crowned with three distinct peaks, I was overcome. Gazing at its dark, looming grandeur which reached toward heaven, the verse sprang to mind, "He has set eternity in their hearts."

I spent one night in a hostel with some Asian girls who giggled incessantly and sprayed their exotic eastern fragrances in the claustrophobic room until a cloud formed. They continued talking and giggling well after lights out, until another young lady sharing the room let out a robust "pssssst-shp!" that must have conveyed her displeasure across the language barriers sufficiently to encourage them to stop. And I thought suddenly and morbidly about how dreadful being in a prison camp and sharing one's sleeping quarters would be.

From Interlaken I traveled to Milan via Spiez. Anise has extended family in nearby Lodi and so that's where we spent Christmas. Although I couldn't understand a word that was spoken by Anise's relatives, and she had to act as our translator for the simplest things, the warmth and hospitality of her Italian family made me feel completely at home. To my surprise, our meals consisted often of rice, and Anise told me that in this particular region of Italy, it is served more frequently than pasta.

It was another "pinch me" moment, sitting there at the table eating *osso buco* (veal shins) and listening to the rolling crescendo of the Italian words and getting a sense of spooky sanctimony projecting from the religious symbols mounted throughout the rooms.

The Christmas traditions were different, too, both from America and Germany. In Germany, the Germans decorate the tree Christmas Eve (sometimes with actual candles) and this is when they celebrate and do the gift-giving. In Italy, we really didn't exchange gifts, but it was a big deal to go to the Christmas Mass. That was another hour of electrified surreality, to be in a church in Italy at Christmastime, celebrating a mass.

While staying with these hospitable Italians, a package arrived for me from home. Besides some really lovely gifts and some currency (yeah!), my parents sent boxed mac and cheese, Rice Krispie treats, and brownie mix. Anise and I divided the spoil among my hosts. (A big thank-you, to my mom and dad!)

We left the gracious Lodi relations on December 27 after a day in the bustling cosmopolitan city of Milan, and hopped a rail to Vienna, Austria. There we saw more castles, more churches, more cafés, and a lot of well-dressed dames in fur coats. And, I was navigating the German language again (albeit with Austria's very different accent). Most of the people whom we encountered in Vienna were friendly and helpful and hid any annoyances they might have had with tourists. We were directed pretty easily to Vienna's Main Cemetery, which houses the remains of several famous composers, including Beethoven, Brahms, Schubert, and Johann Strauss. (And this is to my dad, if you are reading . . . by all means make a joke about them "decomposing" – I would be fearful something was wrong if you didn't).

I'd very much wanted to visit Salzburg, but sizing up our funds and our time, we determined between the two of us that both were deficient. It's too bad. I was very much looking forward not only to a trip down into the city's famous salt mines, but also to seeing the infamously schmaltzy Salzburg *Sound of Music* tour.

From Austria, we again hopped a train and spent a night in a lackluster hostel in a dismal town in Slovakia. I don't think I slept well in this place for fear if I closed my eyes, I wouldn't open them again. Then on to Brno (pronounced just as it's spelled) where we spent a cheerful but relatively quiet New Year's Eve. After that, we made our final destination of Prague and visited Golden Lane and saw Franz Kafka's house.

So . . . here I am, back in Bremen and quite exhausted. I have a boatload of laundry to do but no energy, particularly if only one washer is functioning downstairs. Perhaps I should invest in a washboard and start doing some items by hand.

Maria was here for New Year's Eve, and said that a bunch of students lit off firecrackers outside the dorms, which is a German tradition for *Silvester*. Apparently, many Germans also watch a film called *Dinner for One* which is kind of like our equivalent of watching *It's a Wonderful Life* around Christmas. It wasn't really originally a holiday movie, but turned into one by tradition.

Funny with all my travels – six countries in eighteen days – that Germanland feels like home. After Italy, Czech, Slovakia, and Switzerland (whose dialect of German is nearly unintelligible to my ears), I am now happy to be back to where the language is one in which I can doggie paddle successfully, the terrain is familiar, and I have a rough idea in a restaurant what it is that I'm ordering to eat.

And do you know, men in *Lederhosen* are starting to look suddenly attractive?

#####

Chapter Twenty

Back in Bondage

The Uni Macho
Uni Bremen – 8. Januar

Here are the top three things I miss about the U.S.:

1. Diners
2. English (hearing, speaking, and reading it)
3. Muscular men

The last one, let me clarify. It is just hard on the eyes to look around all the time and see predominantly lanky, lady like young men everywhere wrapped up in scarves and skinny jeans. In the States, we'd call them metrosexuals. I didn't see this trend nearly so much in the south of Germany. There is only one male my age here in northern Germany that I've seen who has a muscular, masculine build. He's a student at the Uni and is quite the gym rat. I call him the Uni Macho. He's pretty good looking, and he's pretty aware of it. He has a bit of an ethnic look about him, so I don't even know whether he's German.

In other news, there was a demonstration at the Uni today. A bunch of Eurogoobers marching against a proposed tuition fee – something like $150 a semester. *Protesting for paying in tuition less than what we'd pay back home for books for a semester!* In case you weren't aware, these students go to school for free here. That's why many of them never leave. Why graduate when school costs little to nothing and the economy's rotten anyway? Not only that, there are great perks to being a student, including fantastic discounts on transportation, hospitality, and a boatload of other things for which those who work must pay full price. Yeah, no such thing as "free" tuition, free health care, free anything. Somebody must pay.

I don't think paying fifty grand a year to go to college like we do at home should pass for normal, either. But taking to the streets because you're expected to cover less than a dollar per day of your education is loony. Entitlement boogers!

"Arrogant, Oberflächig, und die Polizei der Welt"
Northern Germany – 11. Januar

It has gotten so that when I ask a German his or her impressions of Americans, I always – without fail – a can predict the same three words: "arrogant, superficial, and the policemen of the world." (Now, I have finally learned my lesson in all this simply not to ask any more). But the consistency of the response – I mean, literally these three adjectives each time – not only seems ill-mannered, but it shows that they've been conditioned to think this way. It's uncanny.

This kind of treatment seems particularly unfair, I might add, coming from a population that is known for its national obsession with David Hasselhoff.

#####

I sighed as I typed the end of my last blog. I was already turning into Mopey Molly again, spiraling downward. After the merriment of Christmas and my wonderful respite south, I had returned to Bremen sincerely wanting to see the good in it and to try to enjoy some aspects of the exchange experience. I had given myself a pep talk the whole way back on the train, and even a passenger next to me who picked his ears and smelled of *Sauerbraten* had not deterred my resolve.

But even before I'd reached my dorm, the pervasive cold and dark of the region had assaulted my defenses, and I could feel the same dismal chill sinking into my bones. It was raining again. Or sleeting rather. It was January and the dead of winter. I'd be here until July, which meant that my time in Bremen wasn't even halfway through. How could I shake this thundercloud over my head?

And I was lonely. Lonely with the loneliness of unshared thought. Kendra was faithful to keep in touch, but she had her own world of responsibilities and term papers and deadlines. She shouldn't have to babysit me from four thousand miles away.

I sighed again, grabbing a half-eaten Milka bar from the fridge, dropping onto my bed, and flipping on the television. The draw toward something sensual was becoming instinctive now. I sometimes felt that I was spending all my time in Bremen in bed. Sleeping, watching rot television, reading, sleeping, surfing the TV channels to alight "accidentally" on porn, falling asleep again . . .

Occasionally on nights when I'd drunk too much I'd break it up with wasting time on the web and I'd cyberstalk people from childhood. *Whatever happened to that kid from fourth grade who'd had to move in the middle of the year . . . last name? Hinkle? No, Hinkley!* [Type, type, type].

Glancing over by my window sill, I noticed that the plants I'd bought a few months earlier to spruce up the room were brown and withered. They hadn't been watered in weeks, and had been dying even before I'd left for my travels. I'd throw them out tomorrow maybe, when I had some energy.

*****

I'd spent so much of my stipend and the money my parents had sent on holiday travel that I couldn't afford to escape to Nürnberg for a while. I was stuck in Bremen.

One day rolled into another, each looking pretty much the same. Straining to catch a word in fast-spoken, formidable German during class; hunkering down in the library in between lectures; coming home in the damp fog to my little room, alone except for a chill that couldn't be shaken even with multiple cups of hot cocoa and my blankets wrapped around me like some great cotton burrito.

I hadn't touched my Bible or listened to an online sermon from home in weeks. God seemed farther away than ever – He had abandoned me, I felt – thrown up His hands as He'd edged away in disgust.

Without the hope of escaping my holding cell on the weekends, my heaviness increased. The world around me was no longer in color, but in grays and muted tones of dark. While Helene had once referred to Bremen as "The Shadowlands," I never thought of Bremen as being a *shadowy* place. For in order to have shadow, one must also have light. Bremen was simply dim.

I sensed that in my melancholy, I was becoming not just a drag to myself, but also to others. I considered myself an introvert, except for instances in which alcohol abounded, when I could usually shed that cloak for something lighter and airier. But now, lately, even when I drank I seemed simply to become more pensive and withdrawn. And who wanted to be around Droopy Drusilla?

In vain I attempted to pick myself up, shake it off, lift off from the runway. But the gravity of my depression pulled me down hard.

Sometimes after class, I'd hop the S-bahn over to the Irish Pub all by myself, so as not to have to face the confining dreariness of my room. And sometimes there would be a guitar player who'd strum "Always on My Mind" or some other mournful ballad by request, and I'd sit alone at the bar and listen until my pint was empty. And I'd laugh at the wisecracks that the potty-mouthed bartender would make in his Kilkenny vernacular, and wish myself away to somewhere else, sometime else. And my thoughts would inevitably drift to Hank, and what might have been.

*****

"No more green police uniforms over here," Maria said, reading something from a magazine. "The last of them have been phased out and replaced with blue."

"Oh, you know I actually *remember* those uniforms?" Tabitha said, grabbing the magazine from her and holding it close to her face, stretching out across her bed with the abandon of an actual tabby. "Way back from when I was here as a kid. Haha, yep. Urine yellow shirts and parakeet green pants."

"Looks intimidating to criminals," I observed, taking a break from shredding the label on my bottle of Warsteiner long enough to glance at the photo.

"That's probably why they changed them to blue," Helene said perfunctorily, examining her finger nails.

"Nah, I heard that the German women complained. They were tired of hiring male strippers for bachelorette parties and getting a guy who was decked out like a hall monitor," Tabitha quipped.

"Really?" asked Maria.

Tabitha grinned and threw a pillow at her.

Helene tore open a bag of Fritos and began passing them around the room. We had vowed probably a dozen times since our arrival in Bremen that we would speak only German together, and thereby force ourselves to improve our language skills. As many times as we'd made this resolution, we had been faithful to break it.

"You know what they say when you pull apart labels from your bottle of beer like that," Tabitha observed, nodding at my little pile of damp paper shreds.

"What?" Maria asked curiously.

"It's a sign of sexual frustration," Tabitha diagnosed.

"That's not far from the truth," I agreed dismally. I finished ripping the pieces to tiny shreds. "Although it's probably a sign I'm just frustrated period."

The furtive glance exchanged between Tabitha and Maria did not escape my notice. Nobody said anything for a few moments. Finally Tabitha turned to Helene. "So when do you plan to visit Markus again?" she asked.

"The Pied Piper of Hameln"
Am Weser – 17. Januar

I learned something new today. You know the story of the Pied Piper of Hamlin? Well, Hamlin is actually *Hameln*, a German town just a quick jaunt south of Bremen. And in the story, do you remember how the Pied Piper drowns all the rats in the river? Well, if you look up the original tale, that river is actually the Weser River – as in the same Weser that runs through Bremen.

As I tried to dodge the sleet on the way home tonight in the dark after a particularly discouraging two hours spent at the Goethe Institute, trying to make the German language my friend, I must say that I sympathized with those rats. I could just picture them, flopping haplessly into the Weser, and myself right behind them – the only willing participant following the Piper.

#####

I woke up one morning, staring at the golden lions of the Bavarian flag mounted on my wall, bright red tongues rolling out of their mouths like birthday blowouts, and realized all of a sudden that I'd drunk dialed someone from America the night before. Someone from church. *Crap.* What had I said?

My head hurt. It hurt more to think. *Who had I called?* Rummage through thoughts . . . Not the pastor, not the youth pastor. Thank heavens. *Who was it?* Think.

"Oh, no," I groaned out loud, my words reverberating around the cold walls as they exited my pasty mouth. I rolled over and pulled my pillow over my head. I remembered. It was my old Sunday school teacher from days long gone, who'd taught us faithfully, week after week, when my age was still in single digits. *Verna Woodhouse.* She was a saint. Small and soft spoken and ancient as the hills. Literally a saint. I had phoned her up, mournful and plastered and hoping to seek out some solace. She'd been on my mind all evening, in that dreamy, magnified sort of light that drunkenness can cast over people from your past. I remembered her phone number by heart because the last four numerals spelled "halo" on the dial pad.

I lay there in bed, head throbbing and my stomach indignant. No idea what I'd said to her. No idea what she'd said to me. Awful.

I'd always looked back on seventh grade as the lowest point of my life. The awkwardness and uncertainty of puberty colliding with short, unsympathetic middle school boys. It had been a rough go. But now, for sure, this incident had taken the title.

*****

When I opened my student mailbox one afternoon, there was a slender package inside. To my surprise, the return address read "Shady Oaks." Tearing across the top of the bubbled envelope, I pulled out a plastic bag containing a small, delicate locket on a chain. I opened it to see a woman's face staring back at me — a stranger.

Puzzled, I looked inside the mailer and there was a note stuffed deep within it. After the salutations, it read,

> "Gladys Hauger passed away on the third of October. When the executor of her estate went through her belongings, this was found.
>
> Most Truly Yours,
>
> Gerald Firman, Executive Director
> Shady Oaks Retirement & Nursing

Along with the typed note was a handwritten one, in shaky, hard-to-read cursive. It simply said:

> "Molly, this is a photo of me when I was young. It belonged to my late husband. I don't have any children, and I don't want these money-grubbers to have *all* my belongings when I die. You have it. You couldn't get my coffee right, but you were kind."
>
> Gladys

I closed the door of my dorm behind me and read her note again. I sank onto my bed, staring at the youthful face in the locket. And I cried and I cried and I cried.

Chapter Twenty-One

An Encounter

Receiving Gladys's note and the news of her death released something in me. After I stopped crying, I slowly took my Bible off the shelf and began to read. There wasn't any other action in the world at that moment that seemed appropriate, not only in relation to my mood, but out of respect to the sudden discovery of Gladys's passing. And even if I was the most wretched of sinners, even if Jesus was annoyed with me because of my relapse into old patterns, as I suspected He might be, I'd gladly take His anger over His absence.

As I paged through different books, my eyes were drawn to a verse I'd once underlined in Deuteronomy that said, "The Lord will vindicate His people, and will have compassion on His servants when He sees that their strength is gone."

"Will you, Lord?" I asked out loud, still a teary mess. "I'm holding You to Your word here. My strength is gone. I'm thousands of miles from home and I feel like *everything* about this place is set against me. All of it. Nothing is easy or encouraging or familiar or even fun. The people, the university, the culture, the weather, the creepers, the slugs . . . even my shower head is hostile. Lord, please show me this compassion You've promised for Your servants. God, I'm *desperate*."

And then I was reminded of last summer at the conference and the teaching on giving thanks, and I thought about Gladys. And as difficult as it was, as much as it felt like being right-handed and trying to use my left to comb my hair, I began to thank the Lord for the city of Bremen.

✯✯✯✯✯

Julia, my study buddy set up for me by the university, met me in the *Mensa* for lunch that week. While I was hopeful to meet a real German and forge some kind of connection, I was also nervous. As a rule, I detested small talk, and found icebreaker conversations to be awkward and tedious. I was interested in people's worldviews, their backgrounds, and what guided them in life as the standard of truth. But one couldn't start firing away those kinds of questions without the other person generally turning tail and running. It just wasn't done.

Julia had long brown hair that she wore in a braid down her back. Surprisingly, she greeted me with the custom European embrace and kiss on both cheeks that was normally reserved for close friends, and always made me uncomfortable. She had a pleasant smile and a nose ring.

Wait till she discovers that she got matched up with Holly Hobbie, I thought grimly.

Julia was from a town midway between Bremen and Hamburg called Zeven. She hadn't been to the States but had plans to go to New York the following summer. She was studying manufacturing engineering and was in her third year at the Uni. She was a movie buff and liked American television sitcoms.

She asked about my life, and I told her about my sister and my family and how great they were, about my appreciation for vintage television and films, and I told her frankly when asked that I had trouble sitting down to a modern movie. Unless I caught one on the fly and happened to get sucked into the plot by accident, I didn't generally watch many. As for television, I preferred the 1980s cop series *Hill Street Blues* to an episode of a *CSI* drama, and believed that *Frasier* was the last great television sit com ever to be produced.

When she asked me what I thought of Germany, I hesitated. "I find that other parts of Germany are delightful –

everything about them I love. But Bremen . . . Bremen . . . I – I struggle to see the charm."

"Really? Perhaps you haven't seen enough of it to be able to appreciate it," Julia replied.

Okay, we'll go with that one, I thought wearily as I nodded.

As we stood up to say goodbye, Julia gave me hope that she hadn't found me the colossal disappointment I'd feared. "Shall we meet next week?" she asked. "How about the corner coffee shop by Am Dobben?"

"Sure," I said. As I made my way from the Mensa, I thought to myself in a sing-song voice, "I- have-a- German-friend – finally!" I felt both grateful and a bit pathetic.

*****

The following Friday, I was feeling achy and warm. Why was I never sick in the States but felt on the verge of the flu so often in Bremen? Something with the damp weather, no doubt. By the time I got back to the dorm, I was freezing as I sweated. I dug down under the covers and slept until Maria stopped by to return a book she'd borrowed. She stayed to fix me some tea and we sat there and watched an episode of *Unser Kleiner Farm* until it was followed by a racy drama, which we watched through about the fourth commercial break.

I felt considerably better Saturday but was morose to be stuck in Bremen all weekend when I'd been contemplating an escape to the Franconian town of Würzburg, which I'd calculated I could afford the train fare if I were extra careful not to eat much the following two weeks. When Maria stopped by again to see how I was doing, she announced that she wanted to get a new area rug for her room. She asked if I felt well enough to accompany her to the *Viertel*. I didn't feel like leaving my room, nor did I feel like staying there. So I halfheartedly agreed. We made our way through the mud and the fog to the S-bahn, and sat through the lulling trip with its various stops, gazing out in silence through the dirty windows.

At a store which sold handspun rugs and other artsy furnishings, I idly picked up a cobalt-colored vase while I waited for Maria to finish her purchase. As I examined its asymmetrical contours, a voice interrupted my thoughts.

"Pardon me, Miss?" I glanced up to see warm brown eyes belonging to a gentleman of about forty. I searched his face, wondering how I knew him, before concluding that I didn't. "Might you be in need of some prayer?" he asked.

I nearly dropped the piece of bric-a-brac in my hand. I stared at him speechlessly for a moment.

"My name is Freimann, Michael Freimann," the stranger said, holding out his hand.

The thought flashed through my mind, *Is this really happening, or is this a new tactic of the Bremen League of Molesters?*

"I'm Molly," I replied finally, shaking his hand. I stared at him for another moment, blinking, waiting for him to vanish and for me to discover I'd begun hallucinating. "Um. Yes. I – I could use some prayer."

We kind of moved off to the side of the store so we wouldn't be as noticeable, and the stranger lightly touched my shoulder as we prayed. (For a German to touch you while conversing was uncommon in itself.) To my amazement, he prayed as though he had read all my blogs, and then read in between the lines. He referenced depression and the need for new joy, and he even said something about the Lord being pleased with me. While this last thought seemed like wishful thinking to me, the style of the man's prayer was so authoritative – he was stating things to God rather than petitioning Him – that I couldn't help but believe every word.

I expected the man to disappear mysteriously following the prayer – I mean, the whole encounter was too otherworldly to be true. But he apparently was human, not angelic.

Explaining, almost stuttering, how very much I needed that, I conveyed my surprise that he'd happened to ask me.

"God told me to go into this shop when I was walking by," he stated easily, matter-of-factly. "He said I'd find a young lady inside holding a piece of blue pottery, and I was to approach her. And there you were."

Still in shock, I talked with the man further and learned that he was part of a small house church that met in Findorff. He invited me to join them, and said that they were meeting tomorrow.

As much as this was music to my disbelieving ears, I figured I'd better make sure that he wasn't part of some Kool-Aid cult. Seeing my hesitation, he said he'd give me his wife's number and I could get in touch with her if I was ever interested in visiting with them. And with that, he was gone.

*****

I met Petra Freimann at a tea shop in the Schnoor the next week, after a particularly frigid, windy trek from my dorm. She had short blond hair cut just above her shoulders, and wore red, horn-rimmed glasses. Her nails were painted with a bright lacquer that matched her glasses. Within minutes, I felt as though I'd known her a long time.

Listening to my sob story of Bremen and culture shock and despondency, I was relieved to see that she didn't seem offended by my disdain for her city and its environment. She nodded from time to time, and smiled sympathetically sometimes. At one point, she spoke up when I described how I tried, *really* tried, especially coming back off of a high in Nürnberg, to rally myself and keep being optimistic and cheerful, only to find myself sinking backward into the mire shortly after stepping off the train.

"*Unterdrückung,*" she stated knowingly, nodding her head.

"*Bitte?*" I hadn't understood the word.

"You sense a heaviness when you get off the train in Bremen. It is not just the weather. There is an atmosphere here of spiritual oppression into which you are entering. That is in part what you are sensing."

That gave me something to chew on.

After I'd finished unloading my woes, Petra smiled brightly and said, "Well, and now for the good news. What we *do* know. The Lord has not abandoned you as you supposed. He has never left you for a minute. Also, you did not come here to Bremen by mistake. There is purpose in your being here. And, I am not saying I know this for sure, but very likely the Lord has allowed you to go through some wilderness time – like He does with all the saints – before bringing you into a new space of ministry."

"Do you really think so?"

"It is very characteristic in the Bible for men and for women of God to go through various times of testing – and of literal wilderness – before being used mightily by Him. Think of Moses, Elijah . . . even Jesus Christ had to go into the wilderness to face the devil before His ministry formally began."

"So you think that God is putting me through" [I paused to look up a word] "boot camp right now?" I asked, a little incredulously, seeing an easy parallel between being in Bremen and facing the devil.

"It is possible that this is a testing period for bigger things," she answered. "But one thing I know for certain. He is not standing over you, frowning on you with disapproval and shaking His head at what a disappointment you turned out to be. Beyond how you can imagine your parents feel with you far from home, God infinitely more longs for you to be safe with Him. He is so eager to be with you. And that is really the most important thing. Not that you perform something for Him, but that you simply *be* with Him."

And instantly, I was taken back to last spring in Central Park. Petra was telling me the same truth I had given Anise. Why was it easier to give grace to others for certain things, but difficult to believe for oneself?

The conference I'd attended in the summer with Kendra had taught me a valuable tool for testing whatever teaching I heard. When Jesus instructed in Matthew 7 that His followers were to judge what they were taught by the fruit, one minister had explained fruit in one way: "Good fruit glorifies Jesus, and so good fruit will push you toward Him. Bad fruit doesn't have Christ at the center, and ingesting it leads you away from Him."

As I met a second time with Petra, my thoughts were drawn continually to Jesus, and my desire to spend time with Him quickened. So I was persuaded to attend a prayer meeting that the Freimann's were having one Wednesday evening. It was in their home on Regensburgerstraße.

Neue Name (or New Name, as this group of disciples was called) was comprised of a mixture of nationalities and backgrounds, predominantly Germans, but also some British couples, a Sicilian, several Africans, and a Greek woman. When we gathered in a circle that Wednesday, Michael Freimann sat down to the piano and we sang a mixture of contemporary and old German songs and hymns, with lyrics printed on sheets of paper so that we could follow along. As the singing progressed, it was a surprise to see how this eclectic group raised up their hands in worship and broke out in spontaneous vocalization.

At one point, Michael said, "Everybody just praise the Lord in your own language — let the voice of the Bride be heard by the Bridegroom." When we did so, the affect was powerful. Passionate cries of German were harmonized with Greek and English and distilled with an arpeggio of Italian. Again, I thought of Revelation's scene in Heaven with "every tongue and tribe and nation" joining in the song of the Lamb. A shiver of wonder and delight ran through me.

After singing, another man whom I'd later learn also served as pastor of this congregation, had us proclaim a passage of scripture together. It was warmly familiar to recognize the words we were repeating as Psalm 90. (I would come to find out that the congregation of Neue Name regularly did bold proclamations – that reading scripture together was not seen as stale liturgy, but as mighty weapons uttered into the spirit realm against the forces of darkness.)

The time with them felt refreshingly uninhibited. I had been in prayer circles where we followed "grocery lists" of needs, and while I could see some value in that, this was more satisfying in that we seemed to be led in our prayers by God. We prayed first as a whole, then in smaller groups. Michael encouraged us at intervals to be silent before God. After all, what *He* had to say was more important anyhow.

Michael introduced me to the group at one point and asked if I wanted to tell about myself. All I said was, "The Lord is faithful. He led me to your church."

When I left to take the bus back to Luisental, thanking Petra and Michael and remarking how invigorating it was, Petra remarked, "We all have different backgrounds – some here have been raised Catholic, others Lutheran, some Orthodox, some Anglican. And still others with no religious upbringing whatsoever. But we find common ground at the foot of the cross."

As I left this hodge-podge group of people, already dear to me after one evening, I remembered the words of the German martyr, Dietrich Bonhoeffer: "Where a people prays, there is the church; and where the church is, there is never loneliness."[3]

---

[3]Dietrich Bonhoeffer, *Barcelona, Berlin, New York: 1928-1931* (Dietrich Bonhoeffer Works, Volume 10), ed. Clifford J. Green (Minneapolis: Fortress Press, 2008), [pg]. Used with permission by Augsburg Fortress.

Chapter Twenty-Two

Warfare

The week following my introduction to Petra and Neue Name was harrowing. It was as though I were wearing a giant target that marked me for trouble. It started with losing my Bible — which I eventually realized I'd left in the library at the university and reclaimed, but not before I'd had quite a stressful time worrying over it. My personal Bible with all its underlines and notations and cross-references had become an extension of myself.

During the time I'd misplaced my Bible, internet service was down in our dorm for three days, which meant also that I couldn't read my Bible online. And I never realized how much I'd depended on the internet for contact to the outside world until it was taken. Because the internet was down, I was forced to do all my online reading and much of my work at the Uni, which meant staying there well into the evening, which in turn meant that I was riding public transportation home alone in the dark.

While waiting for the bus one evening, I was approached by a man who passionately implored me to let him kiss my feet. I glanced down at my very nondescript brown boots and tried to figure out the appeal that they held for him. The hesitation as I wondered if I had understood his request correctly must have encouraged his hopes, because as I took a step back from him, *he pulled out a leash* that was attached to a collar around his neck and tried to hand it to me. Ears burning as onlookers stared, I shook my head and desperately hoped he'd vanish. He followed me as I tried to scamper away, crying out a chorus of earnest *bittes*. Increasing my pace, he ignored the low "no, thank-you's" I hissed and continued to follow me, causing me growing alarm. Finally, in my irritation and angst I stopped and turned to stare him straight in the eyes. "You make me sick if you really care to know," I spat out in my best German, aware of even more stares. At this, his eyes grew wide and he gave up his quest and slunk off into the shadows. When the bus pulled up moments later, I walked all the way to the back and melted like a slinky down below the seat, trying to hide.

How glad I was to meet up with Petra again, who had invited me for coffee in Worpswede (pronounced Vorpsvayduh) northeast of Bremen, a former artist colony that she was eager for me to see. As we took seats at a table in the cheerful, canary yellow interior of the coffee shop, she filled me in a little more on her personal history. She and Michael were from Thüringen in the center of Germany, but had moved north six years ago.

"It was difficult leaving our home town where Michael and I had grown up and knew everyone, and especially to leave family. Both of us have elderly parents and to everyone else it looked like we were deserting them. We come from a small village and everyone knows each other – we all spoke the local dialect, which of course is different from the *Plattdeutsch* spoken here, and it was a very big adjustment. But God is faithful – and besides, He told us to go here."

"How?" I wanted to know.

"He spoke unmistakably to both of us – separately – but within the same week. He told me to leave my job as a teacher at the *Realschule* and pack up our things and go to Bremen. Michael was a pastor at a local church and between the two of us, we were leaving job security and home to travel to a place where we had neither work nor personal connections." Petra smiled as she took a sip of her tea. "Even our parishioners thought we were foolish when we both handed in our resignations, and a few openly questioned whether we had accurately heard from God."

"What happened after you quit your jobs?" I asked, intrigued.

"The very next day after we announced our resignations, a colleague from the school I'd just left notified me of an opportunity in Lower Saxony, just outside of Bremen. I began the application process and was selected from at least two dozen candidates. In the meantime, we knew of a cousin of Michael's who had a vacation rental home in Utkiek, not far from here. We inquired about renting there just until we could get established. Michael's cousin was agreeable to that, giving us a discounted lease in exchange for having trustworthy and steady tenants for a span of a couple months. After a time, we found our current home on Regensburgerstrasse. Michael was doing some consulting work, but did not believe he was to apply for a formal pastoral position. Within six months, we began holding services in our home. And while the congregation has been relatively small, God has been doing amazing things in our midst."

"We have a phrase we use in America," I told her, listening to her story in amazement. "Faith is spelled 'R-I-S-K'."

Petra smiled. "That saying has a lot of truth. And I think Americans are a little more accustomed to taking risks than Germans. We tend to be a cautious people, quicker to analyze and assess all the factors. This caution is a value that we hold to be dear. To be a disciple of Christ is to be counter-cultural, even in the face of praised values."

I told her about the craziness that seemed to have invaded my life of late, especially since our prayer time, culminating in the foot fetish perv.

"Yes, I definitely believe you are encountering warfare," she assessed. "Let us pray together, but first I want to ask what you know about the nature of the spiritual battle in which we Christians are involved."

"Well, I know about putting on spiritual armor," I replied. "I'm pretty familiar with that passage in Ephesians."

"Let's look at it, yes?" Petra pulled up the Bible on her phone. Then she looked at me. "This is probably easier for you to do in English, no?" She fiddled with the screen and the page came up in my native tongue. "Read the passage, beginning from verse ten:

> Finally, be strong in the Lord and in the strength of His might. Put on the full armor of God, so that you will be able to stand firm against the schemes of the devil. For our struggle is not against flesh and blood, but against the rulers, against the powers, against the world forces of this darkness, against the spiritual forces of wickedness in the heavenly places. Therefore, take up the full armor of God, so that you will be able to resist in the evil day, and having done everything, to stand firm. Stand firm therefore, having girded your loins with truth, and having put on the breastplate of righteousness, and having shod your feet with the preparation of the gospel of peace; in addition to all, taking up the shield of faith with which you will be able to extinguish all the flaming arrows of the evil one. And take the helmet of salvation, and the sword of the Spirit, which is the word of God. With all prayer and petition pray at all times in the Spirit, and with this in view, be on the alert with all perseverance and petition for all the saints.

It seemed like old hat to me. I had read this passage many times, and could remember flannel graph cutouts of the various pieces of the armor being used by teachers at vacation Bible schools when I was a little kid.

Petra pointed to the screen. "This verse here: 'Our struggle is not against flesh and blood, but against the rulers, against the powers, against the world forces of this darkness, against the spiritual forces of wickedness in the heavenly places.' What do you think that all means?"

I considered her question. "I don't know...I never thought about it in depth. I guess I always figured it meant our real enemy is the devil."

"Yes, that is the truth. But do you realize that Satan has a kingdom of darkness, and that just like God's kingdom, he has angelic rulers? His fallen angels – the ones that were part of the rebellion in Heaven and took his side – they did not just disappear. They are still in existence and still in rebellion, and they hold a specific hierarchy within his fallen kingdom. Now, these disembodied persons are called demons."

"Right." I was tracking with her so far.

"Now, look at this verse again. 'Rulers . . . powers . . . world forces . . . spiritual forces in heavenly places.' When I first met you, you had mentioned the heaviness that you felt as soon as you got off the train and returned to Bremen. Did you know that geographical regions of this world are actually ruled by demons?"

I must have had a peculiar expression on my face as my mind whirred and processed this information, because Petra paused and showed me another passage. This was in Daniel chapter 10, and she asked me to read the whole chapter, in English.

When I was finished, she said, "Look here. In this chapter, Daniel is praying and fasting for three weeks, abstaining from all but the blandest of foods. A heavenly being comes to deliver a message to him, and tells him that the moment he began to set his heart on understanding, the answer to his prayer was on its way. However, it was delayed by a spiritual force – in verse thirteen it says that this spiritual force was *the prince of the kingdom of Persia* that stood against the heavenly messenger. That is not a human being – it is a spiritual ruler of Satan's kingdom that was opposing the advancement of God's kingdom spreading through Daniel. Later, in verse 20 this angel leaves Daniel, saying that he must go and fight against this prince of Persia, and then he references another evil ruler – this one, of Greece.

Again, these are demonic rulers scripture is speaking of, not human ones."

Petra put down her phone and looked intently into my face. "Do you see — does it make sense, *Herzchen,* that we are in a war simply because we are in God's kingdom and because Satan's kingdom opposes God? Allegiance to God means enmity with the world, of which the Bible says Satan is ruler of, having usurped the power from Adam in the Garden of Eden. So our enemies are *not* other human beings, but spiritual ones."

"People picket and lobby and demonstrate and vote. But the source of power is not the politicians. It is not even — how do you say it in America? — special interest groups. It is the spiritual power *behind* the political forces that is what matters. That is the essence of what you and I and all disciples of Christ are battling."

"Yes, it makes sense," I said slowly as I swallowed this. "But are you suggesting that there aren't truly evil people out there?"

"I am not denying the existence of wicked people. But it is imperative to understand what Paul is saying here — that our battle is *not* against flesh and blood, but rather spiritual rulers and principalities. That means that as Christians, we should not have enemies in other people. Rather, our enemies are the forces influencing the mindsets of those people. When you understand that all of humanity is involved in a great war, and one is either a part of Satan's kingdom or of God's kingdom, but no one is ever neutral, then one views everything in life entirely differently."

I nodded. She wanted so badly for me to get it. And I *did* get it — partly.

"Do you ever wonder why there seem to be entire mindsets over different groups? And these mindsets aren't godly ones? They don't even seem to fit common sense?"

Immediately, my mind was drawn to yesterday, when I'd been waiting for the bus near the *Hauptbahnhof* and I'd watched, repulsed, as a man who was holding the hand of a little girl, presumably his daughter, paused to ogle the window display of one of the sex shops located near the center of the city. Moments earlier, I had darted across the street corner when there was no traffic coming, and received dirty looks and a sound scolding from a couple of onlookers who were appalled that I had jaywalked (jaywalking, as I said, is pretty much a capital offense in Germany). When I smiled faintly at what I deemed their overreaction, one of the men asked me, did I not realize that I was setting a terrible example for any children who might be watching? Yet the man transfixed outside the sex shop with a little girl by his side drew no condemnation from this same crowd.

Not wishing to offend Petra with any more negatives about Bremen, I instead cited another trend that I'd long noticed in the United States: the obsession with childhood obesity, and the war on trans-fatty foods. This diet dilemma always seemed to me to be a particularly misplaced focus in light of the fact that my generation was literally killing itself off in record percentages with drug addiction, sexually transmitted diseases, and suicide. In fact, since graduation from high school not three years ago, my class had lost four of its members — one due to suicide and three to drug overdose. Why wasn't the focus on the root cause of this, which like every other social ill was rooted in the breakdown of the family unit through illegitimacy, divorce, and abuse? Where were all these highly trained experts of youth culture who obsessed over calories when it came to the depression and despair of our generation? Why was the focus always on things that might have a mite of merit, but were of third-rate importance?

I shared this insight with Petra. She nodded. "That's precisely an example of misplaced priority. Behind the petty things that distract us from the important are these demons. It is not by chance. And if I may add, it seems to be fitting that this is the way that the western world sees the problems: always superficial, with a focus on the material and the physical body, never going deeper. For to examine the emotional and spiritual make-up of individuals and problems is to risk speaking of a Creator. And that goes against the worldly mindsets that govern people and institutions."

Petra continued, "It is not surprising that the world, being the unknowing slaves to Satan, gets taken in by these ruling demons. What is tragic is that Christians get sidetracked and we war against human beings and political factions whom we see as the threats. But the powers behind them are far more important – to recognize this is to be able to strike at the root rather than the branches."

I nodded, trying to take it all in.

Petra added, "I tell you all this not because I want you to focus on the devil, but because I do not want, like the Apostle Paul said, for you to be ignorant of his schemes."

When I left Petra, she asked me to do something before the next time we met. She asked me to read Matthew 12:1-29 and to jot down what I observed in the passage that related to what we just talked about and to the two kingdoms. It was the first "homework assignment" over which I can remember feeling undertones of excitement.

Chapter Twenty-Three

Lost in Translation

"No, that's not quite what I meant"
Vor dem Steintor – 22. Januar

Had a language mix-up today when I went to get my hair trimmed at a place recommended by Julia in a section of Bremen called Vor dem Steintor, or "In front of the stone gate."

The German word meaning "to cut" is *schneiden*. There is a similar verb meaning "to cut" that is *be*schneiden. This latter word is the one I used mistakenly to explain to the stylist what I wanted done. In essence, I asked her if she would circumcise my hair! (I did see her smother a smile before asking me in which style.)

Of course, this mistake wasn't nearly so embarrassing as the one that Helene made over video chat with her folks and the parents of Markus during Christmas break. Helene meant to say, "I want to introduce you, Rolf and Sabine, to my parents." The word for "introduce" is *ein*füren. But Helene used the wrong prefix like I did, and instead said she wanted to *ver*füren them. That is the word for "seduce."

Incidentally, the reason I went for this salon visit was a result of using Tabitha's hair relaxer. She is half Jamaican, and I asked her once if I could try it, thinking it would save me the trouble of using a straightening iron. (Bremen's perpetually drizzly climate is always at war with my hair.) I left the relaxer in too long and the result was damage to it that Maria warned might make my hair fall out. Essentially, my hair suffered a severe chemical imbalance.

The German *friseur* who managed the place came by to inspect my head before his employee applied the shearers. He sifted his fingers through my locks several times in a grandiose manner, and then told me in perfect English, "Your hair eez a dee-sahster!"

"My first-grader could draw that"
Weserburg – 25. Januar

My study buddy Julia and I went to an art museum yesterday called the Weserburg, which sits right on the Weser river. The castle-like building is at odds with its content: outside, it looks picturesque and old-fashioned, but inside is filled with off-the-wall contemporary art. While I'm more of a fan of traditional art, I could get into some of these modern collections. One of my favorite series was of "painted-over" photographs by Gerhard Richter. Just as it sounds, he takes photos and coats them with varnish, then paints over them with oils or enamel. The ones he did of landscapes and outdoor scenery I particularly liked; the ones involving people as subjects were kind of creepy – like something out of a horror dream sequence.

On another note, I found out today that I've secured an internship for next semester. I will be helping to teach English to teenagers at a local *Gesamtschule,* or comprehensive school (equivalent to high school) two days per week, and it counts for a full credit!

#####

"There is a town in Germany where adults actually come to dress up and play 'Cowboys and Indians'" Tabitha read. Her uncle had spotted the magazine article in an American periodical and sent it to her. She read its subheading aloud, "'Why do Germans love American westerns?'"

Helene spoke up. "Markus says that it's just a stereotype. It was more his parents' generation that felt that way. Not the young people today."

"It says here it was a trend that was more popular in East Germany." Tabitha read further before tossing the paper on top of her pile of notebooks. "I find it hysterical that grown men actually spend the time and money to dress up and do this."

"I can understand the allure of the American cowboy," I said. "As a woman, what girl doesn't want a larger-than-life, swaggering superhero to sweep her off her feet?" I separated the label, soggy with condensation, from my beer bottle, and rolled it up in a ball. "Especially one that works hard, smells of rawhide, and is good with his hands."

Maria nearly spit out her Riesling.

"Whoa, I don't think I've ever heard *you* talk that way," Tabitha said incredulously, staring at me.

I shrugged. "It's true. To me, the cowboy embodies everything wild and wonderful in a man." I thought about my own statement for a moment. "So long as he has a good sense of humor and some interests outside of steers and frontiers — you know, a thoughtful side."

"They say the trend today is for women to prefer more feminine features in men," Helene countered. "Less rugged, more soft."

"I just don't believe it," I shook my head. "I've heard that, too. But I think given a choice, most women prefer the confident, macho, man's man."

"As opposed to . . . Edward and Jacob, those little *Twilight* bitches?" Tabitha asked.

This time, it was I who sputtered my beer and coughed, before nodding in agreement. "Too many pretty boys."

"Maybe that's why so many women go for the bad boys," Maria mused. "They want a man who can *be* tender and considerate, but they're attracted to that tough, rowdy masculine side."

I considered this. "Maybe you're right. Maybe they get confused over what they're seeing and they're drawn to the aggressiveness. So they end up with the jerks."

"I think guys who are jerks are super, super insecure," Tabitha offered. "They have unresolved issues and take that out on their women."

"I'd agree with that," I nodded.

"There sure seem to be a lot of that kind," Maria sighed.

We thrashed out some thoughts a bit on the subject, each of us throwing in details as to our perfect male prototype. Sipping our German libations and speculating, a casual observer would think there was an assembly line somewhere that was taking orders on customized men.

*****

Petra came to visit me at Luisental and brought me a small pot of white miniature roses. She took her time in examining all the photos in my room and inquiring as to the subjects within them, and studied my collection of books in detail as well. When she was finished, she sat down at my request in the single chair that I had in my room, while I made her some flavored tea from the variety pack my mom had sent in the last care package.

"I do not think I understood you on the telephone" she said as I handed her a saucer. "What is this special knock that I was to do on the door?"

Briefly, I explained about Stefan the Stalker.

"Ah," she nodded and leaned back in her chair. "Yes, you must be very firm here with the men who approach you."

A hand grenade is about the level of persuasion that's needed with the men here, I thought.

"And how is Julia?"

I told her about our trip to the museum. "I like her. She's very . . . " I searched my German databanks for the correct idiom. "She 'stands with both feet on the earth?'"

Petra smiled. "Ah, that is good to hear. It sounds like an answer to prayer."

"Yes. A double answer is meeting Julia *and* you."

"So what did you think as you read Matthew 12?" she wanted to know.

Eagerly, I told Petra how I'd grown up knowing that passage in which Jesus is haggled by the Pharisees, but this time it was brought into focus more. I told her how it came to light as I read the verses over and over, paying careful attention to the references to kingdom, how there really were two distinct kingdoms – God's and Satan's – and that in this passage, it was clear that the religious people, the Pharisees, had their allegiance to the devil, even though they couldn't see it for a mile.

Petra listened, nodding. "I really think religious people are still Jesus' greatest headache today. Or perhaps I should say 'heartache.' The religious spirit is a big stumbling block for the Body of Christ, as well as to the unbelieving world."

I wasn't sure I understood her entirely. But I wanted to think about that statement.

Petra continued. "Did you notice that the sickness in the deaf mute was caused by a demon? Sickness is a work of the enemy. Physical, mental, spiritual. It is not of God. God is so good. Everything that He brings is life, like it says in John. That is one of the reasons Jesus states for why He came. 'To destroy the works of the Enemy,' and that people 'might have life and life abundantly.'"

Petra's words penetrated my noggin and did a few laps around the perimeter of my brain before slowly starting to sink inward. I thought of the woman bent over with some kind of crazy arthritis, whom Jesus had healed on the Sabbath. Jesus had accredited her illness to Satan, I now remembered. I'd never thought of sickness or mental illness as being a work of the enemy so much as just being something unfortunate that happened to people.

"Of course, Christians are not only at war with Satan, but they're also at odds with the flesh, according to Galatians 5:17."

"Oh, terrific," I sighed, smiling.

"That is a whole study in itself. Let me show you just one more passage in scripture. In 2 Corinthians 10 Paul says, "For though we walk in the flesh, we do not war according to the flesh, for the weapons of our warfare *are not of the flesh*, but divinely powerful for the destruction of strongholds. What would you say that that means, in your own words?"

"Christians exist in physical form like other human beings, but we don't play by the same rules in the battles that we see."

Petra pondered my explanation for a moment, then seemed to concur. "And how would you explain a stronghold?"

My mind went back to the *Burg* towers of Nürnberg, high up on the hill over the city. "A stronghold is a kind of a fortress. A place that is occupied by a specific group. A military stronghold is an area that is difficult or impossible to penetrate by enemies of that army."

"*Genau.* Exactly. What is an example of a spiritual stronghold?"

I wasn't sure. All I could think about was how remarkably like a benevolent drill sergeant Petra was at that moment. And how profoundly my German was expanding by seeing familiar scriptures written in German – the "really *hard* German," as Maria would have called it.

"The next verse tells us what strongholds are," Petra prompted me, pointing to the scripture.

I studied the passage a moment. "Arguments . . . pretensions . . . and thoughts that are contrary to the knowledge of God."

Petra nodded and sat back in her chair. "So you see, *Herzchen,* that the strongholds Paul is referencing here are mindsets. Once we identify our own *personal* strongholds, we can destroy them or take them captive."

I considered for a moment what this personally meant for me. "I think a stronghold I struggle with is feeling like I haven't done enough for Jesus — like I've come short of the mark. And He's disappointed with me and so we can't go any further."

"Let's take that thought captive right now," Petra suggested. "We dismiss it as ungodly and contrary to what scriptures say is true of you — that you have the righteousness of Christ." She seemed to discern where I was already going in my thinking. "And if this thought gets away and comes back to taunt you, take it captive again. You might have to do it a hundred times, but keep doing it. And sooner or later, that thought won't return."

I thanked her. "I read a sermon online once that talked about spiritual warfare and taking down strongholds. But it was focusing on the mindsets of society. The things that dominate our news headlines and the political races. Abortion, drugs, poverty, crime, ethnic wars, *um zu weiter.*"

"What do you remember of it?" Petra wanted to know.

"Just that these strongholds over different nations — addiction, suicide, abuse, genocide, and every other social problem of our time — are not solvable by the world. When the world tries to fight these problems, they only succeed in — [I paused to look up the word in German] — *rearranging* them."

Petra nodded rigorously. "That is right. But Christians have the *divine* power, according to Paul, to destroy them utterly."

I considered that for a moment, wondering if I truly believed it.

"Paul says here that the military strongholds, these fortresses that are hostile to the Truth, can be destroyed utterly by the weapons of the Christians. Otherwise hopeless people whom the world cannot rehabilitate or assimilate back into society can be set free in a single instance by Jesus Christ working through His church. Entire cities that are governed by a mindset can be set free. Again, we Christians are easily sidetracked and we war against human beings whom we see as the threats with the same blunt weapons that the world uses to fight social problems, like lobbying and picketing and boycotting. But the powers behind the problems are never addressed. To recognize this is to be able to strike at the root rather than the branches."

Petra set down her tea cup and rose to go. "I have so much enjoyed talking with you. I can feel the presence of the Holy Spirit here in this room with us now."

She closed her eyes for a moment and smiled. When she opened them again she said, "I have one more assignment for you, *Herzchen*. What are the weapons of our warfare that Paul is referring to?"

My conversation with Petra was taking me to new terrain, and I would need time to process everything that we'd discussed. But I felt that in the brief time that I'd met her, Petra not only had given me a much-needed crash course in basic Christian worldview, but she'd also inadvertently given me a significant piece to the puzzle I had been struggling with in recent months. If those who were in Christ were already seated in heavenly places, were already in His kingdom of light, and had citizenship in Heaven, then Ephesians 6:12 and 2 Corinthians 10:4 connected these dots together in another way. For it said that we are at war with spiritual forces in heavenly places and that we were destroying heavenly strongholds. In order to battle one's enemy, one had to be operating in the same dimension as the enemy.

To be a Christian was *not* so dull as the church had made it out to be. To be a Christian was, in a very real sense, to be an officer in the Special Forces of the King of the Universe, fighting in territory ruled by an evil Enemy, in order to advance the kingdom of Heaven on earth.

In the world's eyes, I realized then that while I might not appear spectacular or super exciting, in Heaven's economy, I was Wonder Woman. There was a role designated only for me, that had been set up before the dawn of creation, that only I could fulfill. I had been offered the keys to the Kingdom.

Rather than trying simply to usher people into Heaven, I was beginning to grasp that the true mission of the church was to bring Heaven down to earth – drawing from its resources, unloading its coffers of gold. It was to be using weapons of might, weapons of dynamite, to rescue the unsuspecting masses who were driving, shopping, surfing the web, eating, partying, planning their weddings, receiving a diagnosis from the doctor, cheering a soccer game – and were all the while targeted for doom.

*****

My mom's tones were quiet coming over the telephone. "I have some sad news," she said. The words seemed to reach me slowly.

Death. It was in the strains of her voice. I braced myself.

"Molly. Molly, Agnes died this morning."

Agnes. My dog. My dog was dead. No. That wasn't possible. Agnes was there in the kitchen, begging scraps of a dish my mom was making, or sunning herself in the light streaming in from the picture window. Agnes was too full of life to be dead.

"Molly? Are you there?"

"I'm here."

"I'm so sorry to have to tell you this news over the phone. We thought about waiting until a better time, but didn't know when that would be. If you had asked about her, well, you'd be upset we hadn't told you right away."

I swallowed. "I – um, how did she die?"

My mom's voice grew softer as she spoke in the gentlest tone she could. "She slipped past me out the door when I opened it to grab the newspaper. Normally she doesn't do that, you know, but she heard a motorcycle outside – it's been unusually warm here the last few days – and she took off to chase it. A car was coming the opposite way and -" my mom broke off. "It was instant."

Tears spilled out and ran down until they dropped one by one off my chin. But I didn't make a sound.

"Are you alright, Molly?

I cleared my throat, trying to pull myself together. "Yeah. I'm okay. How's Anne?"

"Well, your sister's taking it pretty hard. We buried Agnes down by the end of the yard, underneath the willow tree. Anne's gone for a walk now."

"Well." I swallowed hard. "Tell her to call me if she wants. When she gets back."

I got off the phone just in time and the geyser of emotion let loose.

Agnes. Dear, dear Agnes. I'd been impatient with her the day before I'd left for Germany because she'd decided to curl up and take a nap on my load of clean clothes that I'd just pulled out of the dryer. Had I known it would be the last time I'd see her . . .

Last night, she was cozy and content in my parents' house, probably lying down expectantly under the table as everyone sat down to dinner. Tonight, she was cold and dead and alone under the willow tree.

Chapter Twenty-Four

Culture

I was fighting a very real pull to sink back into my former despondency with the news of losing Agnes, especially since I was so far away. A picture of her standing in the doorway, gazing up at me with her affectionate brown eyes and wagging tail, would flash in my mind as I waited for the bus. The dogs the German students brought with them to class constantly reminded me of her. When I did my laundry, I'd think of how surly I'd been to her the last time she'd seen me, and I'd just lose it.

And I was angry at my mom. I knew it wasn't right, but I faulted her for Agnes getting killed. If she'd just been a little more careful . . .

In the midst of struggling with these heavy feelings, the loss of Agnes got me thinking about death in general. Something crept back in my mind from one of the books I'd read the year before, when I was so hungry for the things of God that I'd devoured every piece of Christian literature or commentary into which I'd come into contact.

One Bible teacher I'd read asserted that Jesus' arch enemy was not Satan so much as it was death. When God had created man, He designated man as His viceroy on earth – a kind of personal representative. But in Adam's sin, Satan in the form of the serpent had usurped the authority God had given man. Satan therefore had become "the ruler of this world" and the process of corruption began. It was not only human beings that were corrupted, but also the earth and everything in it. Natural disasters, sickness and disease, and death were all a part of the corruption process that had begun upon the earth. The corruption process could be slowed down through various means, like the way a refrigerator slows the decay of a vegetable, but it couldn't ultimately be stopped or reversed.

Jesus, on the other hand, came "that [we] might have life, and have it more abundantly." He hadn't come just to save us from Hell. He had come to annihilate death and everything that led to it. There was only one source for life, and there was only one source for death. As George MacDonald had put it, "All that is not God is death." Every decision and every choice to move within or without His commandments was a step toward life or toward death.

*****

Ulrich got more than he bargained for when he took our little quartet on a cultural excursion to the Neckar River valley. Maria got deathly sick, while Helene and Tabitha kept the small group dynamics interesting with a tiff.

Everything started out splendidly in our tour of Germany's southwestern state of Baden-Württemberg. We had commenced our three-day trip in famous Heidelberg, where the weather was much milder than in Bremen. By our late-morning arrival, we had felt sunshine on our faces, and that was enough to recommend the entire trip.

In a restaurant decked out in dark paneling, antlers, and tree-trunk tables, cozy and rustic as a medieval hunting lodge, we'd feasted on *Spätzle* (a kind of doughy noodle), *Schäufele* (smoked shoulder of pork), and *Schwarzwaldkirschtorte* (Black Forest Cake).

"You can't even eat this food without spitting in it first," I'd remarked, as we read the tongue-twisting names.

Maria was the only one of us daring enough to try the Schwabian delicacy of *Schneckensuppe* (snail soup) so we suspected this might have been the culprit in her sudden illness.

When her lunch didn't cooperate with her stomach, Maria opted to sit and rest while we toured the magnificent castle and its ruins atop the hill in the city of Heidelberg. Ulrich stayed with her. By the time we returned, she was pale as the blanched stucco of the nearby parish church. Moments later, the offending snails were returned unceremoniously to a watery habitat like that of their origins, this time in the form of the commode.

Retiring to her room, we didn't see Maria again until after dinner when darkness had already closed in over the town. She and I had chosen to be roommates during this trip, but her heaving sprints to the bathroom at regular intervals prompted me to suggest that she might be more comfortable having the room to herself. Tabitha and Helene agreed to let me spread out on their floor.

As we were performing our various feminine bedtime rituals of brushing hair, removing make-up, and applying various washes and creams and moisturizers, Helene offered some random, innocuous observation to Tabitha. It was a statement submitted for Tabitha's approval, of whom it was clear Helene admired. For whatever reason, be it fatigue or just an offbeat mood, Tabitha's response was short and sharp – not very nice.

The silence following this very brief exchange was charged. I brushed my hair and quietly hummed, as if that might diffuse the uncomfortable atmosphere. Instead, Helene retorted something low and loaded under her breath, topping it off with the sarcastic salutation to Tabitha, "Your majesty."

At this, Tabitha got up, grabbed her bag and her shoes, and left the room, pulling the door shut behind her none too softly as she padded out into the hallway in her socks. Wherever she intended to go at that late hour, I wasn't sure. But forty-five minutes later she still hadn't returned, and Helene had already hunkered down under the covers. So I turned off the lights.

The next morning, Ulrich woke us up with a knock on the door. He'd stopped by to inform us that he was taking Maria to the nearest hospital. She hadn't stopped up-chucking all night, and he was concerned about dehydration.

"Where is Tabitha?" he asked, surveying the room behind us and Tabitha's still-made bed. (With his accent, her name always came out Tobby-tah).

Helene and I looked at one another.

"She left last night and I guess didn't come back," Helene volunteered timidly.

Ulrich looked mystified. "Where was she going?"

"She didn't say," I whispered, my mind racing down corridors that led to all kinds of horrible possibilities.

Ulrich whipped out his phone and punched some buttons. Helene and I waited, poised in dreadful silence.

"Tobby-tah?" he said finally. Both of us exhaled. Concern was still embedded in Ulrich's voice. "*Wo bist du? . . . Ja . . . Alles klar.*" He murmured something further, but I couldn't detect it.

Hanging up, Ulrich explained that Tabitha was on her way and would arrive shortly. Apparently, she had gone out with and stayed the night with friends from Heidelberg whom she'd met through her summer speech course.

"Do you want us to go with you to the hospital?" I asked, wondering whether Ulrich's carefully level countenance belied the annoyance that *I* felt over Tabitha's disappearance.

"*Danke, nein,*" Ulrich replied. He urged us to go on and to explore the town of Neckarsteinach, which had been on the agenda for today, saying that he would check in with us around noon.

Tabitha met us as we were finishing our continental breakfast of *Brötchen*, cold cuts, and fruit in the hotel. She mumbled a sulky greeting before running up to our room to grab her belongings which had been abandoned the night before.

Between Ulrich's and Maria's absence, and the estrangement of Helene and Tabitha, who steadfastly avoided one another, it was a rather dreadful ride to Neckarsteinach. Concern over Maria and my travel companions faded to the back of my mind, however, as we approached this medieval town and I glimpsed four different castles situated along the narrow ridge overlooking the Neckar River. High in the hills they arose, and intrigue and wistfulness washed over me at once in a baptism of anticipation.

The first castle we toured, Hinterburg, was in ruins, but one could still see the outer walls surrounding what had once been the palace. The view from atop the hill was spectacular, with the river beneath us, and mountains and trees surrounding us. A foundation stone read HINTERBURG: UM 1100 (A.D.) A staircase leading to the top of the wall was still intact, and the weight of the thousand years of history in which I was standing grew tangible. I could *see* the lord of this castle striding back and forth across his walls, scanning the horizon for signs of a vessel emerging from the bend in the river. Who might be out there – a merchant, a visitor, or a marauder?

Two of the remaining castles, to my surprised delight, had been preserved and were still private residences. Of course, we couldn't see the interior for this reason, but I was fascinated to think that a lineage of nobility still occupied these imposing dwellings. Helene struck up a conversation with a stranger, native to the area, who was more than willing to answer her questions, and in fact gave us a whole run-down on what was before our eyes, just like a private guide. She spoke so quickly, I missed half of what she said, but her enthusiasm was touching. She gave Helene and then me and Tabitha as we gathered near, details of the residences, both of which had been built in the twelfth century.

"Each year there is a *Herbstmarkt* here," the tiny, enthusiastic woman informed us, gesturing at the structure behind us. She went on to explain that one of the two privately owned castles hosts this fall fair, and it is a time when the châtelains (castle owners) invite the "commoners" to mingle with them.

What I wouldn't have given for a peek inside one of these chateaux, particularly the renovated Mittelburg, which was evidently in spectacular shape. And its inhabitants intrigued me as well. *I wonder if they come out to do their own grocery shopping,* I would have liked to know.

Throughout our walking tour, Helene and Tabitha had avoided one another. I tried repeatedly to break the ice, making little jokes from time to time, talking first to one, then the other, trying to get a three-way conversation going. But nothing worked. When Helene and I dialogued, Tabitha would edge over to snap a photo of something, and by the time I got Tabitha talking, Helene would have exited the interaction.

By late afternoon, Ulrich had called to let us know that Maria had been seen, treated, and discharged. She was fine, but was resting at the hotel where we'd be staying that evening. Ulrich suggested that we all meet at a quaint little *Weinstube* overlooking the Neckar.

The cozy charm of the wine bar Ulrich had chosen was marred by the awkward silence that enfolded the four of us when once again, Tabitha and Helene were forced to be in close proximity. I was weary from my day-long vain attempts to create peace, and so I sat in the silence as well. Ulrich asked us questions about the sights we had seen, and we individually gave stilted answers. I could tell that he was reading us carefully, aware that something was up.

Eventually, Ulrich excused himself for the restroom, and I decided to seize the moment.

"Listen, you two," I sighed. "All day long I've felt like a kid traveling with two parents who won't talk to each other. It's bad enough to have a cat spat during a day we've set aside to tour castles, but now Ulrich knows something is weird. *Please* talk to each other and work it out."

Tabitha looked at Helene dubiously. Helene looked down at the tablecloth.

"*Please,*" I said again. "The longer this goes on, the worse it will be, and we have to be together for another six months."

Helene raised her eyes and looked at Tabitha. She looked down, then mumbled, "Why did you snap at me last night?"

Tabitha sighed. "I don't know. I just did. Why did you call me 'Your Majesty'?"

Helene studied her knuckles. "Well, sometimes it seems like you act like you're queen of the world."

Tabitha considered this. "Alright. I suppose you're right."

Neither said anything for a moment. Finally, Tabitha offered, "Well. Hey. I'm sorry I was rude. Just stuff going on back home that was on my mind. No excuse."

"I'm sorry I was sarcastic," Helene returned.

"So are we *Freunde* again?"

"*Freundinnen*," Helene agreed, correcting Tabitha's grammar at the same time.

Ulrich reappeared moments later to find the three of us giggling over something dumb in the relieved atmosphere that followed.

Grief, he must think we're nuts, I thought. *Or at least manic.*

Up until this point, I hadn't thought much about Ulrich's responsibilities in all of this. Really, it was quite an assignment to be in charge of a group of girls barely out of their teens, for one year, an ocean away from home. If any of us got seriously ill, kidnapped, or pregnant while on his watch, well . . . four young ladies running loose in Europe was quite a liability.

Maria had recovered completely by the next day, and was in her usual spirits for our final day of the excursion. Once we were en route to our last destination of Bad Wimpfen, glancing at poor Ulrich, I wondered if it wasn't he who'd experienced the most cultural immersion during our brief trip.

*****

"Julia, have you ever had Girl Scout cookies?"

"I have never heard of them."

"Here, try this. You're going to want to come to America for sure." I gave her a thin mint.

She munched it thoughtfully. "It is different," she said noncommittally.

I sighed contentedly, taking one out of the wrapper. "Oh, I could eat a whole sleeve of these in a single sitting. I'm so glad Anne thought to send them."

We were sitting on a bench outside the university, taking a moment to savor the sunshine which was occasionally peering out from behind the usual canopy of clouds, before deciding peevishly that it did not want to shine on Bremen after all. It was February and around 40 degrees Fahrenheit, which felt positively balmy to me now.

"Molly, you are someone who believes in God, yes?"

Utterly surprised, I felt my spiritual antennae go up. I made an effort, however, to appear nonchalant.

"Yes. I do."

"You seem to be a strong person. I gather you are a pretty independent woman."

I shrugged. I didn't see myself this way, but if others did, I was comfortable with the delusion.

Julia wrinkled her brow. "How does being a strong, independent woman fit in with being a Christian?"

How did we get from thin mints to feminism? I wondered.

"What do you mean?"

"The Bible is sexist, isn't it?" Julia persisted.

"In what way?" I asked.

Julia frowned. Evidently she hadn't expected a cross-examination of her own question.

"Well, women are seen as inferior."

"I'm not sure where you're seeing that in the Bible," I responded slowly, "or I could answer it more specifically for you. On the contrary, I think it is remarkable that Jesus chose to appear first to women, not men, after His resurrection. It was also to a woman that Jesus first openly revealed Himself as

Messiah. And not just any woman. This woman was a Samaritan — a race considered to be lowlifes — and a big-time sinner. She was living with her boyfriend, and had had five husbands before that."

Julia stared at me, expressionless.

"Jesus healed women, He delivered some from demons, and many of them were His disciples." My heart was pounding now. "He never showed Himself to be unkind, patronizing, or demeaning to a woman. Now, how many *other* men can you say that about?"

This time, Julia was definitely at a loss for words. I, on the other hand, was excited, eager. The truth of my own words had warmed me.

She looked as though she still wanted to argue the point, but wasn't sure from which angle she should parry. Finally, she picked up a dosido. "What do you call these?" she asked.

Twenty-Five

Amsterdam

"American Football"
Bremer Mitte – 1. Februar

Ulrich is taking us to a Super Bowl party on Sunday so we can watch the big game on a big screen. Since I don't have a favorite team represented, I'll just say *"Go AFC!"*

"Lamaze"
Luisental – 3. Februar

I've jumped back into running and fitness and joined a gym that is conveniently close to the student dorm. The gym is not very large, but it has some pretty decent equipment and plenty of free weights and machines.

Ever direct and ever wanting to be helpful, the same German man has approached me on more than one occasion to admonish me in the correct breathing technique for lifting. "Like this," he said, demonstrating proper exhaling as he pushed a small stack of weights upward in a shoulder press.

Well today, I nearly screamed while doing the bench press when I opened my eyes and there this man was, inches from my face.

"Now breathe!" he commanded me enthusiastically (in German of course), pushing out his breath in three short puffs to demonstrate.

Exasperated and scared half out of my mind at the surprise of his face so close to mine, I told him that he would make a good midwife. At which he stared at me for a split second, before throwing his head back and roaring with laughter as though it were the funniest thing he'd ever heard.

Anyway, it's nice that he wanted to be helpful. And, it's good to be running again, although humbling how out of shape a body can become in four months.

"Hurray for Schnee."
Bremen – 4. Februar

The title of this blog is actually a rhyme in German – "hurray for snow" (pronounced *schnay*). We got two inches of white stuff today, after being told it *never ever* snows in Bremen. It was so pretty coming down outside my window in Luisental. The whole city went into emergency panic mode, and there were crews on every corner as I took the bus home from the Uni. Even though it was just a light covering, it has changed the way Bremen looks entirely.

"Proverbs 11:11"
Bremen – 7. Februar

"By the blessing of the upright a city is exalted, but by the mouth of the wicked it is torn down." I read this verse this morning and was socked with the knowledge that I have been tearing down Bremen by my steady confession of disdain for it. So . . . I am determined to speak blessings over Bremen – over the beggars in the *Viertel*, over the S-bahn and the smelly buses, over the communists and the wymyn and the tardy professors at the Uni; over Hans Heckelmeyer and over my student dorm;

and even over the creepists who whistle, stare, and verbally harass the innocent!

Hamsterdamn
Amsterdam – 15. Februar

Tabitha and I took a train from Bremen to the Netherlands and met up with three other Dursties in Amsterdam. We were there just for the extended weekend, since neither Tabitha nor I had class Monday.

How to describe this infamous city . . . or our experiences there. There was the arrival at our dubious (as in somewhat skeezy) youth hostel, lunch at an Irish pub, the utterly fabulous Rembrandt museum (yes, "fabulous" might be a traditionally phony word, but no lesser adjective will do to describe this one), being solicited to buy drugs from several of the city's aggressive Prince Charmings (as in grubby-looking stick men with about seven teeth (most of which were black), a stop in a notorious coffee shop, and then the deliciously frightening wax museum.

We were supposed to tour the Heineken museum, but it was closed when we got there and so we browsed a flea market instead. We got a good look at the Red Light District. Seeing the women standing in the windows plying their sorrowful trade made me very depressed.

Staring at all the original works of Van Gogh in his museum was almost surreal – this was the highlight of the trip for me. *Starry Night* and *The Wheatfield with Crows* are my favorite of his masterpieces, but on this visit I was introduced to a number of his others paintings I'd never seen. I left the museum with a print of *The Olive Grove* in tow.

We stopped at one more place in Amsterdam, but it is difficult to write about it. It was the annex in a narrow house at Prinsengracht 267, world famous now as the Anne Frank museum. I can't – or would rather not – describe the atmosphere of being in that space, shared by two families who day after day dared not make noise, nor so much as open the windows for a breath of fresh air or sunshine for fear of being discovered by the Nazis. Then, one terrible day they *were* discovered . . .

Amsterdam is a peculiar city – kind of a Las Vegas meets the Metropolitan Museum of Art. It is a place where depravity collides with creativity, and centuries of rich history serve as a backdrop for businessmen seeking out clandestine sins.

While we were in Amsterdam, I kept remembering a *Twilight Zone* episode in which a man wakes up in a place where he is given every single wish his flesh could desire. A gambler, the man wins at every tug of the slot machine. He is given his fill of booze and cigars, and a giggling gaggle of girls piles into a sports car with him and follows him to his penthouse. After a short time, he suddenly becomes absolutely sick of it all – hates the very sight of each fulfillment of his fleshly desires. He complains to the proprietor that he's bored to tears and utterly depressed – if this is Heaven, he's had enough of it. Could he please be returned to the shabby life he left behind? To which the proprietor asks him why on earth he'd imagine that he's in Heaven? With a sinister laugh, the proprietor informs the man that he's actually in Hell.

#####

Visiting the secret annex that hid Anne Frank and her family filled me with torrid emotion. For the first time in my life, I felt like I knew what it meant to be "grieved in spirit." It was a level of sadness that transcended anything else I'd known. I would not have even described it as being on a normal human emotional plane. It cut deeper – a sadness that one could not shut off nor escape.

Returning to Bremen with Tabitha, I fell asleep in the train and dreamed that I was on another kind of train. It was full of the collective sounds of people and yet it was silent with a blanketing terror. Anne Frank was sitting next to me, and I had my arms around her, trying to comfort her as she wept bitterly over the Nazis' discovery of them, and the subsequent separation of her family, and the fate before her.

Chapter Twenty-Five

The Sinful Mile

Michael Freimann preached an unforgettable message one Sunday on the Tabernacle in the wilderness, and how it was a pattern of, among other things, the nature of man. That man, made in God's image, is a triune being as well. Man is made up of three parts, Michael had said, "body, soul, and spirit."

The Holy of Holies in the tabernacle was the part in which God actually dwelt, just as our spirits are the part of us where God dwells by the Holy Spirit, if we have been saved. The spirit is the part of us that we use to communicate with God (God is spirit, and those who worship Him must worship Him in spirit and in truth).

Our body, of course, is what we use to contact the outside world. And in between the body and the spirit is our soul (Greek word *psyche* from where we get our term "psychology") determining whether our body or our spirit will have dominance. He explained that the body's five senses – sight, hearing, touch, taste, and scent – act as gates that either blocked or allowed in everything good and bad that would either glorify God and transform our spirits, or deaden our spirits and feed the flesh.

The sermon reminded me of a little rhyme I'd once read:

> *Two natures beat within my breast*
> *One is foul, the other blest,*
> *The one I love, the one I hate*
> *The one I feed will dominate.*

I never knew until Michael's sermon that there was a difference between the spirit and the soul. I always believed that they were the same, but Michael pointed out scripture such as Hebrews 4:12 and I Thessalonians 5:23 that reveal that they are indeed distinct. He also said that most Christians don't realize that they need to move from the soulish (intellectual/emotional) to the spiritual.

For the first time it made sense to me how we need not be ruled by our emotions, but that we could "take thoughts captive to Christ" as Paul said we were to do in 2 Corinthians 10. We didn't need to be driven and tossed by anger, by a relationship wound, even by passion for another person. (I felt with piercing conviction now that it was possible not to obsess over Hank, and this not by willpower, but through a choice of obedience carried out by the grace of the Holy Spirit.) It wasn't about keeping a lid on our emotions. To make emotions and thoughts that entered us bow to Christ was to make them bow to the Truth.

Knowing that these emotions, however strong, existed on the soulish level, but were transcended by the spiritual, was a powerful truth that allowed one to step back from circumstances. It was like having a zoom-out lens on one's life, and as you got to see the broader picture, suddenly there was a much clearer awareness of what was really going on – and why.

I thought of my own sins that seemed so easily to entangle. Especially lust. It could be starved or it could be fed. Whichever decision was made was a step to killing or growing its hold on a person's life.

I suddenly remembered Pastor Steve's sermon last summer on "product packaging." That was, the gospel was the "same product" but now we were simply using "different packaging" to promote it for today's audience. His message had struck a wary chord in me, but I didn't know why. It *sounded* alright. But Michael Freimann's message would suggest that God did not need our soulish help – our best ideas and patterned programs

– to win the lost. He wanted us to tune in to Him wholeheartedly with our own wandering spirits and let *Him* show us how and where to go about reaching the lost.

And prayer. For the first time, I was understanding that had I been one of the disciples following Jesus, I'd have echoed their plea to Jesus, "Master, teach us to pray!" Of all the things that they could have asked Jesus to teach them! Not healing, not casting out demons, not walking on water 101, not a workshop on miracles. "Teach us to pray." Yes, because this was a key to the kingdom. *Prayer* was where it was at, and how little I'd seen the church employ it, other than a routine formality that one used to salt and pepper the services. How little I myself knew how to pray, especially as I witnessed this little group of believers at Neue Name travail – praying with actual sweat and tears.

In thinking of Pastor Steve, I decided to email him and tell him about the Freimann's and Neue Name and all the exciting stuff I was discovering. I sent him a message, detailing some of the highlights of my life since I'd left in August, culminating in meeting Petra and the other members of the church here. I told him why it was finally making sense, this morbid veil that seemed to hang like a garment over Bremen. Pastor Steve's response was kind, but there was a cautionary note in his reply.

"I do think we need to be careful not to over-spiritualize things," he had written.

When I read that, a dart when into my balloon. Was it possible to over-spiritualize life? I mean, certainly it was possible to hear or perceive something incorrectly and misunderstand what God was saying or doing in a situation or with a person's life. But scripture said that we were to fix our eyes on things unseen, not on the visible. It also said that our focus should be on things above, not on things of earth. The spiritual realities were far more important than what we were seeing in the natural realm – that the natural realm was less real because it was passing away. The natural realm – what we could see with our eyes — was in fact impacted and a result of the spiritual. This knowledge was the essence of faith.

In the end, I decided not to debate this point with Pastor Steve. He had his seminary degree, and I did not. I doubted that I would convince him on what I was seeing. And I had been warned by Petra, with her uncanny ability to peer into my soul and tell me just what I needed to know for the moment, that while it was okay to disagree with him — even sharply — that I needed to be careful. For to criticize or find fault with Pastor Steve in an unloving way, this man called by God, was to sin against myself.

"If you can't beat 'em, join 'em"
Findorff – 1. März

I've gone and purchased a bicycle. It is an exceedingly ugly one, but it gets me from one place to another and I got it for a song. I've named it Rusty, which is a fair description of it. Since the German word for bicycle is *Fahrrad*, and this is often shortened to simply *Rad*, I call it Rad Rusty. Julia was actually my broker in that she connected me with the person who was selling it. Now the trip to the university is much, much faster — and no bus fumes!

"The Sinful Mile"
Hamburg – 4 März

This past weekend the congregants of my little church family here in Bremen were invited to participate in a time of prayer and fasting with another congregation in Hamburg. Hamburg is about an hour by train, and is twice the size of Bremen — it's actually the second largest city in Germany.

Our reason for going, as I mentioned, was to join our spiritual brothers and sisters in Hamburg. This congregation of about fifty people there, called Lebenstor (Lifegate), frequently joins with Neue Name for worshiping together and just ministering to one another and reinforcing the other's spirits. In this instance, the "Hamburgers" have been praying specifically for some things, and we went to join them as they anticipate breakthroughs. We also did street ministry (for me, it was the first time ever).

One of the ministry burdens of this congregation is for the media. The Bible indicates that the devil is always about the business of using people in positions of influence. (If you've ever found yourself shouting at a news outlet, "You lying sons of Beelzebub!" you're probably reacting to this fact. Okay, likely none of you have ever done that, but I will freely admit that I have, more than once. Or maybe you've watched *Celebrity Jeopardy!* and wondered how these people — rich not in intelligence nor integrity, but simply in good looks — are held up as heroes.) Well, Hamburg is a major media hub, and a substantial portion of its citizens are employed in the media industry. Lebenstor is praying for a spiritual awakening among these particular individuals who influence so many mindsets. In a broader sense, Lebenstor is praying that other forms of media that have been vessels of idolatry and self-worship would be channels to glorify the Lord.

Hamburg is notorious for something else. Situated in its St. Pauli district is the infamous Reeperbahn, center of the city's nightlife and also its Red Light District. In German, the Reeperbahn is known as *die sündige Meile*, or "the sinful mile," and is replete with sex shops, brothels, strip clubs, and the like. There is even a section of it that is blockaded and has a sign warning that women and persons under 18 are forbidden to go further. Petra explained that technically, the street is public, but females who take a stroll past the sign risk having objects launched at them by the prostitutes who work there.

Lebenstor is a house church situated right in the St. Pauli district, and there is frequent prayer going up for those who are like "oxen being led to the slaughter . . . who little know that it will cost them their lives" (see Proverbs 7) as well as the unfortunate slaves who work in the sex industry. (When I say "slave" I mean it both spiritually and in the natural sense — there's an obscene amount of human trafficking and criminal activity connected to the Reeperbahn, as with most involved in this business.)

Reeperbahn literally means "rope walk," and this is fitting for Lebenstor, walking a rope as it seeks to bring life in the midst of a deathtrap.

On a lighter note, Hamburg sits on the Elbe river, which always reminds me of a palindrome that my grandfather taught me: "Able was I, ere I saw Elbe."

#####

My blogs mentioning church activity didn't usually generate as much buzz from readers as the others, but this particular one did. Among the "oh-là-là's" for the Reeperbahn and a handful of indignant remarks from other Dursties valiantly defending the media, there was yet another comment from the unknown "WholesomeInFolsum."

"So, in essence, your trip to the Hamburger meat market was to intercede for two kinds of prostitution — the literal kind, and the media's."

*****

It had been an incredible weekend. What stuck out in my mind was the street ministry we'd done. We had gone out, two by two, following the commission of Jesus to the seventy. For me, etched in my mind were the images of the faces we'd seen. Listening to a transvestite speak of an abusive childhood after we'd prayed with him, and testifying of God's love to a young girl employed in a massage parlor who thanked us over and over for caring, and who'd resolved tearfully to go back home and seek reconciliation with her father. We'd also prayed over a man with a herniated disk in his back, and I'd watched in awe as he bent over, touched his toes, and then was able to walk around without his previous gingerness. The matter-of-factness with which he accepted his newfound healing – a handshake and a single, sincere *danke* – cracked me up.

"Petra, Michael, you *must* come and minister to our church in the United States," I told them on the train ride back to Bremen, still in wonder. "You could stay with me. I'll take you to New York and D.C. and we'll go to Hershey Park and minister there, too." I searched their faces anxiously, hoping my bribe tempted them.

"We would very much like to come to the United States," Michael laughed. "Perhaps next summer."

"But I'll warn you," I said solemnly. "My country is full of *oberflächig, arrogant* Americans."

"We will come prepared," Petra chimed in humorously.

I was silent for much of the rest of the train ride home, lost in thought. All my life, I'd grown up imagining that life in Christ was one thing, that church was a particular thing, and only this year I was discovering it wasn't at all what I'd thought.

Michael had studied church history in depth, and had once put it this way during a prayer meeting. "The Romans took the gospel and made it into a form of government. The Greeks took the gospel and made it into a philosophy. The Europeans took the gospel and made it into a religion. The Americans took the gospel and made it into a business."

The American church had by and large forgotten its original purpose of fellowship — with Christ, and with one another. It had forgotten and been sidetracked with the business of budgets and facility management and programs and marketing. It was busy hiring and firing and forming committees and passing agendas. Somewhere in there, occasional prayer was offered — usually as a means to open or close a meeting or a sermon. But hearing from God — knowing how to listen to His Spirit and glean gems from His word — had gone untaught for the first two decades of my life in any church circles I'd attended.

I had been living all this time with the imitation diamond ring. Yet with this glorious new truth that there was so much more to life in Christ, that it was so much better than what I'd been given, came another foreseeable temptation.

"Jesus, don't let me fall into a new trap," I prayed in my mind as the flat, marshy landscape sped by my window. "I'm eager and excited for your supernatural kingdom to come. But no matter what kind of miracles you do through me or in my life, don't let me get distracted even by the *real* diamonds. Don't let me pursue Your gifts and the fireworks that sometimes accompany You, instead of desiring *You* as the biggest Wow."

Chapter Twenty-Six

Springtime

"Frühling"
Bremen – 21. März

I realize that it's been a few weeks since my last blog, but I've been preoccupied with end-of-semester term papers and other assignments. Yep, just a week away from the end of my first semester in Germany (and yeah, back home you all are more than halfway done with your second, which just doesn't seem right).

One more presentation, this one for my African Women's Studies class, and then I'm done. Next semester starts promptly however, first of the month (on April Fools).

In other news, I have been faithful in my resolve to speak blessings over the city of Bremen, and I must confess, the town is even beginning to look differently to me. Or is it simply that I'm seeing the first glimpses of spring arriving, with some warmer temperatures and a few blossoms on the trees?

"Dis-missed, Schultz!"
Bremen – 31. März

The semester is finally over! Which means that there are less than four months until I return to the States! And yet . . . suddenly – strangely – I am just a tad sad about that fact.

On a side note, Julia tells me – astounded – that I can actually speak German without an accent when I wish. She chides me for being lazy (because I usually lapse right into my regular mode of talking with my American accent). What she doesn't know is *how* I achieve this amazing feat. How I can speak German without any accent is by widening my jowls, crisping off the ends of my words and basically imitating Hogan's Heroes. No kidding. It works, and when I do it, Julia stares at me in wonder, shaking her head.

"Disorderly Conduct"
Schwachhausen – 7. April

One week into my second semester and I think that I can pass at least two of my classes this time around. The others I am not so sure: there's the whole language issue thing, but also the fact that the material is brand new to me, while it seems most of the others who are taking the course have had prerequisite experience.

All the more reason why I am dependent on my internship, which has officially begun at the *Gesamtschule*.

There are about twenty students in the class around the ages of fifteen and sixteen, and they're not exactly driven to learn. Turns out this is kind of a remedial class, and the teacher is evidently not fond of his pupils. Herr Montag is a pencil of a man, German, who speaks English with a British accent. He uses the word "right" a lot. Like . . . "Right. Take out your textbooks. Right. Now read page 47. Right."

The kids are really noisy and disrespectful and don't pay him any mind. He has to shout a lot to get their attention, and occasionally, when this doesn't yield results, he resorts to slamming objects on desks to gain silence for a few moments.

This part always scares the *Quark* out of me personally, and I'm surprised my heart hasn't stopped.

Part of me feels really sorry for him because he gets no respect. Part of me is tempted to join in with the kids taunting him.

#####

Being in fellowship again with other believers was quickly bringing a check into my spirit about some of the miry stuff I'd slipped into over the last few months. Especially the quicksand of pornography, which was particularly easy to step into in Germany.

Michael Freimann's sermon on body, soul, and spirit led me to regurgitating Matthew 5:8 over and over in my mind. "Blessed are the pure in heart, for they shall see God."

"I want to see God," I thought, time after time. "I don't want this stuff creeping in and seizing my life."

"Blessed are the pure in heart. Blessed are the pure in heart, blessed are the pure in heart."

It was a struggle to redirect those thoughts. I wondered at times if I'd ever fully take them captive so they wouldn't have dominion over me. But there was an ultimate prize.

"For they shall see God."

*****

I had not been to Nürnberg since I'd met Petra and Michael. While I missed southern Germany, I realized that I would have missed the Sunday mornings at Neue Name even more.

Neue Name was unique to my experience in that there were several leaders who shared the pulpit. I was coming to appreciate their individual preaching styles and gifting, how they genuinely seemed to like each other, and how they were quick to yield to each other. Each Sunday and Wednesday evening prayer felt like a present from the Lord to me personally.

One Sunday, after being treated to a testimony from a man in the congregation who shared how the Lord had delivered him from prescription drug abuse and restored his marriage, we were given a word from Bruder Rainer.

Bruder (Brother) Rainer had been a Jesuit missionary, and on this particular Sunday he handed us a message that, to me, was earth-shattering.

The premise of his message was about the beginning of life: that we didn't come into being when we were conceived, but rather that we were "God's masterpiece, created in Christ to do good works, which God prepared beforehand so that we could walk in them." We existed in Christ before we were even conceived, and basically were Heaven sent — wearing our "earth suits" as he described our flesh, to move and live and breathe in places and times ordained specifically for us. Not chronological times, but *Kairos* times — as in the right or opportune moments. Our job, he said, was to bring Heaven here to earth. That was the Christian life. Did ever a secret agent have such a glorious task?*

Bruder Rainer was Hungarian, and had a gentle, square-shaped face. His kind, translucent-blue eyes positively lit up each time he said the name of Jesus, and at one point, he got especially animated.

"Do you know — can you even imagine — how good God is? His very nature is good, good, good. Everything that He has for your life is good. The thoughts that He has about you, the works He's already prepared for you, the gifts He wants to lavish on you, the new spirit that He's given you — everything that He says and does and touches in your life is good. So why would we hold any area of our lives back from Him?"

*****

Back at Durst, selection time for rooms was at hand. This posed a question for me, since I'd been torn the previous year over rooming with people from fellowship and rooming with Caitlyn and Anise. Now Anise had told us of her plans to live in the Italian house her senior year, so she wouldn't be with us.

At home, in the absence of me and Anise, Caitlyn had been rooming with a plump sophomore whom she described in her emails as cheerful, earnest, and flatulent.

"She's a nice person," Caitlyn wrote in reply to my condolences. "I burn a lot of scented candles."

But Caitlyn wanted to know, "Are you up for being roomies again next year?"

And after I'd prayed about it and thought about it some, I responded to her that yes, we'd finish our time at Durst as roommates.

"We'll always have . . . beggars?"
Paris – 17. April

Off to France, as Tabitha, Maria and I are taking advantage of having a week free for Easter break. Fortunately, Tabitha and Maria both speak a little *français* so we are getting by okay. I can say, "yes," "no," and "a little more, please" and really, what more do you need to navigate a foreign culture?

We decided to split the time, with three days in Paris and the remaining three days traveling the countryside. So today is day three, and tomorrow we leave for Alsace, known for its rolling hills, scenic villages, cheap-but-good wines, geraniums, and (this time of year) nesting storks – oh, my!

Well, I know that some would argue that three days isn't enough to see a whole city like Paris – you really need about that much time just for the Louvre – but honestly, three days was plenty for Paris. We had a thousand misadventures, tromped down the Champs-Elysées, saw L'Arc de Triomphe, and stared at the Eifel Tower for a good while before deciding none of us felt like waiting in line to go up in it.

Notre Dame was stunning enough, but after so many German cathedrals and then Prague, Notre Dame in some ways felt like just one more gothic church. I actually preferred the uphill hike to Sacré-Coeur, and touring its white travertine arches and portico. The view of the city from the basilica filled me with a sweet calm.

Mona Lisa. I don't know. When we finally, *finally* got to see her it was like, "oh, yeah – there she is" and "Okay, well, that was fun." I don't know. Mona Lisa was a bit of a letdown. But it's not Da Vinci's fault. The painting has been so hyped for so long in so many places – even Nat King Cole's heart-plucking song contributing to the fervor – that when I finally saw her, all I could think was how small the portrait looked in person.

Paris was interesting and historic and artsy – with its loads of architecture and its human statues and its painters selling watercolors along the Seine . . . and the food was good. But it was a compromised enjoyment. Nearly everywhere we went, we ended up thronged by beggars. Worse, most of them were children. Even when I gave one my packed lunch, she kept following me and holding out the free hand that *didn't* have my lunch. It was really, really sad to see that everywhere.

And once, when the three of us were in a French burger chain, sitting on the second story and looking out the windows at the streets below, I happened to lock eyes with an oily-haired man standing there. The moment he saw me, he sent the little boy who was with him *upstairs in the restaurant* to beg at our table. It was awful.

I gave the little guy my burger, untouched and still wrapped. He wanted money but I only had two Euro notes in my wallet – both twenties – and so I withheld them. He stood there for the longest time, saying *"Si vous plait"* over and over until we finally stood up and left. His dirty, brown little face haunts me even now. Maria said later that sometimes the parents beat them when they return empty-handed. I wish so badly that I had the moment to do over again. I'd give him the twenty.

#####

Anise commented on my last blog, "Don't let it haunt you too much, Darlin'. Live and learn."
Kendra had written, "Perhaps the little boy was a divine appointment, and every time you remember his face, you can pray blessings on his life."

*****

So I'd now visited seven countries outside of Germany, including this latest tour de France. As much as the French countryside had delighted me, as well as the stately chateaux we'd glimpsed, I found that I thoroughly preferred Germany. I didn't know why this should be, except that it seemed that the German loveliness and charm was undergirded with something solid and strong. A particular invincibility. Or perhaps it was simply that I sensed inexplicable ties to the country, for reasons unknown to myself.

"Lost in Translation"
Kaufhof – 22. April

Had a funny mishap today at the Kaufhof — Bremen's department store. I was frantically trying to find the housewares section, and spotted a (presumably) Turkish man standing nearby. I should have known not to try to speak broken German with an American accent to a Turk in order to solicit help. There was just way too much margin for error in the whole language thing. But I was desperate because of a time crunch. So I asked him for directions to the "housewares" section. He repeated what I said, then proceeded to give me directions out of the building and via the S-bahn. Only later did I realize that he probably thought I'd asked where Sachshausen (a district of Bremen) is. I just thanked him.

"Officially an Adult"
Luisental — 29. April

I am the last of our foursome here in Bremen to turn 21. For the Americans celebrating their twenty-first birthdays in Germany has been like giving an Alpine skier a ticket to hit the slopes in the Poconos — a little anticlimactic. That is, the marker of one's twenty-first usually is the right to purchase and consume alcohol legally — but here in Germany, we've had that privilege for nearly eight months.

We had a nice little shindig with the Brits at a *kneipe* in the Schnoor. Julia met us out, as did Petra and Michael Freimann. After noshing on some appetizers, Tabitha conducted a short, flattering toast. Everyone raised a glass in *Prost* and shouted happy birthdays at me — it was embarrassing and sweet, and my favorite part was the blend of all the different accents.

Somehow, Herr Montag caught wind of the fact that it was my birthday, and Friday, at the end of our usual raucous time of unproductivity, he slammed some unabridged textbook down on a desk with such force that it raised me a few inches off my chair. (I was distracted by a couple of the students making out in the back and wasn't able to prepare for the terrible *thud*.)

As I sat there in the silence that followed, quite sure that my spirit had literally left my body, one of the girls approached me with a small German fruit torte, decorated with a single candle. Suddenly the whole class burst out into a chorus of "Happy Birthday." Since most of them couldn't pronounce the "th" sound correctly, what came out four times was "happy birf'day," sounding much like a group of preschoolers was serenading me. I absolutely melted.

Later, I thanked Herr Montag for his thoughtfulness. I also considered asking him for a pacemaker for my next birthday.

Wow. I'm 21. It seems so old.

"How do you solve a problem like Molly?"
Gesamtschule Bremen – 1. Mai

I had to lead a lesson in my rowdy English internship today. Maybe the kids were in awe of my different accent, or else how fast I spoke . . . they just stared at me the whole time, frozen in place, quiet as I've ever seen them.

These kids are great. I especially like the Turkish girls. It's funny with the Turks here in Europe. You see a lot of the Turkish guys out and about, but not as many girls. You can tell right away whether a family is traditional or modern, because the wife still wears the burka on her head and follows several steps behind her husband (um, pardon me while I wretch). With the more westernized families, however, the girls dress like their German counterparts and assimilate into the culture. These girls have considerably more freedom to act like normal teenagers. In my class, I have two girls who still wear the burkas and they happen to be my favorite students. They're super shy and are the only ones who aren't disrupting the order. But they're soft-spoken and sweet and diligent and earnest.

Oh, did I mention that the kids in my English class call me *Fräulein* (as in, German for "Miss")? This always makes me think of myself as Maria Von Trapp from The Sound of Music.

#####

Tabitha and I decided to hit Berlin one weekend. I wanted to see Germany's capital before I left, get a glimpse of the Brandenburg Gate. Tabitha was hoping that in Germany's largest city, she'd blend in more with the ethnic population.

Tabitha made for a good traveling companion. She was more outspoken than me, but when it came to adapting to new surrounds and new situations, she was usually easy to please and could go with the flow. She attributed this to her army brat past.

We talked a bit about ancestry and cultural nuances and race relations at one point on the train ride. Tabitha remarked, "My father grew up in Newark and his parents were Jamaican. My mom is white and she grew up in Staten Island. Where the hell does anyone get off calling me an 'African American'?"

Berlin was a hodgepodge of contemporary architecture and glass, mixed with plenty of history and museums. Compared to what I'd been accustomed to seeing in Germany, it was huge and metropolitan and sprawling. We went up the TV tower, its tallest structure, and had lunch within the observation deck.

Between the two of us, we chose a museum, the Brandenburger Gate, plus the Reichstag, seat of the German parliament, to go see. Time permitting, we'd visit the house at Checkpoint Charlie, gateway between the one-time Soviet East

Berlin and the free West. To my relief, Tabitha ruled out visiting Berlin's famous sex shop — "If you've seen one, you've seen 'em all," was her remark.

Unfortunately, after we'd left the TV Tower and were on our way to the hotel, Tabitha realized that she'd left her overnight bag somewhere by the Alexanderplatz when she was snapping pictures. She didn't have any of her clothing, so we stopped to buy some toiletries and I offered to lend her some of my stuff for the following day. But she decided just to wear what she had on for our night on the town — jeans and a tank top — which we'd decided should include a club.

The particular club we decided upon must have had a low tolerance for "our kind." Whether it was Tabitha's threads or what, we didn't know. But the other party-goers kept giving us snide looks and smirks. Even the bartender had a bug up his bum — he appeared very miffed to have to serve us.

When one girl in a tight black vinyl ensemble looked Tabitha up and down, then leaned over and whispered something to her pal, Tabitha said loudly, "Oh, excuse me. I left *my* Catwoman suit at home."

We stayed a little longer with this group of wet blankets, determined if not to get the full experience out of our cover charge, then at least to sour everyone else's with our unwanted presence. At eleven, we exited and warily entered the next club. However, the revelers at this one looked a lot happier to be alive. I actually let loose to some disco and cut up the rug. Some dude in wire rims and skinny jeans saw me and yelled, "She can dance!" which I found hysterical, because I figured the only thing they had to compare to my gyrations was the angry square dance.

Now Tabitha is a member of the most infamous party sorority at Durst, and she has this uncanny knack for being able to open up her throat and down a whole liter of beer at a time. She chugged an entire *Maß* as the onlookers gathered to gawk, and I couldn't help but feel a tinge of pride.

Berlin was unlike all the other towns I'd seen so far in Germany, and like any city, had its own distinct atmosphere. From the time of our arrival, I was overwhelmed with the sense of a convergence of many, many minds, as well as the intellectual liberalism pervasive in so many cities. And I felt a sadness underlying Berlin as well. It was a thick sadness, difficult to pinpoint. Not like the oppressive heaviness of Bremen when I first came into the train station. This was more like a deep sorrow had been pushed down and concealed beneath a kind of frenzied, hipster bustle.

Berlin's Kaiser Dom, nicknamed the "hollow tooth" because of being bombed in World War II, sitting right alongside a newly built modern cathedral, seemed a fitting picture of the personality of the city. One sensed its tumultuous history, and one saw its dogged determination to go forward.

Before we'd left Bremen, I had explained to Tabitha that I very much wanted to visit Dietrich Bonhoeffer's house at 41 Marienburgerallee. On the train, she had asked me about Bonhoeffer and my desire to visit his home (his name was not familiar to her through our German studies). I recapped for her in a few sentences the 500-page story I'd read of the life of this courageous man from an uncommon family, who risked everything he had to take a stand against Hitler, for the sake of God's people the Jews. And I told her of his deep love for his country and the calling he had on his life, and how he shunned the safety of a salaried position in America to return to war-torn, Nazi-led Germany. And I told her about the terrible day when the Gestapo came for him, and how he calmly met with them, and how they drove him away from his beloved family and from his home in Berlin in a black Mercedes, never to return there again.

When we arrived outside the landmark home, the strangest thing occurred. Glimpsing Dietrich's window (which I knew from having seen photos of it was on the third floor of the home), I found suddenly that I felt ambivalent about going inside. I almost felt like I was intruding in someone's private life, gawking. And then in my mind came the words, "Why do you seek the living among the dead?" and I had a sudden picture of Dietrich with Jesus in glory.

Nevertheless, we made our way inside. Every furnishing, every corner hit home the love of this family for each of its members, the warmth of their affection for one another. And as we walked through the downstairs, I could almost hear the voices colliding and overriding and tumbling together during the many joyful gatherings, including the very last one they celebrated for Dietrich's father's seventy-fifth birthday, not knowing that only days later, Dietrich himself, his brother, and his brother-in-law would be arrested. When we went up to his room, masculine and understated, I thought of him penning his famous *Ethics,* and I thought of him in the last days before the Gestapo came, lying in bed and pondering Christ, and dreaming of his fiancée Maria.

But mostly while I was in the home, I kept thinking of his mother, Paula Von Hase Bonhoeffer, daughter of a countess, and the heart of this home. I thought of what it must have been like to raise eight children (including a set of twins, one of whom had been Dietrich), and to be a wife to the country's top psychiatrist. What was it like to live here in Berlin, in the middle of a tyrant's rise to power? To watch one's beloved nation fall apart from within? And what did it feel like to lose three sons, a brother, and two sons-in-law in one existence on this earth?

Never before in all my years studying the rise of Hitler to power and his subsequent suffocation of anything that rose up against him had I so clearly seen the way that spiritual forces were at work behind the man and the people as I did now that Petra had enlightened my understanding with her biblical teaching. I knew that there were multiple failed attempts on Hitler's life, but to read of the plots in detail, and how they each backfired under the strangest, most inexplicable circumstances . . . clearly one saw now the powers at work "behind the scenes." To further observe how Hitler swept in, anointed himself as Germany's savior, took on the role of a benevolent father, and then manipulated the good things – (the values of the German people) – and used their loyalty to authority and hard work against them . . . not to mention the way he could sniff the wind and pick up exactly when to strike and in what format . . . really hit me how he was the definition of a false Christ.

Nor had I known that Heinrich Himmler, leader of the SS and Hitler's right-hand man, was heavily involved in the occult. This explained where the Nazis got their horrific ideas of torture and human experimentation – literally, straight out of Hell.

When Petra had posed the question a couple months prior as to what were the weapons of the Christian's warfare, I had cheated. I'd read commentaries. And so when she'd later asked me about what I'd discovered, I had rattled them off one by one, as if a catechism: *Love, faith-filled prayer, righteousness, and truth.*

"It is a good start, *Herzchen*," she had surprised me by saying in response. "There are more."

And so I'd searched the scriptures, perplexed as to what the commentators I'd read might have missed, until Kendra unknowingly referenced 2 Chronicles 20 in an email that she'd sent. When I'd read the passage, I was blown away by the fact that when the worshipers went forward from among God's people, God set up ambushes against the enemies of Israel and the two armies annihilated one another. All Israel had to do was worship – then stand and watch as God took down their foes. Afterward, they collected the spoil – for three days.

Worship, I therefore learned, was a weapon of warfare. Sincere, spirit-and-truth worship could take down a stronghold. Just like each time Moses had raised up his hands toward the heavens, the army of Israel had prevailed. Just like

Paul and Silas singing in the prison – their version of "Jailhouse Rock" had brought the place down.

Chapter Twenty-Seven

The North Sea, and a Baptism

There was a "Stefan the Stalker sighting" one afternoon. It was the first clear day that Bremen had seen in over a month, and I was on my way to the Unisee, a nearby lake. Suddenly, I saw him ahead and of course there was nowhere else to go or to look and then we passed one another on bicycles. He gave me a look that was at once quizzical and grim. I considered it a mercy that I'd not run into him again near Luisental, what with the two of us living in dorms of close proximity. I'd often held a curious dread as to whether he wasn't peeking at me from behind his own pair of ugly magenta curtains, scowling and perhaps muttering maladies.

I wondered what it was about stalkers that made females feel somehow guilty. When I saw him whizzing past me on his bike, culpability started closing over me like a cloak. But I shook it off and refused to wear it, and pedaled away quickly to enjoy the intermittent sunshine.

One day in mid-May I took a solo trip up to the North Sea. It was blustery and overcast, and the brackish water was bitterly cold. Still, it was the sea. I'd come prepared with layers of clothing and even a hat and gloves, as well as a thermos borrowed from Julia and some Pringles.

I huddled up on the beach and read halfway through Frances Burney's *Evelina* until I couldn't feel my fingertips, and the gusts of wind stung and blurred my eyes with tears. Deciding I'd subjected myself enough to the elements, I packed up. Before I left, I headed down to the tide, my steps sinking and grinding into the sand. I gazed out at the thousands of rippling divots made by the wind atop the great sea's surface, and thought of the vastness of the ocean. As I did so, a line of poetry suddenly came into my mind:

> *Gray rocks and grayer sea*
> *And surf along the shore;*
> *And in my heart a name*
> *My lips shall speak no more.*[4]

*****

Markus came up to visit Helene for nearly a week in early May. I was glad to see him. Besides the fact that I found him likeable, his presence brought to mind the happy early days I'd spent in Bayreuth.

"I still cannot believe of all the wonderful German cities to choose, your college placed you here," he told me, grinning in pity as he gestured. We were hunkered down in Helene's room, eating chips and listening to "Wish You Were Here." Outside, it was drizzling.

"Me neither," I agreed, shaking my head dolefully. "But, I have to say, there have been some good things about being here."

"That's a change from all that you've said before," Helene remarked in surprise, handing me a soda as she perched herself on Markus's lap. "I remember how you once said you wouldn't want to live in Bremen, even as a slug."

"Yeah, I was a little hard on it," I agreed.

Helene's phone beeped. It was Maria downstairs, trying to get into the building. "Be right back," Helene said before jumping up and heading out the door.

---

[4] Charles G. D. Roberts, "Grey Rocks, Greyer Sea," in Jessie B. Rittenhouse, ed., *The Little Book of Modern Verse: A Selection from the Work of Contemporaneous American Poets* (Boston: Houghton Mifflin, 1917), 61.

Markus waited until the door had closed behind her and the rapid *thwack-thwack* of her footsteps was heard down the corridor. He smiled at me, then nodded toward the receding steps. "I am serious about her. I want to see her again. After this year in Bremen is finished."

I smiled. "Guess she'd better keep working on her German, then. She might be coming back here for a long time."

*****

While out shopping for some seeds for her garden, Petra asked me when I'd received the Baptism in the Holy Spirit.

"I'm not sure," I replied. "I don't know what it is."

Petra was appalled. "Don't know what it is?" she gasped. She had picked up a flower pot in her hand and stood frozen, poised. Her expression of horror, combined with the suspended flower pot, looked as though she might bring it down on some culprit's head.

Thus began the understanding that throughout most of my life, when seeking to carry out the commissions of Jesus, I'd been trying to fly an F15 fighter jet over enemy turf without armament. It was as though I'd had a vague sense of where the targets were, but I didn't have the weaponry with which to make a dent in them. And in the meantime, I had been getting shelled and bruised myself.

Petra walked me through several scriptures,[5] starting with Luke 11:13 in which Jesus says, "If you then, being evil, know how to give good gifts to your children, how much more will your heavenly Father give the Holy Spirit to those who ask Him?"

"So you see, Jesus says here that it is possible to ask for and have more of the Holy Spirit."

---

[5] Luke 11:13, John 20:22, Acts 2:1-4, 16-18, 32-33, Acts 8:15-17, Acts 10:47, Acts 19: 1-2, 5-6

I nodded.

She then took me through several passages in Acts, culminating in chapter 19: "Paul . . . found some disciples and asked them, 'Did you receive the Holy Spirit when you believed?' They answered, 'No, we have not even heard that there is a Holy Spirit.' So Paul asked, 'Then what baptism did you receive?' 'John's baptism,' they replied. Paul said, 'John's baptism was a baptism of repentance. He told the people to believe in the one coming after him, that is, in Jesus.' On hearing this, they were baptized into the name of the Lord Jesus. When Paul placed his hands on them, the Holy Spirit came on them, and they spoke in tongues and prophesied."

I didn't know what to make of the passage, but Petra pointed out that Paul had to ask them whether they received the Holy Spirit when they believed. If this was automatic for every believer to receive at the moment of salvation, then why would he have to ask them? Upon their negative response, Paul places his hands on them and the Holy Spirit comes. Obviously, there were two different phenomena going on with the Holy Spirit.

She explained it this way. Jesus breathed on the disciples after they saw Him resurrected, and said "Receive the Holy Ghost." Then, he told them to wait in Jerusalem for the Spirit. Why would he have told them to wait if they'd just received the Spirit? Because the in-breathed Spirit that every believer receives the moment that they believe in Christ as Lord is for *salvation*. The outpoured Spirit given at Pentecost was for *power* (as stated in Acts 1:8).

Petra led me through some other scriptures. She then asked whether I wished to receive the baptism of the Holy Spirit. I still didn't fully understand it, but I sure wanted it. I nodded, a little scared. But when she prayed, nothing visibly happened.

"Believe in faith that you have received something, that 'no good thing will God withhold.' Thank Him for it. Remember

Jesus' promise. 'How much more will the Father give the Holy Spirit to those who ask.' Don't doubt His word."

I went home, overwhelmed and mystified.

Three nights later, I was sitting on my bed, reading my Bible and listening to some worship music. A package had arrived from home, and when I contemplated how much trouble and expense my parents were going through to send me to Germany, but also to remind me of their love for me while I was away, I was reminded of all the spats I'd had with my mom, the lingering anger over the forbidden trip to California the previous summer, as well as my recent bitterness over Agnes' death. Even though parents could be a strong irritant, they were a gift from God. My mom and dad were good people doing their best, and sometimes we clashed. I was very fortunate to have them.

The outcome of my life didn't hinge on one forbidden trip to California to see a guy, I felt the Lord was saying gently. Surely I understood after all that I'd been through in the last two years that He was certainly working everything for my good, through every situation, whether the situations themselves were good. Submitting to my parents' judgment and authority on an issue wasn't going to ruin my destiny. If anything, it would only serve to bring in a blessing.

And Agnes running into the street was, after all, an accident. It could easily have happened to me, and what guilt I would have suffered. What guilt my *mom* must be suffering! I'd never even thought of that until now.

As I glanced over the contents of the package, including a heartfelt card, I told the Lord that living at home with them could be trying, but I was really sorry that I had such a chronically crappy attitude. Would He forgive me? And would He forgive me for being so self-centered not to even wonder how *they* must be feeling, what with me away from home and the dog being killed and probably already suspecting the depression I'd been under?

And all at once, no sooner had I uttered that prayer out loud, something happened in my room that reminded me of the night at Keller's.[6] I knew that the presence of God was right there – upon me and around me. In fact, it was so tangible that I felt as though someone gently, gently pushed me back, so that my head was leaning against the wall and tilted upwards. It was an awkward pose, but I didn't dare move for fear that He'd vanish.

"Lord, You are welcome here," I said after several moments. "Thank You." And then He was there even more, and I felt suddenly rapturously joyful and peaceful in a way that was almost like being tipsy – except that my mind was crystal clear. I praised Him out loud, not caring a bit who heard the hallelujah's echoing in my room. And then all at once, speech was pouring forth that I didn't recognize. It wasn't German, and it wasn't Spanish. But it was a language with its own cadence and stresses like any other. And on my face, gentle as could be, a breeze stirred.

*****

This time, instead of emailing Pastor Steve about what God was up to in my life, I sent a message to my campus minister, Pastor Lawrence. I was so excited, that I just had to tell one of my shepherds back home what had happened to me. Kendra and Petra and my parents had already heard, and all responded with varying degrees of warmth.

Pastor Lawrence responded, however, rather coolly to my news, using some doctrinal terms I had to look up to understand what he was saying. In essence, not only was he not rejoicing with this experience I'd described, I discerned that he didn't believe that what I'd told him was trustworthy. On some level, he doubted my word.

---

[6] See *College Bound: A Pursuit of Freedom*

I read his message – frozen in place – my emotions slowly going from eager to evaporated. The wind was knocked right out of me, like he'd punched me low and square in the gut.

Had Jesus felt this?

I got up and paced my room. Pastor Lawrence's gently condescending, frigid words returned again and again to my mind, and each time they did, the life seeped right out of me. Why did some people need a doctrinal label to squelch an experience with Christ and shape it into something tidy or ordinary? It was bad enough, I reflected, that everyone seemed comfortable with the fact that the Bride of Christ had been dismembered into denominations, for which Paul had rebuked the church in Corinth. To me, what I was learning was simply practical application of what was in the Bible. So much the better that it was exciting for the first time. Why did some in the church get so upset about teaching what was in the Bible?

"Probably because they've been taught not to believe it by those who've influenced them, and in turn *they* haven't experienced it," Kendra responded to my question when I put it before her over email. "Think about it this way: if someone has invested their whole life in ministry and only gotten a five-dollar return of Christianity in the process, and then along comes some young chickadee who hasn't lived half as long as they have, hasn't gone to a Bible college or seminary, who claims to be walking in this supernatural stuff . . . well, I can't imagine that it would be well-received. One would have to be extremely humble to receive that news."

"I just can't believe a *pastor* would be so insecure," I maintained. "Could be so *ungodly* even."

"Oh, Molly," was all she said.

Nevertheless, Pastor Lawrence's words roused doubt in me. What if my baptism in the Spirit was just part of my imagination? What if I'd wanted God's Manifest presence so badly that I'd imagined it? The breeze I'd felt on my face could be explained easily enough. Maybe I had somehow faked the words that had spilled from my mouth that I'd presumed were tongues. Or worse – what if something evil and unknown had enticed me to babble in this unknown language? There were some religious groups that I'd stumbled upon online that asserted this must be the case.

I was distressed. Why had Petra told me about the baptism in the Spirit? Why had she introduced these foreign concepts and these controversial subjects? Things were going so great and I had been growing. Why couldn't I have just learned how to move more in love and understanding of people?

Feeling restless and overwhelmed, I hopped on Rad Rusty and sped off to the Weser, hoping to sort out all these seismic thoughts. I felt deep down, far below my intellectual arguing with myself, a flickering awareness that I had indeed unearthed some kind of treasure. That there was *much more* to the Kingdom of Heaven, and it was for now. For this lifetime. But standing at the entrance of the field that looked so rugged and expansive, yet concealed the buried treasure, where did I begin? Was it all authentic? Wasn't it possible that Petra was sound in some areas, but had maybe gone off the deep end in others? How did I know *she* wasn't in error, and Pastor Steve was in the right?

"If anyone lacks wisdom, let him ask for it," I was reminded again by James.

"Lord, please enlighten me as to what is really going on. If what I experienced and this whole baptism and speaking in tongues thing is from you, I absolutely want to have it and understand it. But if it's not – if it's of my own flesh or even something sinister, I want nothing to do with it. Somehow let me know, Lord."

"Grounds for a New Wardrobe?"
Vegesack – 15. Mai

Julia told me about a town and a museum just north of Bremen that she thought I'd enjoy, what with my interest both in maritime history and old architecture. The town is called Vegesack and the museum is situated in Castle Schönebeck. Julia, Tabitha, and I were going to all go together, but Julia had to duck out last minute and take a train bound for Zeven, having gotten word that her mom had been hospitalized with appendicitis. Tabitha and I wanted to wait for another time to go with her, not the least because frankly, Julia would have made an excellent guide. She urged us to go without her though, pointing out that it was forecasted to be a clear day and that those were at a premium in Bremen.

So off we went to Vegasack, pronounced like "Faygazok," but Tabitha and I kept calling it "Veggie-sack" and "Vegas-act," because we are nerds like that.

Now the Castle Schönebeck wasn't exactly what I had in mind when I'd heard the word "castle" – it was a three-story brick and half-timbered structure – imposing and dignified and lovely, but with a rustic, thoughtful personality. To my great surprise, I noticed that on each of the large wooden doors that bordered the entire first story, there were small *heart-shaped* cut-out windows! This made the structure seem more like an American primitive farmhouse than a German harbor town castle. Set among woods and fields and a creek, with a mill on its grounds, I was struck by its idyllic beauty. Setting off its loveliness were a number of enormous, wizened trees surrounding it, which leaned over like strong but elderly men, stretching out their ancient limbs to heaven in imploration and worship. For a split second, when I first took in the scene, I felt that I'd been transported back to Pennsylvania, with its misty meadows bordered by quiet woods.

"This is part of Bremen?" I remarked to Tabitha, incredulously.

"I know. I feel like I'm on the set of Unser Kleiner Farm," she replied dryly.

Tabitha was a good sport as we ventured inside to check out the pictures, models, and sketches of seafarers. I was much more into the whole whaling/fishing/maritime history than she was, I suspect.

After leaving the grounds of this unexpected bit of Bremen, we were meandering around the town near the harbor, taking in all the boats and sails, when we decided to get some chow. Now within the town there was a lovely, vanilla-yellow two-story restaurant with an elegant Biergarten and great, majestic windows inviting us to come inside. But after a short debate outside, we decided to be economical and sensible. We instead grabbed a wrap from a street kiosk and some *Knoblauchsose* and head down to the water – to sit by the dock of the bay...

Well, we took a seat dockside and were savoring every bite of our meaty, carmelized-onion, rib-sticking wraps. In addition, we'd both been craving a coke, and since the only size we could find in town at a little market was a two-liter bottle, we decided to share – each of us taking a swig from time to time before setting the oversized container between us.

Our quiet, waterside reverie was interrupted by a shuffling noise behind us. A man was stooping down to place some coins in Tabitha's *Rutgers* cap, which had been tossed behind her, upside-down. As we stared at him, rising up from this act, looking at us with a peculiar expression that we couldn't quite discern, it dawned on Tabitha first what was going on.

"Thank you, but we are *not* beggars," she declared with sardonic pride, handing him back his currency.

The man looked astonished, then haughty. "But . . . " he gestured in a sweeping motion toward us. "You are sitting here on the *ground,* drinking cola straight from the *bottle* . . . and wearing *exercise clothing*," referring to Tabitha's ensemble.

"We're not beggars," Tabitha maintained. "But thank you for the kindness."

At this, Fritz the Philanthropist straightened himself, turned on his heel, and strode away.

It probably would have been just as well not to have said anything, and to let him live with the delusion and feel good about his charitable contribution. But the moral of the story is, I think this incident is grounds for a new wardrobe.

#####

Tabitha, Maria, and Helene were going to the Irish Pub in the Schnoor that Saturday evening and asked me to join them. I was tempted to go just to get out and be with people – the air wasn't so frigid and it was becoming more pleasant to be outdoors. And they were persuasive. What else could I possibly have to do on a Saturday night? But I'd had this idea while biking home from class about having a romantic evening with the Lord. Just me and Him and some candles and worship music. Reflecting on Who He Is. A honeymoon celebration between the Bride and Bridegroom.

So alone in my room, I read some Psalms out loud, praying them, marveling all over again at what I was reading. And when an upbeat song played, I danced in the spirit, grateful the Lord didn't judge my moves, confident He wasn't even snickering, but rather honored and pleased.

When a medley of "Agnus Dei" and "Holy, Holy, Holy" came through my line-up, I dropped to my knees. There, overcome with His majesty and His goodness, I began to praise Him, calling out His names, one by one as they came to mind. I was worshiping with all of Heaven and with nature. And when I ran out of words, the heavenly language poured forth instead, effortlessly, in peals. More natural than trying to speak English. It was like a faucet of silver was streaming off my tongue. My face was flushed like a schoolgirl's, but a soft wind brushed against it.

I laughed out loud in delight as revelation dawned. "Thank you, God." I whispered. "Thank you."

Chapter Twenty-Eight

Petra's Story

Petra had told me that my baptism in the Holy Spirit was in essence for other people. That the power I'd received was for ministering to others. However, for me it was clear that it was much more than that. One of the craziest things that happened to me afterward was that when I read the Old Testament, every time that I read of the Israelites falling away from God, or being chastised for falling away from Him, I was grieved. It got me so upset that I'd actually get weepy as I read.

And those Israelites, those fickle, quarrelsome Israelites, plagued with their short memories and tendencies toward trusting in false gods – well, now I did not see them as such a peculiar race after all. Instead, I saw myself mirrored most uncannily in their actions.

Something happened in me much later in regards to reading the scriptures and seeking the Baptism in the Holy Spirit. One day I suddenly got really, really *angry* over the fact that I'd never known about this, never been taught it, never heard it mentioned growing up in the church. I was angry over the fact that there had to be so many others like me out there, living in ignorance and deficiency, and believing it must be the norm. But this anger was a peculiar kind of anger. It didn't *feel* like my usual anger, which was often laced with blame, or had sarcastic undertones. There was no bitterness in it toward a certain individual. This anger was singular in that it seemed like a natural manifestation of the fact that I'd only just now received this precious gift that was for all believers, but it had been withheld for so many years. If my Spirit Baptism could be likened to a coin, on one side of it was overflowing joy and thrill. But on the opposite side of the coin was grievance. The outrage was a flashing, passing, *clean* kind of thing, more like a tangible extension of some part of my realization of what I'd received than an actual emotion.

"Escaping the Natural Gravity of Dorkdom"
Bremer Mitte – 15. Mai

When I was a kid, and especially in junior high, I dreamed that one day I'd outgrow my dorkiness, and especially my apparent magnetic draw for weirdos. Now that I am (officially) an adult, I relinquish that dream. It is not to be so.

The latest confirmation of this is what happened outside the Bremer Hauptbahnhof ("train station") today. I was *proposed* to – on one knee, no less – by an intoxicated, genial young man.

Julia and I had gone to a movie, and the cinema is located a stone's throw from the Hauptbahnhof. After it was over and we'd walked out, Julia realized that she'd left her phone inside on the seat and ran back to get it. I told her I'd meet her over at the kiosk, where I'd help myself to a wrap with *knochblauchsosse*.

Well, as I waited for the finishing touches on my wrap, that's when my Prince Charming appeared – in the form of an inebriated Brit in fatigues. He was stumbling by with his more sober buddies, and I made the mistake of answering wryly in English when I overheard him make a sideways comment about me. Perhaps English was just music to his ears, like it was for me when I was in Nürnberg and ran into the Americans. Perhaps it was my jerk magnetism, I'm not sure. But suddenly, there he was, down on one knee grasping my hand while I awkwardly tried to pay for my wrap at the same time. The steady stream of people walking to and from the train station was slowing to watch the dramatics. I was conscious amid the terrible awkwardness of it all that his fellow soldier pals were sheepishly trying to scoot him along.

I managed to untangle myself from his amorous grip and flee, sprinting, foil-wrapped baguette in hand as though it were a baton. Julia was already heading my way and I nearly ran into her. She had witnessed the whole debacle from afar and was laughing.

"I thought the British soldiers had cleared out of northern Germany?" was my puzzled remark in response to her guffaws. (I'd remembered reading somewhere that they were forbidden in some of the pubs in Osnabruck and Bremen because of too much alcohol equating to too much broken furniture. Which in turn made me wonder if the American forces in the south of Germany had an equally bad reputation?)

"Oh, no. They still have a presence here in the north, although the last are expected to leave by the end of the decade," Julia replied in between giggles.

All I wanted was a wrap. After today, I do wonder if there is in fact something in me that's like a flashing billboard for screwballs, and insists on getting myself in these predicaments.

"Sloppy Father's Day"
Luisental – 18. Mai

It is Father's Day in the land of Schiller and Schiffer, and I am quarantined to my room. This is because in Germany, Father's Day (which is celebrated every year on Ascension Day) is actually the biggest booze fest in the nation, and is an open invitation for men of any age to take to the streets with their personal stash of beer, mixers, schnapps, and anything else that's fermented. Many of them actually cart around little wagons with their alcohol inventory inside, and literally drink until they pass out. We were warned that for females, it can be dangerous to go out in the midst of all this drunken debauchery.

So much for a card, taking out the trash, or letting dad have a quiet day with the TV clicker in his man cave. These German men know what they want – and it's ethanol!

#####

Petra was direct like most Germans, and I had already come to appreciate how refreshingly real that was. She was a bit like that spoil-you-rotten aunt who could whisk you away from your parents' place because they knew they could trust her to your care. Meanwhile, you could tell her in the safety of a midnight movie and a mimosa that you'd snuck out the night before and went skinny dipping in the swimming pool of the local motel, just for the thrill.

Once, when she and I were planting bulbs in her backyard garden, I confessed to her that, "I know the Proverbs 31 woman – the wise matriarch and businesswoman – is held up as the standard . . . but don't most of us girls just wish we could be the naughty Proverbs 7 chick, at least for a little while? Be the 'desperate housewife' of the Bible?"

It was the only time that I saw her laugh so hard she had to remove her red-rimmed spectacles, then remove her gardening gloves, to wipe her eyes. I wondered if my question hadn't hit close to home.

"*Herzchen*, you are a realist as much as you are a romantic," she laughed. She put her glasses back on her face and added, more to herself, "Just like Christ."

"Petra," I asked her suddenly. "You've pointed out many times how spiritually dead the German church is. How did you and Michael escape . . . (I ran over to look up a word in my *Wörterbuch*) its *religiosity* and come to have a real faith?"

Petra grew suddenly serious as something heavy and painful flickered across her face. She stared at some point off in the distance. Immediately, I wished I could rescind the question.

She appeared to take a deep, noiseless breath. "I don't mind telling you, *Herzchen.* Many years ago, Michael and I had a son. The only child we had. His name was Mathias. When he was six months old . . . "

She was still staring off into the distance, across the painful years. I didn't move.

"He . . . he had been diagnosed with — with a sickness I don't know how to explain it in English, but the blood vessels constrict." Petra motioned with her hands, looking to see if I understood. I nodded. "He was in and out of the hospital, had numerous surgeries. When he was six months old, we lost him."

I drew in my breath.

"I was *so angry* with God. How could He do this to me? How could a God who claimed to be loving and kind take a woman's only child away from her? If this was part of God's character, I figured I wanted nothing to do with Him."

She looked down at the patch of earth beneath her for a moment, then closed her eyes. "I lost all interest in living. I didn't want to be around other people. I didn't want friendship, I didn't want consolation from outsiders. Even family members I could handle only a little at a time, and then I wanted them away. The only thing that got me through my days was work. I could teach, and I did so like there was not anything else. My students I held at a distance. My interaction with them was remote and rigid. But as long as I could give my work all my attention, all my strength, I could fight my way through the long hours with something else to fix my mind upon." Petra smiled gently in remembrance. "And time. Time did not ease the hurt. In fact, as we passed the one-year mark of losing him, life seemed to grow even more unbearable.

"I could not stand to hear of or talk of children. Whenever I'd see a baby coming towards me on the street, being pushed in its stroller, I'd have to quick cross over to the other side of the road or turn a corner. It was too much to bear."

I swallowed. I stopped studying Petra and averted my gaze to the ground as well.

"One evening about fifteen months after Mathias's death, Michael was working late into the night, which was not unusual for him. We were both consumed with our work, frightened to leave it for even a moment. It allowed us an excuse to avoid one another. Things were very bad then between me and Michael. He was in pain, too, and neither of us had anything to give the other. No energy, no encouragement. We were too overcome with grief, with loss. Physically, I was wasting away and had lost more than ten kilo. At night I could not sleep without taking pills. I do not think Michael was hopeful at that point that I would ever come around, as I was becoming more withdrawn from him by the day. Any attempt he made to reach out to me, even to suggest grief counseling, I rebuffed. It was *my* grief. I clung to it now with a fierce loyalty. Like it was the only friend that understood. And I felt relief when he was not home. To be in the same house with him meant that I had to deal with *his* grief as well. It was too much.

"This was a very terrible time. Looking back, I was very bad to Michael, and very selfish. But I had not the strength nor the will to be anything else. I had nothing to give him, nor he to me.

"That evening while Michael was working so late, I tried to read something. But the words were making no sense on the page. I had finished all my schoolwork and really had nothing to do. I decided then to clean my house. Nineteenth hour and there I was taking every little *Schnickschnack* off my shelves and tables in the living room, dusting them one by one." Petra smiled. "I had put on the television for some company. One-sided conversation. And do you know? The program on the television was a drama about a couple who lost their child and their process of coming to terms with the reality."

Petra shook her head. "I could not move. Could not look away. I wanted to see what the woman did. Wanted to know how she lived her life with her heart buried alive. She was an actress. It was not real. But I had to see. She was me. And so I stood there in my living room, watching this drama. And when it was over, I must have turned off the television set. But I don't remember doing it. But I remember sitting down very calmly on the sofa. And then the grief hit me. Very hard. And I wept and I wept. And I asked God angrily, "How could You do this to me?" Petra shook her finger. "Where were you at when my son died?"

"And do you know what?" she turned to look at me. "God answered my question. I saw Him. There He was in front of me. I could not move. Was not aware any more of being in my living room. But I saw Him. I saw Him not in the flesh, but at the moment that Michael and I were told by the doctor that there was nothing more that they could do. That our son was slipping away. And I saw Jesus. It was like seeing my life on a film screen. He was watching us and He was weeping over us. His whole body was shaking."

Petra sighed. "It is not something that I can explain very easily, this vision. Nor can I explain how bitterness can just leave like it did after my avalanche of tears. How in an instant after such a long time of knowing nothing else, knowing only wretchedness, peace comes in thick and sweet. It is a transaction that takes place in the spirit realm. One that makes no sense. Christ was in the room with me. He was hugging me and holding me so close. He really *was* closer than my skin.

"I felt like we stayed together – Christ and me – for a period in which time just stopped. And in that instance, I realized that Christ had *not* done this to me. Had not taken my baby away from me. And the bitterness that was killing me – literally killing me physically – vanished."

Two children burst out of the house next door, chasing one another. I glanced over at Petra.

She watched them for a moment, then continued quietly. "As a pastor's wife I knew the story of Job. I had thought of myself as Job all that time, especially in the loss of his children. I even knew that it wasn't God who'd taken Job's children from him, but Satan who had destroyed them. But I felt it unfair of God to allow it. But now that *I* had lost my child, I thought Job a fool for saying, 'Though He slay me, yet will I hope in Him.' I am sorry to say that, but I did."

"Well that was arrogance, *Herzchen,* and until Christ showed up in the room with me that night and embraced me, never did I truly understand the story of Job. Of the self-righteousness of Job's statement, 'Though He slay me, yet will I hope in Him.' How disgusting it must be to the heart of God to take the blame for so much evil and sorrow in life, when He has given this earth to men to cultivate and to care for and they have told Him, 'Get out!' And I realized that I *was* like Job, in that I was horribly, horribly self-righteous."

"At that moment, my theology was pulled out from underneath me. I was left holding onto nothing. Just me and Jesus in that living room. And just like He replaced my bitterness with His peace, He replaced my empty theology with practical power. It was no longer a belief system, no longer a set of principles that fled when reality came. It was true knowledge that what happens on this earth is *not* always God's will. Most of what happens in fact is *not* His will. The devil is the ruler of this present world. Christ came to buy back the authority and give it to those who believe in His name. Most Christians I knew, including myself, did not exercise that authority for which He'd so dearly paid. I could persist in blaming Him for the illness, for the death. Could return to my bitterness and hold it between Him and me. But it would be living a lie. And I knew that to believe a lie was to covenant with the devil. The very one who'd made it his mission to destroy my son in the first place. Well I did not want to stay on that foolish path for a moment longer."

Petra took up her little hand trowel and began to dig in the soft, rich earth again, hands working swiftly as she spoke. "When Michael got home that night, he found me sitting there on the sofa, perfectly calm. He could hardly believe it when I asked him for forgiveness. And I told him that if this book were true," she gestured toward her pocket testament, which was sitting on the glass table on the patio, "that it must be true for now or not at all. That I was done seeing sickness and death win. That I was done with unbelief. With thinking miracles and healing were for another time, but God no longer gave out that kind of power like He did to the disciples. What was the point in wasting another moment with an impotent religion if that were true? And so I told God I wanted to see these miracles. That I was letting go of my anger toward Him because it was not right. It was not profitable. But that in return I desperately wanted to see His kingdom come, *His* will be done here on earth like it is in Heaven where babies do not die. That I wanted to see a *real working* faith in return." Petra laughed. "I don't know if I was reaching for His promises or just testing Him. I really was not in a calm and proper mindset. But He had mercy on me. And so, as feeling began to return to my heart, I began to pray for the sick around me. And the more I did that, the more the feeling returned. And, do you know? Some of the very sick people I knew began to get well. Not every one. But some. The more I did it, the more it happened."

"That's amazing," I finally spoke.

Petra agreed with a nod. "It was so amazing that I began to pray in the local *Krankenhaus.* I'd go on weekends and pray with whatever families would allow me. For cancer patients, for those in surgery, but especially for babies and small children. And do you know what happened?"

I shook my head, mesmerized.

"My prayers were so successful that after a time, the hospital kicked me out. Patients were recovering rapidly from serious illnesses and being discharged. And the hospital told me to leave."

"What? No way. Why?"

Petra smiled. "Why? Because there are two kingdoms. The hospital administrator approached me and told me one day that due to regulations, they could no longer allow me to come in to the hospital. And that was that.

"Well, at home Michael was witnessing such a change in me that he didn't know what had happened. All our married life he had been a pastor, but now he saw his wife really living out the faith. Not just knowing what the Bible said. But living it. Walking out the gospels. Praying for the sick and injured and depressed in the supermarkets, at the bus stops. Starting to live the book of Acts. It changed him, too."

"I will tell you something else, *Herzchen*. Something that is too precious to share with most people so I do not share it. But I want to tell you. One day, a few years after Mathias's death, I asked God to see my little *Jung*. Oh, I knew I'd see him one day in eternity. In the — how do you say in English, 'sweet by and by.' But I missed him so badly. I wanted to see him in the now. The not-so-nice now that I was living without him.

"Several weeks later, I was lying in bed. I do not know whether I dreamed it or if I was partially awake. But I can tell you it was the most real thing that has ever happened to me. Mathias appeared. He wasn't a baby, but a little boy. I knew it was him. He had a big smile on his face. He called me. 'Mama! Mama!' he said. He told me that he was with other children and that Jesus was there. That they were all playing and running and laughing. That he couldn't wait to see me but not to worry. And — and something else. Something too dear, too wonderful to share with my mortal tongue. Then he said that he had to go back. His friends were waiting for him. That he would see me and his *Papa* very soon and not to be sad."

Petra removed her glasses yet again, then her gloves, and wiped her eyes. "Still I cannot tell that story or remember it without many tears." She laughed at herself.

My heart, which had been swept up within me, was now was lodged in my throat, so that I was momentarily unable to speak. I stood there for a moment, then touched Petra's shoulder. I did not know what to say. So I said nothing, but went back to helping her plant the bulbs, which blurred and doubled before my overflowing eyelids.

Chapter Twenty-Nine

A Series of Surprises

"On the Wing of a *Schmetterling*"
Luisental – 22. Mai

It's kind of nuts, but I am starting to dream more in German than I am in English. I realized this all of a sudden one morning when I woke up, and *then* I realized that the German language is starting to become much more agreeable with me. That is, while I'm far from mastering it, it's becoming more intuitive. I no longer have to grapple so stridently with the German sentence structure of verbs coming at the end of clauses and sentences. Even the dreaded genitive case is becoming a little less sinister.

Here are a few of my favorite German words and their translations…

Gemütlichkeit – coziness, comfortableness but the German word carries with it a sense of overall well-being.
Lebenslustig – roughly equivalent to "fun-loving," the German literally translates to "lusty for life"
Schmettterling – butterfly

With that in mind, I penned a quick sonnet to the mother tongue of the fatherland. Here it is:

"Deutsch ist Reizend" ("German is Lovely")

Oh German *Sprache*, how I love thee!
Let me count the ways,

How you glue syllables to infinity,
And use umlauts in a craze.

I love the slang from different states
And such varied dialects,
Irregular verbs sure complicate,
As do your nouns, which have a sex.

I once thought you harsh and coarse
Even guttural to my ear,
But now you're my favorite *langue de Norse*—
Oh, what changes in a year!

#####

Sophia came with us for prayer at the Weser. She was Greek and had grown up in the Orthodox Church. She'd begun to attend Neue Name after Petra had approached her in a *Konditorei* and asked her whether she had shoulder pain, then proceeded to pray healing over her after Sophia had acknowledged this fact in surprise. She was a fiery little woman, a widow with six grown children and innumerable grandchildren growing up all over Europe and America. What an unlikely trio we were, sitting there . . . an American girl just past adolescence in a screaming orange Syracuse sweatshirt; a middle-aged German woman in Birkenstocks and funky red horn-rims; and a wiry little Greek grandmother swimming in her oversized hooded parka, with only her hands and her wizened face visible. Kendra had remarked one time that "the Kingdom of Heaven looks pretty funny." I thought she was right.

Sophia talked a lot, and very fast. From time to time, Petra tried to pull me into the conversation and tried to make sure I was grasping what was being said in Sophia's rolling accent. But both the substance and the language were flying over my head a bit. At the end, when Petra summarized it, I caught the essence of their conversation.

In Luther's reformation, Sophia articulated, the Protestants had thrown out the baby with the bath water. Rejecting anything that had a hint of Catholicism to it, they'd neglected or even flagrantly omitted teaching whole portions of the Bible.

The church, she had said, had undergone a *reformation* following the Dark Ages. But in reality, it was in need of a *transformation.* Only Christ could put His church back together. And that was called a restoration. We should pray for that, she said. And we did.

*****

"June, she'll change her tune"
Bremen – 4. Juni

I never thought I'd say this, but with seven weeks left in Bremen, I actually am feeling a definite sadness about the time coming to an end. I'm just starting to get to know people and make some real friendships, and it will soon be time to say goodbye to it all.

Will I miss Bremen itself? I don't think so. At least not the slugs nor the damp walks to the public transportation, nor broken dorm appliances and the cold atmosphere. I won't mourn the creepists, either.

But the people I've gotten to know now will be synonymous with Bremen, as will the good experiences, which lately have been making up for all the bad. So I guess there is something about it that I certainly will miss.

And, I will miss Germany itself. I've grown very fond of this land. It has some wonderful attributes that I have come to appreciate. If there's one characteristic in particular that I find valuable in Germany, it would be order. The order of schedule, of time, even obeying cross-walks! Order is a good thing. It brings stability and clarity and calm, among many other things. Order in its proper use brings out the best in people and in organizations.

And, the Germans are a fine bunch. While I've seen a lot of Gloomy Guses (or Gerhards, rather) here in Bremen, it's definitely something about the region itself that casts a gray shroud over the people. At least, so I believe. And the rest of the country isn't so morose as the land where the Fischköpfer live.

My Harz Delight
Quedlinberg – 9. Juni

Many months of eating nothing but cold cuts have paid off. With the money I've saved by living on a pauper's diet, I was afforded a trip to the Harz Mountains, a little over three hours by train southeast of Bremen. Julia had mentioned this particular geography of Germany with which I was hitherto completely unfamiliar (isn't "hitherto" a great word? It's quite Germanesque); the two of us traveled there this past weekend.

As I was saying, I'd never even *heard* of the Harz mountains or its towns, but let me tell you, this part of Germany just made me swoon. (Bavaria, you'll always be number one in my heart. But I didn't know another could wow me so profoundly.)

Now the Harz Mountains are home to Grimm's fairy tales. This is where the brothers collected most of their stories. It is the land of silver mines and of steam trains, of villages with cobblestone streets and half-timbered houses with steep-pitched roofs and tiny dormers. It is a place of dark forests and rushing streams, and has about it an aura of mystery. A dwarf might pop out from an overturned log at any moment, scuttling away with its treasure.

The Harz's highest mountain is the Brocken, setting for the infamous scene in Goethe's *Faust*. Mephisto (representing the devil) takes Faust to the top of the Brocken, and there beholds a revelry of witches and goblins. Julia and I hiked the Brocken, and toward the end, all I could think of was pity for poor Faust, who didn't have the modern benefit of well-crafted hiking boots. (I myself was sporting sneakers, which were slightly better – back home, I do not generally do hiking, considering it more akin to torture than a hobby.) Having studied the literary masterpiece of *Faust* both my freshman and sophomore year, Goethe's lines came back to me, both in English and in German. Particularly, as the treeless summit of the Brocken drew nearer, the line sprang to my mind, "Tonight the mountain's mad with magic!"

But I was totally swept away by the beauty of the mountains and plunging valleys and the tiny towns dotting the land. The town of Wernigerode in the center of the Harz just stole my breath away (if the half-day hike to the Brocken did not.) Street after street of half-timbered houses, and a castle replete with gargoyles outside and gorgeous tapestries and carved furnishings within.

I don't know if I ever slept as well as I did after yesterday's full day of hiking. I now know what it means to be weary to the bone.

Today, Julia suggested that we go to Quedlinberg, a medieval town that survived World War II and was also part of Soviet-occupied East Berlin. We took one of the region's famed steam trains, and even though we were seated for the trip, I felt muscles I never knew existed staging a protest because of yesterday's activity.

It would be tough to find a town more chock full of charm per square meter than Quedlinberg, and fewer Americans than I've ever stumbled upon in any other town we've toured. Kind of nice not to see so many tourists. Being with Julia helped me to blend in as well.

Interesting fact about Quedlinberg – it was ruled by women for 800 years! Here, in 900-and-something, King Heinrich I was crowned king of Germany. It was the first time Germany had been ruled as a single entity. When he died, his widow Mathilde founded a convent for the aristocracy, and her granddaughter became ruler of the town as its Abbess (that is, the woman who's head of an abbey of nuns for those of you in state schools, haha). And so it continued to be governed by an Abbess throughout the centuries until Napoleon invaded and nullified the Abbey in 1802.

On another note, I feel empowered now that Julia taught me a phrase to say when I don't know or can't remember a particular German word. "Mir ist das Wort entfallen." Translated, "The word escapes me." Much better than saying, "I don't know" or "I forget." Now I can eloquently express my ignorance.

#####

Comment from an unknown user by the moniker of Leigh: Are you making fun of public universities? If so, that is really ignorant!
Comment from Anise: Leave it to the French to spoil a good system of feminist government.
  Of course, I omitted from my blog the story of how I ended up alone with a homeless guy Friday evening while Julia

went to the restroom in the train station. He walked with a limp and his one eye looked in the opposite direction of the other, so that it seemed like he was watching for the train even while he was staring at me at the same time. I looked away.

He fixed his good eye on me and asked me in a hoarse cackle whether I had a cigarette. I had to disappoint him. He then mumbled something unintelligible in his dialect and shuffled away.

I wondered to myself in that instant, what would have happened if I'd responded like Peter and said, "Cigarettes have I none, but in the name of Jesus Christ be healed!" Well, the thought flashed through my mind, but I didn't have the faith or the boldness to act. And the opportunity passed.

He then seemed to think of something, and turned, limping slowly toward me.

"*Woher kommst du?*" he croaked. Where did I come from? Evidently, my American accent gave me away again. I must employ the Hogans Heroes imitation more diligently, I thought.

He was close enough that I could smell him. Grease. Human grease and armpit sweat, with a hint of urine. I tried not to wrinkle my nose or in any way convey the repulsion that rose up at his presence. He leaned toward me and started to say something to me in his crackly voice, but was cut off by Julia's voice, sharp and curt, asking him to leave.

Giving her a look as though he'd been slapped, he stared for a moment. Then he looked offended, and with some real dignity, straightened himself. He hobbled away.

I felt very sorrowful all of a sudden. I remembered reading the story that Jim Cymbala of the Brooklyn Tabernacle had shared about the homeless man who approached him, who smelled worse than any stench he'd ever smelled in his life, even with all the years of working with the homeless in New York. How the man buried his head in Jim's chest, crying uncontrollably, and it was all Jim could do to put his arms around the man and not be sick. How Christ then spoke to Jim and said to him, "That's the smell of the world I died for."[7]

This man with his pitiful appearance and powerful odor had a history unknown to me, but God had seen him before the foundation of the world, had known him before He created him in the womb.

This would be more appropriate if Michael Freimann were present, I thought grimly. *He and Petra would know what to say. What to do. They'd at least be able to* talk *intelligibly with him.*

But Michael wasn't there. Just me. I stood up.

"Was there something you'd like me to pray with you for?" I called after the man, taking a couple of steps after him.

He turned again, the one eye blazing at me and the other rolling toward the platform. He muttered something. I repeated my question, standing there about four feet away.

"You can pray for *Zigaretten,*" he barked hoarsely, laughing, so that he started coughing.

I closed my eyes and extended my hand toward him. Praying in a foreign language for a cynical stranger in a public place was a little disconcerting. But instantly I pictured Jesus standing there, arms extended towards the man, embracing him even, and I prayed boldly, simply in German, "Our dear Lord, please meet this man's needs. Every need. Heal him. Pour goodness into his life. May he find rest in You. Amen."

When I opened my eyes, I saw that the man had bowed his head. Now he was staring at me, a different expression on his face than what had been there before. I dug in my wallet and held out five Euro.

"Danke," he said in a low tone, still staring with the unreadable expression. He took the bill and stuffed it in his pocket, and then limped past me and past Julia and then out of sight.

---

[7]Jim Cymbala, *Fresh Wind, Fresh Fire* (Zondervan, Grand Rapids, MI; 1997, 143)

I didn't dare look up to meet Julia's gaze. I didn't know what I'd find there. Bewilderment? Scorn? Disapproval?

A sleek train appeared before us, sailing out of nowhere, whirring and whistling and letting out an extended grunt before coming to a stop. Wordlessly, we'd climbed on board.

*****

"When in Bremen, do as the Fischköpfer"
Unisee - 17. Juni

Something unprecedented happened yesterday. [Drum roll] Are you ready? The sky above Bremen was perfectly blue *all – day – long*. Not a wisp of cloud in sight. Temperatures were warm and the air was faintly breezy. It was a Perfect Day.

Now, well before yesterday this day had been forecasted, and I mean it had been *broadcast*. All of Bremen knew that the sun was coming and rushed out to meet it, prepared. Nobody went to class (that is, none of us Americans went to class and I'm pretty sure no Germans did either, and I would bet that most of the professors failed to show up too). I'd never seen so many people outdoors at one time. It was like there was a rush on Vitamin E.

We've seen glimpses of sunshine, to be sure, but never a day where it just shone all day, without any threats of withdraw or moodiness. It was glorious.

Tabitha, Maria, Helene, and I decided to capitalize on every ray and so we headed over to the Unisee (Bremen's big lake). We had heard that the Unisee is a nude beach in these rare instances of warm climate, and yesterday, well, we witnessed it.

For the health and well-being of any readers, I will omit details of what we saw. An allusion to older men with enormous bellies drooping over a gaudy hint of fluorescent-colored spandex will probably paint a general picture for you. But I won't disclose who from among our group of Americans decided to put into practice the cultural norms and let the sun hit more of their flesh than would be normal protocol back home.

#####

"What did you think of it?" Julia asked, taking the book I held out to her.

Günter Grass's *Die Blechtrommel*. In English-speaking circles it was known as *The Tin Drum*. A scathing picture of Germany and of war and of the blackness of the human heart, allegorized in the life of Oskar Matzerath, a drummer from Danzig who decides on his third birthday not to grow any taller. I had found the tale grim and dark and comical and graphic. Reading it was like watching a bad wreck from which one couldn't look away. Grass was a master craftsman with words. He had the ability to fashion in the air vivid descriptions and blast lasting impressions on the imagination. Yet all the while the residue leftover seemed to leave a grimy film over the soul. Grass's work had left me amazed by his genius, yet feeling dirty and starved at the same time.

The world lauded those who could allegorize, caricaturize, or satirize with poignancy. I admired these artists as well. But who offered a solution to fallen mankind? To the sickness of the eternally diseased human heart, of which Jeremiah wrote? To the terrible isolation of the individual?

Something else had troubled me the entire time I'd read *The Tin Drum* — something that had nothing to do directly with the book itself. In the back of my mind, I kept thinking how Grass's grotesque description was not even a picture of humanity at its worst. It was really simply a picture of humanity. This was frightening. Because what did the church I'd known in America have to offer such a stricken world? What were we doing, practically speaking, to liberate an addict who'd been in and out of rehab for years? What had my serving in the soup kitchen done to resolve permanently the destinies of the people we'd encountered? Not that it wasn't a nice gesture — serving people and all. But again, what was the church in America doing that any rotary club or secular support group could not? Where was the transformation of lives, from the dead to the living?

When Jesus and then later his followers in the church had encountered the poor, the mentally ill, swindlers, and even the deranged, there was in every case an instant transfer for those who wanted it, from the kingdom of darkness into the kingdom of light. As Paul had stated to the church in Thessalonica, the gospel had come "not only with words, but in power and in the Holy Spirit and with full conviction." That was the difference — what had been missing from most of my church experience growing up, and then later with the congregation near Durst — was that the gospel had only been words. No power. Very little of the Holy Spirit. Miniscule conviction.

Now that I'd seen the gospel in action, and not just with words, I could not fathom why there was such resistance toward it from Pastor Steve and Pastor Lawrence. It made no sense. It was like they were handcuffing themselves to a theology that in essence was a broken down, leaky rowboat. They believed wildly that this inadequate vessel would take them safely across the roaring, hostile waters of the Atlantic Ocean. While all the time, a sleek jet was available to them for passage — only they didn't trust it. They'd heard those things could be dangerous. Sometimes went off course. Had been hijacked in the past.

And the worst of it was that my pastors — and thousands like them — were persuading millions onto the decrepit boats as well, when they could have been soaring in the skies instead.

I had to know why.

*****

Michael listened to my question thoughtfully before responding.

"What you are describing . . . these ministers of the gospel with their lifeless sermons and their impotence in really seeing the kingdom of heaven come . . . I think that there are many factors why this is so prevalent. Why it's the current state of the crippled Western church. A life completely yielded to God cannot help but bear much fruit. Those who hunger for Him, then surrender to Him and obey — above pride, above politics, above pleasing people, above personal preferences — these are the ones that manifest the power that changes communities and even the world."

"Pastor Steve is a really *good* man, though," I said. "I've known him a long time. He genuinely cares about people. I don't think he's willfully holding back the truth."

"All of us are enlightened when the Light touches us," Michael replied. He sat in silence for a few moments, thinking. "There are many factors that influence individuals, including just plain bad theology, passed on by Bible professors and even well-meaning mentors. This happened to me. My Bible was in many ways a history book for a long time. Of course, at the time, it never occurred to me that my way of thinking might be off course." He fell silent again for a moment, carefully sifting through his thoughts. "One universal inhibition I see is that we really do not believe our own theology until we experience it. Petra has shared with you our history. When I first started out as a pastor, I knew my Bible. I had been a good student and a good disciple, I thought. And, I truly cared about the welfare of my flock. I wanted to see them living holy lives, peaceful lives. But had someone asked me to pray for a blind man to be healed right there in front of me, I would have been paralyzed. I might have tried, but there would not have been any faith attached to my prayer. Yet this is the work that Jesus commanded His followers to do. Sooner or later, I had to stop bringing this book," he gestured toward his Bible, "down to my level of experience. And I had to start bringing up my experience," he raised both hands in unison, "to match the miracles that Christ and his followers did. It was a process. There were many opportunities for failure and ridicule. I did not always see results when I prayed for certain things. But I continued. Had I given up, my faith would have dried up to where it had been before – or worse. But I kept believing that it was possible to live and move in the supernatural because the Bible said so. That in fact operating in what was humanly impossible to do was the only task worth doing."

My eyes widened at this thought. It had never occurred to me that much of what constituted my good deeds all my Christian life might just have been self-reliance.

Michael continued. "The disparity between the miracles recorded in the gospels and in the book of Acts, and that of my own faith-deprived church, was not because God had changed, but because I had been content to operate without Him."

*****

One day when I returned from the Uni there was a message awaiting me on the computer. It was a moment totally surreal, and yet completely natural at the same time. The name on the left of the line was Hank Bobek. I stared at it for a moment, feeling something akin to dread. Then, fanning my face rapidly with my hand, I clicked on the message.

Dear Molly,

Life has been dull without you. I know you're in the process of conquering Western Europe and its male population, but I reserve my old corner of friendship in your life. I'm coming to Germany in two weeks and thought I might drop in for a visit.

Your pal emeritus,
Hank (alias WholesomeinFolsum)

P.S. Do you have any suggestions for a birthday gift for my nephew? He's turning two next week, and I don't know what to get him. He's kind of into eating dirt and beating the family dog with a stick.

Thirty

Prelude to Farewell

"I wonder how – or *if* – I should clear up this misconception," I messaged Kendra. "I don't know where Hank gets this idea that I'm some sort of man-eater. It's quite the opposite of reality. I mean, I'd sure *like* to be . . ."

"Well, if he's going to be there in two weeks, maybe you'd better wait until you can talk to him in person," Kendra advised. "It seems that there have been plenty of misunderstandings between you two, and discussing it in person would be better than over a computer."

"Maybe I should ask Stefan to drop by while Hank's here to fuel the illusion a bit."

"Yeah, I'd better get back to praying for you," Kendra said.

*****

"I'm not sure whether I can take sorority life when we get back," Tabitha lamented, popping the top off a Beck's as the four of us sat around her room. "I've spent an entire year roaming Europe, living pretty much on my own. I know I can't take orders from someone. But even as a senior, I don't think I can give them. The whole Greek set-up is just goofy to me now. I swear I'll break out laughing at exactly the wrong time."

My kinship with Maria, Tabitha, and Helene, which had survived the tests and nuances of a different culture, had grown dear to me. In many ways, I felt as though they were my army buddies. None of us had known each other well back home, yet overseas we had weathered a great many obstacles together. The persistent, dogged endurance of a year in dismal Bremen had drawn us together, even as we'd learned to survive and appreciate some of the city's good points.

Senior year would be upon us almost as soon as we got back home. And exactly a year from now, I'd be flung out into the real world. I felt I'd gained little insight into what I wanted to do with the rest of my life. Were Ms. Viviano to sit down with me again, I suspected our conversation would have proceeded much the same way. The most exhilarating work I'd ever participated in had been the street ministry in Hamburg, in the St. Pauli District. I tried to picture the expression on her face when I told her that what I seemed to have the most aptitude for was praying over prostitutes and the homeless.

"If I could just minister to people and write, I'd be totally satisfied," I told Kendra. "Perhaps the purpose of my life is to be sponsored by a sympathetic and reasonably well-off husband. Do you think God calls certain people to be trophy wives?"

Bible reading had become a staple again in my life. Not that I always felt like it, because sometimes I was tired or lazy or distracted with the trivial stuff around me. But spending time in the Word — that is, with Christ — was clearing out the grime and dust in the highways of my mind. I was beginning to pick up on His specific thoughts for me, for my situations. And I was coming to notice and mind the distinct difference in the days when I *didn't* get that time with Him. Meditating on scripture not only fueled me in preparation for the day, but it was also truly an act of putting on my warrior's armor, going into battle prepared. Wherever it cropped up in my life and in the world at large, through sickness, rejection, grief, relationship breakdowns, fear, disaster, poverty and every other degradation of humanity, I was learning to turn to my spiritual armament in response.

And in turn, I was learning to wield those weapons. Petra was showing me in her gentle, solid teaching that I'd only scratched the surface of what was available to me as a believer.

That Christ had already paid for everything, and there was a storehouse of riches that I was only just now learning how to open. That the key to being effective in my walk with Him was learning to listen to His voice. My mission was to do in the course of a day – in the course of a lifetime – only what He instructed me to do. No more, no less.

Love, truth, righteousness, faith, prayer, worship, thanksgiving and the rest of the arsenal at first glance seemed too mild to tackle the forces of Evil. But the Source of them was irrepressible and inexhaustible. What a boost to know that I was already on the winning team.

Maria and Helene and Tabitha had all in turn been offered prayer by me for various physical and emotional distresses in their lives. They had heard me testify of my faith. Sometimes, they even applied a nickname when my "religiousness," as they deemed it, manifested in various ways – "Sister Molly." I accepted the appellation graciously.

*****

Auf Wiedersehn
Bremer Gesamtschule – 20. Juni

I'm wiping away the water from my eyes as I've just returned from my last day with my *Gesamtschule* Rowdies. [Sigh]. I'm sure going to miss those kids.

For my final class, I wanted to bring in some American treat that they wouldn't normally find over here. Since my parents had sent along a package of graham crackers recently, I took in those, cemented together with peanut butter (you *can* find decent PB here, but I haven't been able to locate any graham crackers). Root beer was the only exotic beverage I could think of to give them to try, but alas, I couldn't find any. So, everyone feasted on graham crackers with peanut butter and then everyone was really thirsty and asking Herr Montag for special favors like going to the vending machine, and all in all, my snack pretty much disrupted things on a grand scale for Herr Montag.

I suppose it was an appropriate way to close out the year.

As a means to work on their language skills (or perhaps simply to punish them) Herr Montag had each student write me a brief poem, employing their best English. This was a challenge for them, and the best gift ever for me. I'll share one, written by a boy named Jens:

To my Favorite *Ami*

Thank you for visiting our school.
Truly think we you are cool.
I am sorry you not like Bon Jovi
You taught me the English word for 'sowie.'

Short, sweet, simple, and sincere. I'll never forget these kids.

#####

Maria would be gone to Switzerland during Hank's visit, and she offered her room for the couple of days we'd be in Bremen. I was sorry we couldn't run off to Bavaria immediately, but I had a class that I couldn't afford to miss. Anyway, I was very eager for Petra and Michael to meet Hank.

In my mind, I was already imagining Hank and me in Nürnberg, Hank and me in the Alps, even Hank and me revisiting my stomping grounds in Bayreuth. He was only coming for a week, but I'd already envisioned us in some sort of German *Casablanca*, seeing half of the country in that time, discussing the kingdom of Heaven and literature and art, lost in the charming backdrop of it all. One would think that I'd learn my lesson eventually – that life never turns out the way I picture it, and the rosy portraits I paint in my imagination usually outshine reality. It was better not to anticipate these things – what wasn't a let-down with the opposite sex was usually slightly uncomfortable in the moment. But the hopeless romantic within me refused to obey my own logic.

Still, the thought of any romance-infused interludes made me squeamish. Friendship really was much more satisfactory. Unless of course we suddenly got engaged while he was over here. That could work, too. But anything in between – the whole girlfriend/boyfriend awkwardness – I just wanted to skip altogether.

Perhaps we can elope while he's here for the week, I thought. That would be the easiest solution to all this.

"I'm really glad Hank's coming over here with a mindset for friendship," I told Petra later. "I'm convinced I'm way too neurotic to be in a relationship. I'll either make it into an idol, or I'll kill it with over analysis. Either way, if there's romance in it, it will have to be destroyed."

"I am looking forward to meeting him," she said smiling. "He must be rather special to hold the interest of one such as yourself."

*****

"So Bremen hasn't exactly been the ultimate destination?" Hank suggested. We were on the telephone. He had asked if it was alright to call me. I was aware of the cost, and felt like I had to put my responses together quickly.

"No. It hasn't. But it's gotten slowly better."

"When you said they have *The Simpsons* there, I figured, it couldn't be *too* bad," Hank said easily.

"Well, it does have that," I conceded. "*The Simpsons* and *Little House on the Prairie* and *Hogans Heroes.* Not to mention a brand of pornography that's pretty violent."

"Pornography *is* violence," Hank observed.

"So why the sudden decision to come to Germany?" I asked archly, directly.

"I figured I'd stock up on Cuban cigars and switchblades — you know, stuff that's contraband back home."

"Uh-huh," I said.

"Truth be told," Hank's voice took on a rare, earnest tone. "I figured our friendship was worth it. If you'd told me that it wouldn't work, that you didn't want me to visit, I'd have respected it and just zipped around as a tourist by my lonesome for a week. It still would have been a good time."

"Ah," I said.

"But it would be more fun seeing it with you."

*****

He would be landing in Frankfurt right about now, I guessed, glancing at the time. I'd already gone through a series of emotional pendulum swings that day, Holden Caufield style. One second I was practically ill with anticipation over his visit. The next moment I simply wished he weren't coming at all. Then I couldn't wait another second to see him. Then I was annoyed with him for stirring up such emotional intensity.

At the moment, I was looking forward to seeing him. Mostly, I couldn't wait to hear his thoughts on everything German. His thoughts on the Germans themselves. And above all, I couldn't wait to tell him about what I was coming to know of Christ.

There was plenty of time until I had to make my way to the Bremer *Hauptbahnhof* to meet him. My room was reasonably clean, my mini-fridge had been fully stocked for the first time ever, and my smudge-resistant eye make-up had been applied.

So I grabbed the remnants of a *Milka* bar from my fridge, plopped onto my bed, and opened up my Bible to where I'd left off in Romans.

The coarse, heavy curtain had been pulled aside from my window, which was flung wide open. A light, temperate breeze sailed into the little room, ruffling the Bavarian flag and lifting up its corners. Somewhere from within the building, I could hear laughter. And outside, the sun was beginning to peek from behind the clouds.

THE END

Author's Note

In many ways, this book is more of a memoir than it is a work of fiction. What has been fictionalized are the characters; also, the sequence and timing in which the events occurred has been shuffled, rearranged.

My desire in writing this book is to see those with backgrounds similar to my own bridge the gap from knowing something of God to really engaging Him. To graduate from spiritual milk to meat, as Paul said to the church in Corinth. To realize that there is so much more than what many of us have grown up being taught in the western church. What is encapsulated in this novel is only the first layer or so of a depthless treasure.

The American church has been segregated by denomination and doctrine, and up until recently, most of the persecution I've witnessed and experienced as a Christian has come from *within* the institutional church. However, that is rapidly changing with our current social and political climate, and I expect the atmosphere of this nation founded on Judeo-Christian beliefs to grow increasingly hostile toward followers of Christ. While seemingly unpleasant, we know that this persecution will strengthen and refine the true Bride of Christ, and ultimately advance the Kingdom of Heaven.

The difficulty will be for Christians who have areas of their lives not yet surrendered, and who do not know the tremendous freedom that comes with total abandon to Him. I hope that this book is an encouragement that there is *so much more* to be enjoyed in Christ, and that for us, eternal life has already begun.